My Brother
DANNY

To Linda Weathers

with best wishes.

Ernie Baker

Gifted to the Ocme
LIBRARY because he
was a member for
years in the 1900's.
by Ken an Linda

My Brother

DANNY

A NOVEL

Ernest Baker

iUniverse, Inc.

New York Lincoln Shanghai

My Brother Danny

iUniverse books may be ordered through booksellers or by contacting:

iUniverse
2021 Pine Lake Road, Suite 100
Lincoln, NE 68512
www.iuniverse.com
1-800-Authors (1-800-288-4677)

This is a work of fiction. All of the characters, names, incidents, organizations and dialogue in this novel are either the products of the author's imagination or are used fictitiously.

ISBN-13: 978-0-595-39923-9 (pbk)
ISBN-13: 978-0-595-84312-1 (ebk)
ISBN-10: 0-595-39923-1 (pbk)
ISBN-10: 0-595-84312-3 (ebk)

Printed in the United States of America

Acknowledgements

The author is grateful for the counsel and suggestions provided by Kelly Wilson, D.V.M., a member of the staff of the Brinker Veterinary Clinic in Lake Orion, Michigan. I appreciated the editorial review of the novel made by Kathryn "Kit" King, and also the input that Father Richard Herbel of Saint Augustine's provided. I also owe a special vote of thanks to my friend, Sid Houghton, for editing this novel.

The Michigan Apple Committee generously supplied the photography for the cover of the novel, for which I extend my sincere thanks. Whenever I needed technical assistance with the computer I used to write this novel, my neighbor, Frank Gambino, came to my rescue. The Lake Orion Public Library was a valuable resource, which I utilized whenever I needed to clarify facts or to do some research. And I am especially indebted to my wife Mary Lou for her indulgence, as well as for her encouragement in writing this novel.

CHAPTER 1

Sweet Sixteen

"Good morning, Papa."

My grandfather, John Daniel Malone, heard me ride up to his horse barn on the John Deere utility vehicle we use to run around our family farm and apple orchard. It was a few minutes after 6:00 a.m. My grandfather, who I call Papa John, was already up, and I saw him approaching me with a big mug of coffee in his right hand, and a smaller one in his left for me. The coffee was obviously hot, because I could see little wisps of steam swirling from both cups as he walked toward me.

When Papa heard me drive up, he knew that I was there to ride my quarter horse, Star. The date was Friday, October 17, 1980. My alarm clock had been set for 5:30 a.m. that morning so that I could exercise Star. I knew I had a full day ahead of me, which would be followed by a busy weekend...and a very special week coming up. There simply would not be another opportunity for me to ride Star for at least a week.

"Here's a warmer-upper for you, Colleen," my grandfather said as he offered me the coffee. "Do you have time to drink it, or are you in too big a hurry?"

"I think I'd better saddle Star and get going, Papa. Mom will have breakfast ready by 8 o'clock and we want you to join us."

I did take a few sips of the coffee while I saddled Star, which only took me a couple of minutes. As soon as I was up in the saddle, I could tell from the approving look on Papa's face that he was pleased that I was going riding on this crisp, Michigan fall morning.

Papa and I have a special relationship. He gave me Star on my 11th birthday, and next Monday, October 20, I will be 16.

When I ride Star, it's the best part of my day, and I'm fortunate to have an 880-acre farm and orchard available for me to ride my horse around. Papa John was the third generation to operate our farm and orchard. Now my Mom and Dad, my brother Danny and I live in the big farmhouse where Papa John and my grandmother Mary used to live.

When my grandmother died eight years ago from cancer, the 80-acre farm next to our farm was for sale. Papa bought it, and he lives there by himself in a small ranch house. He could have stayed with us in the big centennial farmhouse, but he wanted his independence and he and my mother occasionally rub each other the wrong way. Margaret, my mother, is of German descent…her maiden name was Goetzinger…and she is a strong-willed, confident woman who very capably manages the finances of the family farm, which includes a large apple orchard and farm market. The Goetzinger side of my family are also farmers, and have apple and cherry orchards on the west side of Michigan, north of Grand Rapids.

My mother and father have known each other since they were nine or ten years old because they would see each other when they attended regional and state horticulture meetings with their parents. After my father graduated from the School of Agriculture at Michigan State University, and my mother had graduated from Western Michigan University in Kalamazoo, they started dating and decided to get married. They'll celebrate their 20th wedding anniversary next year.

My Dad, Edward Malone, is a tall, muscular man and I think he's very handsome. He is of Irish descent, and loves being a farmer. For someone with an Irish heritage, he's unusually quiet, while my mother, on the other hand, is outspoken and far more aggressive than my Dad. She has very strong opinions…one of them being that I'm too young to date boys, but that will hopefully change after I turn sixteen next Monday.

My mother is also not fond of pets. When Papa John moved to the adjoining farm, Mom decided that there would be no more pets allowed in our home. My two cats…Frick and Frack…got moved to the barn, and my plan to get a puppy was cancelled. Frick and Frack like living in our barn, however, as they are free to roam not only the barn, but the apple orchard as well. They catch a lot of mice in the orchard, which pleases my Dad, as mice can cause a lot of damage to apple trees.

While riding Star, I thought about all of this and a lot of other things. I thought about how lucky I was to have my grandfather, Papa John living nearby. When I was seven years old, he put an apple seed in the palm of my hand and said, "Colleen, if you plant this apple seed it will grow into a tree that will produce bushel after bushel of apples for many years. If this little seed can do that, just think about what you can do with your life." Well, Papa and I planted that seed and it has grown into a tree that's now taller than I am. Last year we picked the first apples from that tree and we named them "Col-Jons"...which is a combination of my name with my grandfather's name. When you plant an apple seed you never know what variety of apple you're going to get...you might even get a brand new variety. So, if our "Col-Jons" turn out to be an especially good apple, Papa John says we'll start taking cuttings from this tree to graft onto rootstocks. That way we could raise a lot of them. Maybe we could even patent "Col-Jons" as a new variety if people like them. Wouldn't that be exciting!

Papa John recently celebrated his 67th birthday, and fortunately this wise, wonderful man is blessed with good health. He's still able to handle his share of the farm work, as well as helping with the pruning and spraying of the apple trees.

At harvest time, he's especially good at supervising the migrant workers who are hired to pick our apples. Papa has known some of them for 30 years or more. The migrant workers like Papa a lot. He takes a personal interest in them and their families, and he frequently gives candy or toys to their children. The housing we provide for the migrant workers is located near Papa's home and sometimes in the evening, he'll saddle several of his horses so that the worker's children can ride them around in the corral next to his barn.

Papa knows a lot about animals...especially horses. Besides Star, there are seven other horses in his barn, and several of them are for sale. Most of them were bred, raised and trained by Papa. He's also feeding a small herd of cattle, which will be ready to go to market next year. Papa shares his home with Oscar, an old tomcat, and a golden retriever bitch named Song.

The harvest will soon be finished. All the early varieties of apples have been picked and delivered to a packinghouse in Belding. Some of our apples have already been sorted, bagged and shipped to grocery stores, while other bins of apples have been put in controlled atmosphere storage. When our apples come out of this type of storage, they're just as fresh and crisp as when they were first put in the "CA" storage rooms.

When I remembered to check my wristwatch, I couldn't believe it was already 7:30 a.m. I gave Star a fast rubdown and then I turned him out in the fenced-in pasture in back of Papa's barn where he could cool down and graze with the other horses. Then I rushed home, parked the utility vehicle next to our house, and ran upstairs to shower and dress for school. By the time I got back to the kitchen, mom and dad, Danny and Papa were already eating the scrumptious feast that mom had prepared. They didn't wait for me as I guess they figured I'd be late. No surprise there.

Breakfast is always a hearty meal at the Malone house, but this morning's was especially so! That was because this would be Danny's main meal of the day. He would be playing football that evening, and would only want to eat a light lunch before the game. After the game, Danny and several of his buddies would probably go to a restaurant for burgers or steaks. That was their regular routine on game days.

I was simply famished. Just looking at all the food on our kitchen table made my mouth water. The hour I had spent riding Star had really built up my appetite. First I piled several potato pancakes...which Mom calls rie-belkuchens...on my plate, then I ladled applesauce on top of them, because I like applesauce on my pancakes instead of syrup. Then I added several strips of crisp bacon and a plump, golden brown wurst. There was just enough room on the side of my plate for a scoop of scrambled eggs. For a special treat, Mom had baked a streuselkuchen, a coffee cake with a topping made of butter, sugar, flour and cinnamon. Danny practically devoured the whole cake by himself, but I managed to grab one slice.

All we talked about during breakfast was the homecoming football game to be played that evening against our high school's main rival...East Kent-wood...a team that was undefeated. This game would most likely determine whether East Kentwood or our high school, the Rockford Rams, will win the conference championship. Rockford was also undefeated this season.

After breakfast, Danny and I left for school in his red '78 Olds, a used car he bought last summer from a Grand Rapids car dealer. Around our high school, it's referred to as "Danny's Hot Wheels." He's already received several speeding tickets, and one more could result in him having his driver's license suspended.

The day passed quickly and at 7:00 p.m., the stands on each side of the Rockford High School football field were packed with supporters for both teams. And, as predicted, it turned out to be a close, hard-hitting game. At halftime, the score was tied 14 to 14, and neither team scored any points in the third quarter. Halfway through the fourth quarter, Danny caught a pass and ran 45 yards for a touchdown. Once in the open, no one on the opposing team could catch him. Rockford won 21 to 14.

Danny not only has exceptional ability as a runner, but he also has big shoulders and strong arms from lifting and moving thousands of bushels of apples over the years. In addition to being a standout football player, he's also the star of the high school track team. Danny has already won letters in track his freshman, sophomore, and junior years. He's expected to win a fourth letter next spring competing in the 220-yard dash, and as the anchor for the relay team.

Sports writers with various newspapers on the west side of Michigan are speculating as to whether or not Danny will set a new state high school record in the 220-yard dash, as he tied the existing record last spring. The state track finals will be held in late May at Western Michigan University's track and field in Kalamazoo.

Unfortunately, Danny takes his God-given athletic ability for granted and avoids training…especially football practice…whenever he can get away with it. Mr. Dow, the Rockford High School football coach, claims that Danny is one of the best athletes he's ever had on the team, but all his efforts to try and get my brother to dedicate himself to a more rigorous training schedule have failed.

That's because Danny is quite satisfied with his status, and doesn't work out or train any more than he has to in order to stay on the team. For the past two years, he's gained more yards than any other halfback in our high school conference, and is being recruited by several colleges. Although he hasn't committed to any college as yet, he's confided in me that he's definitely decided on Michigan State University.

The day following the football game, Saturday, October 18, was a picture-perfect fall day…a little on the cool side with just a few, small scattered clouds in the sky. Everybody was up early…except Danny…as it was going to a long, busy day. This is the peak-selling season for our farm market. There's fresh apple cider that must be pressed, donuts to be made, and shelves that will have to be kept stocked in the farm market with various size baskets of different varieties of apples. Mom had hired several extra people to help with all this, as well as to wait on customers. She had decided that Danny should be allowed to sleep-in after the big homecoming football game and, knowing this, Danny didn't get home until early Saturday morning. After the game, he and several of his teammates celebrated with a steak dinner. Then they drank a case of beer in a local park, which I found out about later in the day.

I was also excused from working in our farm market today because I was going to the home of one of my classmates, Ukadean Scott, to help finish decorating our sophomore class float, which would be in the afternoon's Homecoming Parade in Rockford. I consider most of my classmates to be friends, but I'm especially close to eleven girls in my class because we've known each other since the first grade. Some of our other classmates refer to the twelve of us as "the dirty dozen" but I don't like that reference at all. I think someone who's envious of our friendship came up with that label. Ukadean is included in this so-called "dirty dozen", but she's an especially close friend because she lives on a farm about a mile down the road from our farm. Her mother and father are divorced, and Ukadean and her two brothers live with their father, Franklin Scott. Ukadean's mother lives in Chicago with her third husband. I've overheard my mother refer to Ukadean's mother as that "loose woman."

Mr. Scott is really a neat, nice man and a very successful farmer. During World War II, he was a tank commander in Europe. He was captured by the Germans and put in a prisoner-of-war camp. Somehow he managed to escape, and made his way back to the allied lines and eventually rejoined his unit. He was discharged from the army as a major, and has lots of medals that he won for bravery. When he got out of the army, he bought his 120-acre farm and became our neighbor. However, Mr. Scott actually farms more than a 1,000-acres. He rents land from other landowners and farmers. He mainly grows special wheat that is ground into flour used for making baked goods, as well as navy beans and soybeans. The Scott home is surrounded by big silos and a number of storage barns. This is where he keeps his tractors and all the other equipment he uses for his farming operation. My dad claims that Mr. Scott can fix any kind of machinery, and on a few occasions, he has helped my father fix something that dad couldn't repair himself.

As soon as mom and I put the leftover breakfast food away, and the dishes in the dishwasher, I got my bike out of the garage and pedaled it to the Scott farm. Lots of my classmates were already present, and when I arrived…Ukadean, Cynthia Smith, Wendy Van Raalte and Patty Veldheers…all greeted me virtually in unison by shouting, "Colleen!"

Even though the five of us were together at the football game last evening, our first priority was to find out if something has happened in the meantime that we don't all know about yet. Such things as, "Who else has a date for the dance tonight? Who are you riding with to get there? How late are your parents going to let you stay?" Very important issues to 15 and 16-year-old girls!

As soon as our little gabfest was finished, we turned our attention to our class float. It was really impressive! On Mr. Scott's flatbed trailer, which was attached to his big Dodge Ram pickup truck, was a gigantic pumpkin about eight-feet-high. He and several boys in my class made this pumpkin by tightly stretching painter's drop cloths over a pumpkin-shaped frame. Then they spray-painted it a bright orange color. The stem they added to the top helped make it look like a real pumpkin. We all agreed that if it were a real pumpkin, it would be in the Guinness Book of World Records! It was one "cool" float.

On opposite sides of this gigantic pumpkin were faces painted in the simple style that most people use when they carve their pumpkins at Halloween. One face had a turned-down, sad-looking mouth, while the face on the opposite side of the pumpkin had big happy grin. This was to carry out the theme we were using for our float…"Don't worry, be happy."

The entire pumpkin sat on a pivot so that a member of our class can stand at the front of the float and slowly turn it around. That way, the people on either side of the street along the parade route will be able to see both the happy and the sad face of the huge pumpkin as it rotates.

All that was really left for us to do this morning was the final decorating. This consisted of adding pom-poms, hanging a crepe-paper skirt to hide the underside of the float, and painting the signs to be attached on each side of the float reading, "Don't worry, be happy!"

This afternoon, when the float is in the parade, there will be two couples dressed in Raggedy Ann and Andy costumes standing at the back of the float. They will toss Kraft caramels to the spectators along the parade route. These Kraft caramels will be in two bushel baskets…each mounted on top of a three-foot-high base, one on each side of the float. The back of these bases is open to provide a place to store extra bags of caramels.

What a float! Everybody was excited because we believed we had the winner this year. The homecoming parade was to be held that afternoon, starting at 3 p.m. from Rockford High School. Just prior to that, the judges would select the winning float. Our Parent-Teachers Association sponsors the competition and the class with the best float receives $300.00, which goes to the class treasury. Second place gets $200.00, third place receives $100.00 and fourth place wins $50.00. This is a big deal at my high school and winning this competition gives you bragging rights, at least for a year, as to which class has the most "school spirit".

It was almost noon and our float was finished and ready to roll. Everything was done! We all left the Scott farm to go home and have lunch, so that we could be at the high school by 2:30 p.m.

I rushed home on my bike to grab something to eat. Danny was now up and dressed and I made sandwiches for the two of us, though for him this was both his breakfast and lunch.

"What's the theme for your float?" Danny asked while we were eating our sandwiches.

"Don't worry, be happy," I replied.

This was the first time we had talked about the class floats, and I was glad my brother was interested in knowing what my class was doing. He seemed impressed when I told him about the huge pumpkin, and how it turned on a pivot and how we would be tossing caramels to people along the street.

Then I asked my brother, "What's the theme for the senior float?"

"I think it has something to do with world peace," Danny answered, "but I'm not sure." He hadn't been involved with his class float because he was on the football team. As soon as we finished eating lunch, Danny and I left to go to the high school. When we arrived, there was a mass of cars and people around our school. Danny finally found a place to park on a side street since the school's big parking lot was already full.

"When the parade's over I'll meet you here at my car," Danny informed me. "We're going to have to hurry home for dinner, and then I'll drop you off at the school before I pick up Monica."

Danny's date for the homecoming dance was Monica Fouchey, the Homecoming Queen. Monica and my brother had been going together for about a year now, and some of their friends think they'll probably be married someday. I really like and admire Monica because she's not only very pretty, but she's also a good athlete. She can swim faster than any girl in our high school, and is captain of the girl's swim team. Monica is also great at diving, and when she dives off the high board, everybody stops to watch her. Monica and my brother have quite a lot in common when it comes to sports, and they usually get a lot of attention when they're together as a couple.

Off in the distance I saw the huge, fake pumpkin on our float and I rushed there to see if our class won the prize for the best float. We did! All my classmates were gathered around the float and were excited and delighted. "We won! We're number one!" was being shouted by lots of my classmates. Usually the senior class wins this competition, but not this year. Out float was far and away the most impressive because of its size and I learned that the judges thought that our theme…"Don't worry, be happy"…was a terrific idea.

I saw Mr. Scott…Ukadean's dad…standing in the bed of his pickup truck and he had a big grin on his face. He seemed to be especially proud that the sophomore class won. The real truth of the matter is that, without his help, we probably would not have won. He did most of the work in building the frame for the pumpkin and the pivot on which it turned. Besides that, it was his flat-bed trailer that was the base of the float and he pulled the float in the parade with his truck.

Promptly at 3:00 p.m. our high school marching band started playing, which meant it was time for the parade to start. The band leads the parade, and the sophomore class float gets to follow right behind the band because we won first prize in the float competition.

Behind our float came the senior, junior and freshman class floats and they were followed by two school buses carrying our football team. Most of the football players were leaning out the open bus windows talking or shouting at other students clustered around the buses. Next in line in the parade was the homecoming queen, Monica Fouchey, and she was sitting on the top of the back seat of an open convertible. Monica looked as gorgeous as a movie star in a dark, peacock-blue satin gown with a sparkling crown on her head. The rest of the parade consisted of a dozen or more antique and classic cars…and bringing up the very rear was a fire engine. The fire truck's shrill siren was blasting away, and I was sure glad that it was at the end of the parade.

What a lot of fun it was being part of a parade! There were at least sixty sophomores walking beside or in back of our float. First we wound our way through a residential area, then down Rockford's main street returning to the high school through a different residential area. There were lots of people along the parade route waving or calling to us as we passed by. The two Raggedy Ann's and Raggedy Andy's on our float were busy tossing caramels—especially to the kids yelling, "*Me! Me! Me!*"

As soon as the parade was over, I ran back to Danny's car. Luckily, I got there before he did. As soon as Danny arrived, we went right home to have dinner and to get ready to go to the homecoming dance, which would be held that evening in the high school gymnasium.

At 7:45 p.m., Danny dropped me off at the high school, and he went to pick up Monica. Lots of students, as well as recent graduates, were already present in the gym, which was festively decorated with streamers and balloons. The music was so loud that you had to shout to be heard. I tried talking with friends, but soon started dancing with different boys in my class as well as several older boys that were either juniors or seniors. Danny found me during the evening and true to his promise, he danced one dance with me. That made me especially happy! I think the world of my big brother, and I believe he is proud that I'm his little sister. I seem to be the one person Danny can talk with in confidence, and as a result, he shares a lot of his concerns and thoughts with me.

Danny drove me to the homecoming dance, but I had to find someone else to drive me home. I arranged to get a ride home with Ukadean's dad and at midnight, Ukadean and I met Mr. Scott in front of the high school. When we arrived at my home, I thanked Mr. Scott for the ride as well as for his help building our class float. "Mr. Scott, you're a really special dad so far as I'm concerned," I told him, as I climbed down out of his big pickup truck.

The next day…Sunday, October 19, 1980…was a delightful, weather-perfect fall day, which meant that lots of people would be coming to Malone's Farm Market to buy apples, pumpkins, donuts and cider. From 1:00 p.m. to 5:00 p.m., there was a steady flow of store traffic and I could hardly wait to see the "closed" sign put on the front door at 5:00 p.m., because that meant my 16th birthday party would soon begin.

At 5:30, my eleven special girlfriends started arriving. The twelve of us ("the so called dirty dozen") have been celebrating our birthdays together since we were in the first or second grade. It just wouldn't seem like a birthday unless we celebrated together.

Dad soon had our gas grill in the backyard fired up while everyone else gathered in the kitchen. Our spacious, comfortable farmhouse was built nearly eighty years ago. Over the years, it has been renovated several times and enlarged, with the kitchen being the largest room in the house. Up to 20 people can be seated comfortably at the kitchen table, and a serving counter divides the food preparation area from the table. Usually the food is placed directly on the table, but when there's a bunch of people like today, the food is served buffet style from the counter.

Mom and I got up earlier than usual this morning to prepare all the food for my party. We made a big batch of German potato salad, two-dozen deviled eggs, a green bean casserole and a huge cake with a carrot cake batter…my favorite!

The only thing already on the kitchen table was my birthday cake. Mom put an apple crate upside down in the middle of the table and covered it with a red tablecloth. Sitting on top of this base was my beautifully decorated cake with

16 candles spread around the edge. It made a colorful and neat centerpiece for the table.

Dinner was soon ready. Dad brought in a large tray heaped high with big, juicy burgers. We all lined up, filled our plates and found a place to sit around the kitchen table. I was so hungry I think I could have eaten my burger raw! When we finished eating, everybody sang "Happy Birthday" to me. Then I blew out the candles on my cake, closed my eyes and made a wish. Then I cut it into 16 pieces. As I put each piece of cake on a plate, Danny added a scoop of vanilla ice cream. It tasted great along with a glass of fresh apple cider. Nobody was going to leave my birthday dinner hungry or thirsty!

Then I had the fun of opening my birthday presents. None of my friends were allowed to spend more than $10.00 for a birthday gift. That's a firm rule that we have. Even so, they came up with a lot of neat things, which I really appreciated:

> Ukadean Scott—$10.00 worth of McDonalds gift certificates
> Wendy VanRaalte—Book of poems
> Patty Veldheers—Earrings
> Cynthia Ossenfort—$10.00 worth of passes for the Rockford movie theater
> Mary Lou Keyes—Scarf with kittens in its design
> Sara Johnson—$10.00 gift certificate for use at a local beauty salon
> Susan Seaton—Fold-up umbrella
> Heather Miller—A pen and pencil set
> Kathleen Yates—Stuffed animal (bear)
> Joyce Kallman—Book for writing personal notes
> Amanda Burkhardt—Cologne

At 10:00 p.m. my mother announced that it was time for everybody to go home. "All of you have to be in school early tomorrow morning and you girls need your beauty rest," Mom proclaimed. "Thank you for coming and for making this a really special birthday for Colleen," she added, while shepherding everybody towards the front door.

There was a chorus of "Thank you" and "See you tomorrow, Colleen," from my friends as they departed. Most of my girlfriends have already celebrated their 16th birthday, and have their driver's licenses. Seven of them drove to my house, and the other four got a ride home with one of them. I stood on the front porch watching seven cars pull out on the road. I thought about how much my life and my girl friends lives were changing now that we were 16-

years-old. Being able to drive a car somewhere by your self was simply awesome!

It was Monday, October 20, 1980…I was 16 years old today! It was a regular day at school and I had to keep telling myself to pay attention in class. I couldn't help thinking about all the things that had happened this past weekend…starting with riding my horse Star last Friday morning. This had been the most exciting weekend of my life.

When I got home from school, I helped restock our farm market. Then Mom and I prepared dinner. Papa John joined us, and when dinner was over I received some more birthday presents…a new winter coat from Mom and Dad, and a beautiful sweater from Danny. Actually, Mom and I had picked out the coat and the sweater several weeks ago when we went shopping together. Aunt Amy, my dad's younger sister, and Uncle Joe, her husband, sent me a bracelet. They live in Baltimore and they have four young children. We only see them when they come to visit every couple of years. There were also some birthday cards for me to open and most included either a ten- or twenty-dollar bill. These were from Grandmother and Grandfather Goetzinger, as well as various cousins.

Then Papa John slid a small box across the table to me. When I opened the box, I started to cry. It was my grandmother Mary's engagement ring. Papa John explained, "Your grandmother said to give it to you someday, and I thought today was a good day to do it."

I ran around the table and put my arms around my grandfather, hugging him as tightly as I could. "Thank you, Papa," I said and I meant it from the bottom of my heart. "I'll never forget my 16th birthday!"

Autumn is an incredibly busy time at the Malone Farm and Orchard. Apples and crops must be harvested and either sold or stored for future sale, and the farm market is open from Labor Day through Christmas. And, with Danny and me in high school and both of us involved in outside activities, our lives are truly hectic. It's really hard to find time to get everything done, even though it's early to bed and early to rise seven days a week. Fortunately, we have some dependable people to help with the many chores, and Papa John takes a big load off my father particularly by supervising the migrant workers that pick the apples.

Papa John and my father are counting on Danny taking over some day, but Danny's confided in me that he doesn't want to be the fifth generation to own and operate our farm and orchard. He's hoping he can play on a professional football team when he's finished college, and then get into the business world.

When Danny and I talk about our future plans, he always says, "You like farming more than I do, Colleen, why don't you take it over?"

Following the homecoming game against our archrival East Kentwood, the Rockford High School football team won all three of the games remaining on its schedule. As a result, Rockford placed first in its conference but failed to win the State Class A High School Championship. My brother scored two or more touchdowns in each of the last three games, and was named to the All-State Offensive Football Team by several newspapers. Danny gained more than a 100 yards in every game he played.

Football season ended, but the days continued to absolutely fly by and fall quickly evolved into winter. During January, February, and early March, our family spent several weekends in northern Michigan. Danny and I usually skied at Boyne Highlands near Petoskey, while Mom and Dad did a little cross-country skiing. But they mostly "chilled out," relaxing with friends or catching up on their reading. These were good family times together, and some of Danny's and my Rockford High School classmates were also on the ski slopes or calling in the evening just to talk.

In the spring of 1981, Danny did quite well in the high school track meets. He took first place in every 220-yard dash event and the relay team won all but one of its races. The one loss was due to a dropped baton. When the state high school track meet was held at Western Michigan University, Danny again tied the state record for the 220-yard dash but didn't set a new record as several sports writers had speculated he would do. Danny wasn't especially disappointed, as he felt he had done the best he could, all things considered. Not only did he have to keep up his schoolwork, but he also had to help with the never-ending work that has to be done with a large farm and orchard. He certainly had a lot more activity and pressure to contend with than most high school seniors.

That spring though, something happened that was quite embarrassing for Danny as well as for the Malone family. After the senior prom, Danny decided to take Monica for a ride in his car around the local Country Club golf course. He had never done this before in his own car, but he had been a passenger in a car the previous spring that was driven around the golf course by one of his buddies. Danny's buddy drove down the fairways, spinning his car on the wet grass by accelerating the car then turning the steering wheel sharply to the left or right. They thought it was very exciting and, fortunately, they managed to do this without getting caught or doing any damage to the golf course fairways.

Danny found the service drive open to the Rockford Country Club golf course, and took off down one of the fairways on the wet grass. As soon as he reached about 40 miles per hour, he hit the brakes and jerked the steering wheel to the right, which caused his car to spin around in a circle several times on the wet grass. Very exciting, I suppose, but it sure didn't turn out well. On one of the fairways, when he put his car into a spin, Danny unfortunately didn't see a deep sand trap in time…and his red Olds ended up in the trap, sinking into the sand. Danny tried to drive the car out, but the side of the trap was too steep and his car was axle-deep in the sand. It would take a tow truck to get the car out.

Danny…still in the tux he wore to the senior prom and Monica in her formal gown and high heel shoes…started walking back to the service gate to go look for help when they saw a police car coming towards them with its lights flashing. A homeowner who lived next to the golf course had noticed the headlights of Danny's car when he was driving around the golf course, and the spinning headlights had especially caught his attention. The man called the police, and now a patrol car had Danny and Monica in its headlights.

Danny was lucky that he didn't get a ticket. And, fortunately, the police officer didn't go and check the inside of Danny's car, or he would have found several empty beer cans under the front seat. The officer recognized Danny, and assumed that the Malones were members of the Country Club, which we are not.

Danny asked the officer if he would please drive him and Monica home. However, the officer couldn't drive them to their homes, as he had to respond to another situation. Instead he called for a taxi to come pick them up. This was probably a better course of action than calling our dad to come and rescue them, as it was approaching 2:30 Sunday morning. Another half-hour passed before the taxi arrived. After dropping Monica off at her house, it was after 4:30 a.m. when Danny finally crawled into his bed. He didn't sleep well and he was up, dressed, and in the kitchen by 7:30 a.m. to tell dad about his misadventure following the senior prom.

Dad listened quietly as Danny explained what happened. Dad kept his cool and after a quick…but silent…breakfast, the two of them left for the Rockford Country Club to wait for the arrival of a tow truck. Clarence Calvin, a long-time friend of Dad's, operated a garage in town and he had several tow trucks. Dad called him before he and Danny left for the club and they arranged to meet Mr. Calvin in the parking lot at the Country Club.

After Dad and Danny had waited almost an hour in the parking lot for the tow truck to arrive, they finally decided to walk to the fairway where Danny's car was stuck in the sand trap, thinking that perhaps Mr. Calvin had already gone there.

Soon after Dad and Danny got to the car, a reporter and photographer from *The Rockford Times* showed up...but still no tow truck.

Danny refused to answer any questions or to have his photo taken with his car, but the photographer took a picture of the car anyway. The photo appeared on the front page of *The Rockford Times* the next morning. It was a side view of Danny's red Olds showing the wheels stuck deep in the sand trap. The caption for the photo read, "Danny Malone scores another touchdown on a golf course."

When the tow truck finally arrived, Siebert Medley was driving it. He was a high school dropout, but Danny recognized Siebert because they had gone to grade school together. It so happened that Mr. Calvin was unable to drive the tow truck himself due to a family emergency, so he called in Siebert, who worked part-time at his garage.

In trying to locate Danny's car, Siebert had driven all over the golf course, and had even driven over several putting greens. To make matters worse, it had rained early Sunday morning and the tow truck left deep ruts in a number of fairways and huge trenches in several putting greens. In addition, while pulling Danny's car out of the sand trap, Siebert smashed a small tree, crushed several shrubs, and drove four sprinkler heads deep into the ground. He unfortunately did a lot of unnecessary damage to the golf course. Siebert knew nothing about golf, and didn't think much about any of this until the golf club announced several weeks later that they were going to sue him, the Calvin Garage and the Malones for $16,500.00, to recover the cost of repairing the course.

In early July, when it was time for Danny to appear in court, mom went with him, along with our attorney, Douglas Graham.

As soon as the court proceedings started, Mr. Graham began arguing that the tow truck company, which was owned by Mr. Calvin, should be responsible for the damage to the golf course because the driver of the tow truck could have driven in the rough or on cart paths rather than in the middle of the fairways. He especially had no business driving across putting greens.

Mr. Calvin was present in the courtroom and he stood up asking if he could please say something. The judge recognized him, and Mr. Calvin admitted that the driver of his tow truck had not used good judgment. He said that Siebert didn't realize how valuable golf courses are, and that he had filed a claim with his insurance company asking them to pay for the damage done to the fairways and the greens.

Mr. Calvin's insurance company had notified him just that morning that they would pay $14,000.00 of the $16,500.00 the country club claimed it would cost to put the golf course back in the condition it was in before this ridiculous incident.

What a relief it was for Mom when she heard this! A big smile crossed her face, and I'm sure she felt like kissing Mr. Calvin out of gratitude.

After paying Danny's court costs of $450.00, Mom and Danny left the courthouse in downtown Grand Rapids and returned home. I never learned…nor did I ever ask…how much we paid Mr. Graham. The country club accepted the $14,000.00 as a settlement for the lawsuit mainly because Monica's father, Richard Fouchey, served on the board of the club and talked them into accepting that amount.

This episode of Danny's was obviously ridiculous, yet, I never heard Mom or Dad criticize, scold or blame Danny for trespassing on the Country Club property, or for driving his car in a reckless manner. I found this fact quite interesting and wondered if this would have been their reaction had I been the one who had ended up in a sand trap on the Country Club golf course.

Prior to the court date, Siebert Medley was occasionally discussed while we were having lunch or dinner. Mom called poor Siebert the "Village idiot", and claimed "That the guy was a few sandwiches short of a picnic." Dad was a little kinder, referring to him as a "Nitwit" and saying "That his elevator didn't reach the top floor." I didn't think these remarks were necessary or appropriate, and was disappointed when my mother and father said them. I could only conclude that, whatever their opinion of Danny's escapade, they either kept it to themselves or only discussed it between the two of them. Danny, though, was mainly concerned that this episode might affect the football scholarship he had received from Michigan State University. Fortunately, it didn't. The people at MSU were probably never aware of the incident.

Danny left in early August for football practice and his first year at MSU. Before he left, he and Monica spent a lot of time together, as she was going to attend Northwestern University, the college her mother and father had attended. I couldn't help but wonder whether or not this separation might eventually result in an end to their relationship.

Time would tell!

CHAPTER 2

The College Years

Football practice at MSU was quite different from what Danny had experienced in high school. The players were bigger, stronger and certainly more dedicated...especially to physical training. He soon learned that he was going to be designated a red shirt freshman, which would extend his eligibility to play football. This was done because there were other backs that were either just about as fast as, or bigger than, Danny on both the offensive and defensive teams. And they had several years of college playing experience. Danny was disappointed of course that he probably would not be participating in any games his freshman year...unless several backs on the team were injured. Obviously, if that happened, it would change his status immediately.

In the third week of practice, Danny suffered a broken collarbone and two broken fingers on his left hand during a scrimmage game. While he didn't want to get injured, it did enable him to get a reprieve from practice. Knowing Danny, I suspect he took full advantage of this situation, and stretched his recuperation a week longer than really necessary. He did not relish football practice in high school, and I suspect he carried that attitude on to college.

East Lansing is less than two hours away by car from where we live. Even so, it was difficult for Mom, Dad or me to get away on Saturdays to attend a football game at MSU with the apple harvest and farm market operation requiring our full attention. Early in November though, the apple harvest was finished. Mom arranged to have several dependable people take charge of our farm market the second Saturday in November so that she, Dad, Papa John and I could go to East Lansing to watch Michigan State play football. This was our first visit to MSU since Danny had gone away to college, and I had never been to a college football game.

When I walked into the Spartan football stadium, all I could say was, "Wow, this is just awesome!" I was really impressed with the size of the stadium, which was already packed with thousands of people when we arrived.

It was good to see Danny again, and he seemed really happy to see his family. After the game, he showed us his room in the ivy-covered dorm he lived in. Then we went to a nice restaurant in Lansing where the five of us had dinner together.

Dad was in a good mood…especially after drinking several bottles of beer. He started telling about his life as a student at MSU, and he told us about a few things he did in college that we'd never heard about before. I noticed Mom's raised eyebrows, and I could tell by the expression on her face that she'd never heard about some of these antics before either. We were all surprised to learn that Dad had once participated in a panty raid on a sorority house. After he made this confession, he seemed a little embarrassed, and he quickly explained that this was a popular activity when he was a student at MSU, and lots of guys were involved. So he claimed! I also realized for the first time where the devilish streak that Danny sometimes exhibited came from…*it came from his father!*

Danny came home for Thanksgiving. Except for dinner on Thanksgiving Day, we didn't see him much as he spent most of his time that weekend with Monica and several of his "buds" from high school.

Our lives…mine, my parents, as well as my friends…all seemed to be guided or governed by time. A time to sleep, a time to wake, a time to go to school, a time to eat, a time to study, a time to work, and very little time to play. Time delineated our existence. I got up by 6:00 a.m. every morning, had breakfast promptly at 7:00, and then it was off to high school. Several times a week after school I managed to find time to ride my horse, but the rest of the time I studied for my classes, did my homework assignments, and helped my mother with the housework and preparing our meals. Most Saturday and Sunday afternoons, I waited on customers in our farm market, and I was glad when Christmas arrived because that meant the store would close until the next selling season. Hallelujah!

We spent some weekends up north during the winter months. Mom and Dad talked every year about going to Florida in January or February, but they never did. Danny joined us one weekend at Boyne Mountain near Petoskey, and I really enjoyed the time that we spent skiing together.

My mother finally gave me permission to date boys, but this was limited to Friday and Saturday nights only, and I had to be home by midnight. I never wanted to test my mother by staying out past the midnight deadline, as I knew she really meant it. The consequences of breaking the rules would have meant being grounded for several weekends, and I certainly didn't want to risk having that happen!

Danny came home for a six-week summer vacation before he had to return to East Lansing to start football practice again in early August. While he was home, he spent time helping with the cleanup of the brush left in the orchard from pruning the trees. Apple trees require some pruning every year. It's necessary to open up the foliage so that light and air can get to the center of the tree. Lateral limbs have to be cut back and trimmed so that they are able to support the weight of the apples, as long limbs can easily break. Then there are the suckers, the shoots that grow straight up from a limb taking strength from the tree, which must be removed. All these branches, which are trimmed off the trees, fall to the ground and have to be picked up and run through the chipping machine.

Our chipper is a scary machine. You put brush very carefully into a chute. As soon as the brush reaches the grinding mechanism, the powerful blades grind it into little chips. These chips shoot out the back end of the chipper and get collected in a big enclosed wagon. When the wagon is full, we pull it to the back of the orchard with a tractor, and the chips are added to a huge compost pile made up of these decaying chips.

I've lost work gloves when they got caught on a limb that I placed in the chute of the chipper, and Danny once lost a wristwatch that was pulled off his wrist when it snagged on a limb he was putting in the chipper. I still remember the loud "whang" when his watch hit the blades of the grinder. His wristwatch sprayed out the back of the chipper in tiny pieces.

During his freshman year at MSU, Danny met and dated a number of girls. He still had a relationship with Monica, but his interest in her seemed to be fading. A case of out-of-sight, out-of-mind, I guess. They did get together a few times while he was home for the summer, but he also went out with a Grand Rapids girl that he met at MSU. Danny also started playing poker…once or twice a week…for nickel and dime stakes. He was apparently a pretty good poker player, because he told me he usually won a few bucks. Maybe it was just beginner's luck.

Time quickly passed that summer. In early August, Danny returned to East Lansing for football practice and the start of his sophomore year at Michigan State. A few weeks later I started my senior year at Rockford High School.

We talked with Danny on the phone once or twice a week, and learned that he had been assigned to defense, to play either a cornerback or free safety position. Danny stands six feet, four inches tall, and weighs around 190 pounds. At MSU, there were other backs that were heavier, and for short distances, could run as fast as Danny. The coaches decided to convert Danny to a defensive position to utilize his speed and height to either intercept or block passes. Danny, though, didn't seem enthusiastic about playing defense. In high school he was considered a football "hero" because he regularly scored touchdowns and usually gained 100 yards or more as the ball carrier in every game he played. This got reported in the local newspapers and on the local radio and television sports programs, which made Danny a kind of celebrity in our community. He enjoyed that recognition, and he apparently thought that playing on the defensive team would not only under-utilize his ability, but would also result in less recognition. Particularly since he still had hopes of becoming a professional football player after he finished college.

Another factor...and a big one...was his tackling. Danny was not a hard-hitting tackler when he played football in high school. Rather than lowering his head and tackling his opponent legs, he was like a leopard catching its prey. He usually grabbed a player around his waist or shoulders and pulled him down. And he did it very successfully.

In spite of his initial reaction, Danny adjusted to his new position as a cornerback and did quite well his first year playing football at Michigan State. During the season he broke up a lot of pass plays, intercepted a number of passes and ran two interceptions and two fumbles back for touchdowns. He thus received considerably more recognition than he had first anticipated.

He also managed to get through his sophomore year without serious injury. Near the end of the season though, in a game with Minnesota, he was knocked out briefly when he tackled a big fullback, and was carried off the field. He stopped Minnesota from scoring, but in doing so suffered a mild concussion. This kept him out of the game the following weekend against Northwestern University in Evanston, Illinois. This was disappointing for Danny, as he wanted Monica to see him play in a college football game.

My 18th birthday on October 20, 1982 came and went without any party. There was a birthday cake of course, and presents from Mom, Dad and Papa John. Birthday celebrations that included my close girl friends...the "dirty dozen"…were now a thing of the past. I hated to admit it, but I missed those parties!

Ukadean was still my closest friend and confidant. We talked on the phone frequently and got together sometimes to study and to help each other with our homework. It made a difference because we were both near the top of our class in grade points. I helped her with certain courses, and she helped me with some subjects that I found difficult.

I was also giving a lot of thought to college. Where did I want to go to college, and what should I major in?

The past two years we had not had a good apple crop…in fact, we harvested only about half of what was considered a normal crop year. This was mainly due to very cool weather in the spring, which kept most of the bees in their hives. Consequently, there was not a good pollination of the apple blossoms, and this resulted in far fewer apples on the trees. Hearing Mom and Dad complain about the significant reduction in our income caused me to decide to stay at home and commute to college. I think Mom and Dad were relieved when I told them that I had decided to live at home and drive to and from Holland, Michigan to attend Hope College.

As soon as Papa John learned of my decision, he said he wanted to buy me a new Chevrolet coupe for a high school graduation present so that I would have dependable transportation to and from classes at Hope College…about 40 miles southwest of Rockford.

Ukadean was really thrilled when I told her that I was planning to enroll at Hope College as we had discussed this possibility. She screamed when I told her and she said, "Colleen, guess what?"

"What do you mean, guess what?" I answered.

"I've decided that Hope College is my first choice, too," explained Ukadean.

"Wow, we'll be able to ride to and from Holland together, and maybe we'll even be in some of the same classes." I said.

Ukadean looked at me for a few seconds with a quizzical look on her face. Then she surprised me by saying she was planning to live in a dorm at the College. She hadn't really considered staying at home and driving back and forth to college every day…even though it wasn't a long distance.

I then started pleading with her to please think about it, as she could ride with me in the new Chevy Papa John was going to give me as a graduation present. She said she'd think about it, but it was obvious she had no interest in my offer.

Spring of 1983 was a significant time in my life…with high school graduation being the main event. Our senior trip consisted of a long weekend in Chicago. The "dirty dozen" made a feeble attempt to hang together when we toured various museums, but boys were busting up that old gang of mine. The class chaperones had their hands full trying to make sure that nothing more serious than holding hands took place.

I accepted the first invitation that I got for my date to the senior prom. Later I got several more invitations, but my date, Steve Hurley, was fine with me. I'd been on dates with Steve before and he was fun to be with and had a good sense of humor. I never really wanted to have a steady boyfriend in high school. Seeing my brother and Monica going steady their junior and senior years was not the example I wanted to follow. I found it more interesting to date different boys, and luckily there were plenty of good-looking, really neat guys in my class. Two of them asked me…after several dates…to go steady with them. But I nicely explained that I didn't want to get into that serious a relationship. I must have handled it well, as I remained friends with them. I considered it a nice compliment that they would want to go steady with me…and I told them so.

In late May, Ukadean and I went to Holland to visit Hope College and to enroll in classes for the fall term of 1983. My Mom went with us. I wasn't really sure just what I wanted to do when I finished college, but either a career in business or teaching appealed to me.

Chemistry was one of my favorite classes in high school, and I thought perhaps I could someday teach that subject. So I enrolled in college level chemistry, a biology class, and several other courses. When we finished enrolling, Mom kind of shook her head and said, "Colleen, you sure have given yourself a full plate. I hope you haven't taken on so much that you don't have time to have a little fun too."

Hope College is a four-year, liberal arts undergraduate college with an impressive history. Settlers from the Netherlands founded Holland in 1847, and four years later they established a school to meet the needs of the young colony. This pioneer school evolved into the Holland Academy, which was chartered as Hope College in 1866. While it is affiliated with the Reformed Church in America, and has a great religious heritage, the student body consists of diverse church affiliations. My family and I are Lutherans because my mother made that decision when she and my father got married. Ukadean Scott and her family are Methodists.

A few weeks after Ukadean and I enrolled at Hope College some really incredible things happened. First, Ukadean's oldest brother George approached Papa John about buying his farm. George was engaged to be married, and was going to continue working with his father after the wedding. George was looking for a place to live close to his dad's farm...and if he could add more acreage for them to farm, so much the better.

Papa John had stopped raising cattle and had sold all of his horses except one. The one he kept, of course, was my horse Star. After several weeks of negotiating, Papa John and George agreed on a price. My grandfather had been seriously thinking about selling his 80-acre farm for some time, as he wanted to move to a senior residence in Holland, actually quite close to Hope College, where several of his friends lived. Now this was going to happen.

This marked a turning point in my life too, as I now had to decide what to do about Star. I knew there would be few opportunities for me to ride Star when I started college, so I decided to sell my horse. It was not an easy decision, but it was the right one, all things considered. When the new owner drove away with Star in a horse trailer I felt terrible. The tears flowed and I was down in the dumps for a week.

Then, in late July, the other shoe dropped and, as they say...*it was really a big shoe.* A developer from Grand Rapids approached my Mom and Dad about purchasing 580 acres of our farm for a golf course and housing development. It would make us rich if we accepted the offer. Selling this land, on which we raised various crops, would reduce our family farm to 300 acres, but we would still have the orchards, our home and the farm market. Danny was home from college when this happened, and he urged Mom and Dad to take the offer. He made it emphatically clear to them...for the first time really...that he had other plans for his life, which did not include being a farmer and raising apples.

Dad responded favorably to the developer, saying that we would consider selling the 580 acres of farmland. A series of meetings followed. Our attorney, Mr. Graham, and Mr. Billings, an accountant, became part of our negotiation team, as there were a number of issues to be considered. One issue that Dad insisted had to be resolved before any final purchase agreement was signed, was the use of chemicals for spraying the apple trees. We could not have homeowners objecting or possibly taking legal action to stop the spraying, so it was essential that there be a buffer zone between the orchard and the homes to be built. While the developer didn't see the spraying of the apple trees as a problem, my father and our attorney certainly did. This became something of a sticking point because it would make it necessary for the developer to change the preliminary plans for the layout of the golf course around which the homes would be built. Dad wanted the golf course, rather than homes, located right next to the orchard.

And so the negotiations went on for months. Danny returned to East Lansing in early August, and a few weeks later I started commuting to Hope College…driving to and from Holland by myself, as Ukadean had decided to live in a dorm. Halfway through my first term though…with the sale of the 580 acres progressing…Mom and Dad urged me to get a room in a dorm. With winter approaching, they were concerned about my driving through the snow and sleet storms, which we get plenty of every year in our area. These storms sweep in off Lake Michigan. Fortunately, a room became available in the same dorm that Ukadean was living in, and I took it. My car stayed home, but I moved to Holland.

Meanwhile, at Michigan State, the football season was not going at all well for Danny. In mid-September he suffered a serious knee injury, which required surgery. This put him on the injured reserve team. It was really doubtful if he would get to play much at all during his junior year at MSU…his second year on the team.

When he came home for Thanksgiving, Danny seemed different somehow. I noticed that there were a few times when he seemed upbeat and happy, but most of the time he was unusually quiet. Not at all like the brother I knew. He apparently had a lot on his mind. He was still wearing a brace on his knee, and he used his crutches occasionally when his knee really bothered him.

After we finished our Thanksgiving dinner and the table was cleared and the leftover food was put away, Danny and I sat at the kitchen table and talked for several hours. We discussed our schools, our courses and teachers, and we talked about a lot of little things that simply popped into our heads. He told me that he was able to spend more time studying since he didn't have to practice or play football. As a result his grades were improving, and to my pleasant surprise he said he was thinking seriously about getting an MBA degree after he got his Bachelors Degree in Business. He speculated that if the deal went through to sell a big section of our farm, there should be plenty of money available to pay for both his and my college educations. We really had a good talk because we were both very interested in what the other person had to say. And, best of all, I really felt close to my brother again.

On Saturday morning, I walked past Danny's room on my way downstairs to have breakfast. The door to Danny's room was ajar, and I could see him sitting at his desk next to a window. He was lost in thought…just staring out the window at the orchard.

I knocked on the door and said, "Hey bro, what you thinking about?"

He waved his arm, signaling me to come join him, and I pulled a chair up next to his desk. For ten seconds or so Danny just sat there looking at me…then he asked, "Why do I really play football? I've been asking myself that question a lot lately."

"Why, I always thought you really liked playing," was the first thing that came to my mind.

"Well that's true. Sometimes it's really exciting. I do like the competition involved in the game, and it's always fun when your team wins. But it seems like everybody has always expected me to play football—my friends, the coaches, my family, Monica, just about everybody I come into contact with—and I wonder if I'm actually doing it mainly for me, or is this something that I'm expected to do? It takes a lot of dedication and training, and I'm not sure that I want to maintain that commitment any more. Maybe the injuries, and especially my knee surgery, have put things a lot more in focus for me. Football has really dominated my life for the past six years, and I've reached the point where I realize there's a lot more to life than playing games. I'm just not sure I want football to keep on being the main focus of my life, and I wonder if my dream of someday being a professional football player is really a possibility? That's why I've been giving so much thought to it lately."

Now I realized why Danny had seemed somehow different this weekend. He was doing a lot of soul searching, trying to decide what he was going to do in the future. I looked around Danny's room. It reminded me somehow of a museum. There were shelves full of trophies he'd won playing football and winning track meets. The rest of the wall space was covered with frames filled with photographs or with newspaper stories about Danny's sports achievements. He had accomplished so much in just a few years, and now he was seriously considering taking a different road than the one he had been traveling.

I didn't know exactly what to say. I knew Danny had to make up his own mind, so I simply and sincerely said to him, "Danny I love you, and I'm proud of you. Whatever you decide to do I'm still going to love you and I'll always be proud of you."

Danny responded with that big wonderful smile of his, and said, "Let's go have some breakfast. I've got to get back to school and if I hang around here much longer Dad's going to put me to work doing something. There are a lot of things I have to do before I start classes again on Monday."

He seemed relieved that he had got this out in the open. I could tell it was really weighing on his mind as to whether or not he was going to continue playing football at Michigan State. I felt pleased that I was the one that he was sharing his concerns with, and he knew that I would keep what he told me in confidence.

Early in 1984, the sale of the 580 acres of our farm to the Grand Rapids developer was completed. We learned that this was really prized property for developing. The Rogue River flows along one side of the land, and the rolling terrain would provide many beautiful sites for homes. And, since we are only a few miles north of Grand Rapids, there would be a lot of potential sales of homes to people who worked there, but wanted to live in the country. The final price agreed on for the land was $11,400.00 an acre. This meant that the Malone family would receive more than $6,600,000.00...a colossal amount of money. We were rich beyond our dreams and my comprehension. Dad said he felt like he had won the Michigan Lottery. Plus, we still owned 300 acres, on which was located the orchards, our home and the farm market, as well as the housing we provided for the migrant workers.

An incredible amount of the money we received had to be put aside to pay the taxes. Trusts were set up for Danny and I, and part of the money went to Papa John, as well as Dad's sister Amy. My Aunt Amy is five years younger than Dad, and she met her husband when they were both attending Western Michigan University in Kalamazoo. We don't see them very often because it's hard for them to get away with their four young children, and Amy's husband, Joe, has a very demanding job with a big engineering company in Baltimore. Aunt Amy loves living on the east coast, and her letters make their life there sound very exciting. I'm glad she's so happy. With the share of the money she received from the sale of land, she and Joe should be even happier. They have needed a larger home for some time, and now they would be able to buy it with their unexpected financial windfall.

Danny and I were home for Easter dinner in 1984. Aunt Amy, Uncle Joe and their four children came for the weekend and my grandfather Papa John drove over from Holland. All of us were informed by Dad that he wanted to have a family meeting following our dinner and I kind of wondered what it would be about.

Mom served us a wonderful meal when we got home from church. We had the traditional ham for our Easter dinner along with homemade applesauce, a salad and several cooked vegetables. Mom also made her special cabbage casserole, which is a big favorite of mine. The ingredients for her casserole include shredded cabbage, red apples, chunks of ham, a sweet-sour sauce, butter and cracker crumbs. When I was a little girl she used to make it with chunks of hot dogs instead of with ham, and I loved it.

The family meeting, as it turned out, was all about our family, especially our ancestors. Dad wanted us all to know more about who our forbearers were, and what they did over the years to develop and maintain our family farm. He thought it was important that we know something about them in order to really appreciate the money we were receiving from the sale of the 580 acres to the developer.

Dad started the meeting with a prayer thanking God for our many blessings. After that he explained that he had asked the Malone family to come together today so that we could hear what he and Papa John knew about our ancestors. "We've never taken the time to do this before" he said, "and Easter Sunday is an appropriate time to do it. If it were not for the generations that preceded us, we would not be sitting here today around this kitchen table. I really felt obligated to do this, because I thought you should know more about who they were, what they did and how they lived. We need to respect and honor them because it's the only way I know that we can express appreciation for our good fortune. I hope you agree."

I interrupted and said, "Hold everything. I want to get my tape recorder." I ran up to my bedroom and brought back my tape recorder so that there would be a record of our family history…at least as much as Dad and Papa John could tell us.

Dad began by telling us about Elijah Malone, who migrated from County Westmeath in Ireland to New York in the mid 1850's. He worked in New York, saved some money and used a lot of it to bring three of his brothers to America. Elijah enlisted in the famous New York Irish Brigade and fought in the Civil War. Neither Dad nor Papa John knew much about his service in the Civil War except that he was wounded several times and was a second lieutenant. I found the lack of information about Elijah Malone disappointing. I thought to myself, someday I'm going to do some research on the Irish Brigade to see what I can learn. According to Dad, after the Civil War Elijah moved west…where he helped to build railroads and became a foreman in charge of a work crew. Papa John added that he had been told that Elijah developed a good reputation because he was a hard worker, very dependable and was not a drinker. He explained that, unfortunately, many of the Irish who worked on the railroads squandered their hard-earned money on whiskey.

We were told that Elijah's youngest brother, Daniel, moved from New York to Grand Rapids, Michigan shortly after the Civil War. Elijah sent him most of the money that he earned, as there were no trustworthy banks out west where Elijah was helping to build railroads.

Sometime in the early 1870's, Elijah came to Grand Rapids to visit his brother Daniel. At that time, Elijah was about 40 years old, and Daniel was around 30. Both were still single. Daniel wanted to become a farmer, and he talked Elijah into looking at a farm that was for sale somewhere around Grand Rapids. Elijah was not impressed with this farm and they didn't buy it. However, the seed had been planted and the idea of becoming co-owners of a farm began to take root. Elijah wrote his brother after he returned to his railroad construction job that he should continue to look at farms whenever he learned that one was available for purchase. Dad said that we don't know how many farms Daniel checked out, but in 1875 they bought the first 400 acres of what is now our family farm.

Elijah and Daniel moved into a small house on the property and quickly earned the respect of the neighboring farmers as they worked long hours to improve the farm…clearing brush to provide even more land for crops. Daniel had taken advantage of every opportunity he could to educate himself as soon as he arrived in America, and he had also taken courses at a school in Grand Rapids to learn as much as he could about farming. And he didn't hesitate to seek advice from other farmers who he believed knew more about farming than he or Elijah did.

Several miles east of our farm, there was a one-room country grade school where Sarah Polley was the teacher. Daniel met Sally, which is what everyone called her, when he went to a picnic at the local Grange Hall. Sally and Daniel were the same age and soon they became friends. Daniel sought information from Sally on a variety of subjects, as she was well educated and had a sizable library. Daniel asked Sally to marry him and she accepted. According to our family bible, which originated with them, they were married in 1878.

Daniel and Sally had five children, three daughters and two sons. Their oldest son, Thomas, was Papa John's grandfather and Dad's great grandfather. Unfortunately, Elijah never married, but he lived his entire life with Daniel and Sally and his share of the farm was willed to Daniel when he died in 1899.

The original farmhouse was expanded and remodeled several times, and then Daniel and his two sons, Thomas and John, built a new house starting in 1900. When it was finished in 1902, the original house was torn down. The house they built is basically the home we live in today, with a lot of major changes and improvements made over the years—especially after World War II.

In 1902, Thomas Malone married Anna Martin, the daughter of James and Helen Martin. James Martin had a large apple orchard, and he convinced Thomas that our farm would be an ideal place to raise apples. There was already a small orchard on the farm, but the fruit from these trees…apples, pears, peaches and cherries…was used mainly for family consumption. Thomas and his brother John decided to plant an apple orchard and make it a commercial enterprise. Starting with a 1000 trees in 1904, they had expanded the apple orchard to more than 6000 trees by 1910, also adding 280 acres to the original 400 acres that Elijah and Daniel had purchased. There was a good market for apples leading up to and during World War I, as well as in the early 1920's. The farm and the apple business prospered, and Anna provided extra income from her egg business. Thomas and John built her a large chicken house, as she wanted a flock of hens. Anna sold the eggs or else used them to trade for goods at the grocery store.

Daniel's brother John married when he was in his early 30's. Tragically, his wife died in childbirth and the baby was also lost. John had several romantic interests during his lifetime, but he apparently never found the right woman because he never remarried.

Anna and Thomas Malone had three children. A daughter died shortly after childbirth, a son Michael died of pneumonia when he was five years old and their son John, who was born in 1913, survived. That John is my father's father and my special grandfather, Papa John.

Dad then turned the telling of our family story over to Papa John who proceeded to tell us what it was like for him growing up on our farm. As soon as he was old enough he said he was expected to share the workload. He started out by sharing with us a treasured memory of his childhood. He said, "I particularly enjoyed helping my mother gather eggs and hatching chicks the old-fashioned way, with a brood hen. In the early spring, when the hens would show signs of nesting, we would save up eggs. When we had collected about 15 eggs, my mother and I would put them in a nest box in the chicken house, and a sitting hen was allowed to settle in. That date was marked on a calendar."

"For the next three weeks the hen sat on the nest with amazing faithfulness. She would leave the nest for food and water only a few times during this period. She instinctively knew to roll and rearrange the eggs regularly so that the embryos would develop uniformly. As a young boy it was amazing to me that a hen could sit so long with nothing to do. I wondered what she was thinking about. Did she know that the eggs would eventually hatch, or did she simply think eggs were good to sit on? My mother told me not to disturb the hens so I would watch as unobtrusively as I could, because I found it fascinating.

A few days before the incubation period was up, my mother would tell me to go and look under the hen to see if any eggs had begun to hatch. Any fluffy yellow chicks I found were removed from the nest and kept warm in the house, because we didn't want the hen to leave the nest prematurely. When we were satisfied that all the eggs had hatched that were going to, we reunited the hen with her chicks. She was then transformed from the quiet, silent sitting hen into a clucking mother parading about with her small flock under foot. Papa John claimed that this experience taught him that some of the most amazing things in life are not always the most immediately obvious. Stillness and silence can often cloak powerful mysteries in life, and, if we are patient, they will show themselves to us."

My grandfather never ceases to amaze me with his insight and wisdom.

Papa then went on to tell us about all the horses and mules they had when he was a young boy. They were needed to pull the wagons, the tree sprayers and the plows. He said his father was particularly proud of a matched pair of horses that pulled the buggy whenever they went to town or to church on Sunday. Once in a while Papa's father would let him take the reins—starting when he was about eight or nine years old. And that, he claimed, was really a thrill!

When Papa was in grade school, he rode a horse named Sam to school. He would tether Sam in the schoolyard, but occasionally the horse would get loose and head for home. This usually happened in the fall when apples were ripe, as Sam knew a delicious snack was waiting if he could get into the orchard before someone caught him.

I listened to Papa's description of various machines, tractors, automobiles and trucks that were purchased starting before World War I and during the 1920's, 30's and 40's. Frankly, he lost me for a while when he got off on this subject, because he described the make, model and horsepower of nearly every one of them. I was amazed that he would remember all this.

When Papa started talking about personal things...like courting his wife...he got my full attention again. I learned that he met Mary Ann Taylor, who became his wife and my grandmother, when they attended Rockford high school. She was one grade behind Papa, but whenever there was a school dance or a party somewhere he always invited Mary Ann to be his date. Sometimes she accepted, but he said there were a few times when he got around to asking her too late, and she went with someone else.

Papa told us that he graduated from high school in 1931, and the early 1930's were rough years. Times were tough, really tough. He explained that since they had a few cows, chickens, a big vegetable garden and an orchard they never lacked for good food, but there was very little extra money. Lots of apples went unsold, many bushels were given away or left to rot on the ground. "Apples actually became a symbol of the depression in the early 1930's, because there were so many men standing on street corners in the cities trying to sell a few apples in order to survive. I will never forget the depression, although we didn't have it nearly as bad as a lot of folks," Papa commented.

According to Papa, a big night out was when he invited Mary Ann to go to a drive-in restaurant for a burger and shake and then to see a movie. He called that a $3.00 date, because that was all it cost to pay for the food, their movie tickets and two boxes of popcorn. They also enjoyed canoeing, attending fairs, and having picnics on the shore of Lake Michigan. I think Papa enjoyed telling us about this period of his life when he was a young man, as he seemed to be dredging up a lot of happy memories that he wanted to share with us. He said that, even though times were really tough, they still managed to have fun and enjoy themselves doing simple things that didn't cost much money.

Papa said that when he proposed to Mary Ann on Valentine's Day in 1933, he was really afraid she might not accept, as he had several rivals who also wanted to marry her. To his relief she said "Yes", and they were married in June of 1933. My father was born in 1936—the same year that my mother was born.

In 1940, another 200 acres was purchased from a man who had inherited land that was adjacent to our orchards. He was called into the service and he offered to sell his property to Papa at a bargain price. It was an especially good opportunity for the Malones, as the apple orchard was enlarged and the temporary housing for the migrant workers hired to help with the apple harvest was built on this land after World War II.

It was a really interesting afternoon, and before we knew it, three hours had passed. Around 5:30, Dad said we'd better call a halt to our meeting because Danny and I had to get back to college that evening. Aunt Amy and her family were flying back to Baltimore from the Grand Rapids airport on Monday morning, so they would be staying overnight. I told Dad that I thought this meeting was a great idea. It made me realize that I had given very little thought or consideration to the Malone generations that preceded me, even though there were photos of some of them on the walls in our living room.

Danny and I decided to have a snack before we left, and while we were eating ham sandwiches and other leftovers, I invited Danny to come to Holland during the Tulip Festival in early May. I told him that I wanted him to meet some of the friends I'd made at Hope College, and I thought the diversion would be good for him. Because of his knee injury he was not participating in spring practice, and I also figured it was not likely that he would be playing football in the fall. Danny at first started making excuses, but I persisted. Papa John supported my invitation by asking Danny to stay with him at his senior residence. The persuasion worked, and Danny agreed to come to the Tulip Festival the second week in May.

The Tulip Festival in Holland is a big event, attracting more than a million visitors annually, and includes many special events and entertainment by well-known performers. I had been to this festival several times when I was in elementary school and high school, but Danny had never been to one. Little did I realize or anticipate when I invited Danny to come to Holland for this event that it would have a profound effect on his life.

A few weeks later, on Thursday evening, the phone rang in my dorm room. It was Danny calling me from Papa John's apartment at the senior residence telling me that he was in town and ready to enjoy the festival. We decided to meet at the Maas Center at Hope College early Friday morning for the Taste of Holland breakfast buffet. Later we watched the Klompen Dancers perform and walked around the Marketplaats to check out all the products, food and souvenirs offered in this Dutch Market. After lunch we went to see a show at the Civic Center, then drove around town in Danny's car taking time to visit the Veldheer Tulip Gardens, the Deklomp Wooden Shoe factory, where Danny bought me a pair of wooden shoes, and then Windmill Island. The tulips were in full bloom in every color imaginable, and they were everywhere by the hundreds of thousands. It made you feel good to see so much beauty.

It was a delightful day, perfect weather to be outside, and Danny and I were having a great time together. Danny was enjoying himself far more than he had anticipated, and he told me several times that he was glad that I insisted he come to the Tulip Festival. Following a stop at the famous Malt Shop for a late afternoon snack, we headed for Pretplaats, which is Dutch for Fun Gathering Place. All during the day, I ran into Hope College students that I knew and I proudly introduced them to my big brother.

When we arrived at the Pretplaats, I saw Abigail Zondervine there with some other girls who were students at Hope College. I had met Abby, which is what everyone called her, when we were both taking the same biology class. I knew she was a sophomore, but beyond that I knew nothing about her. When I introduced Abby to Danny I detected something—you could almost call it an electric spark—because they both seemed to me to actually "light up" the moment they were introduced to each other.

Abigail Zondervine is a very attractive blonde with cute bangs that accent her pretty face. She's tall. I'm just over five feet ten inches tall, and Abby's an inch or two taller than me. She has a figure to be envied, and I had noticed that guys usually turned around to look at her again when they passed her on the college campus or in the halls of a building. Abby received a lot of attention from males, but she was either unaware of it, or else simply ignored it. Maybe it was a little of both. She certainly wasn't stuck up though, as she had a warm, pleasant personality and was cordial to everyone who spoke to her.

It was obvious to me that Abby and Danny clicked the moment they met. They were soon involved in a two-way conversation, leaving the rest of us to talk among ourselves...discussing the Tulip Festival, what things had impressed us the most, and what we were going to be doing tomorrow. Danny and I planned to go to Kallen Park Friday evening, where there was going to be live entertainment and fireworks. I soon learned that Danny had invited Abby to join us and she had accepted. As it turned out, it was a nice evening and I enjoyed being with Abby and Danny...even though the two of them were really absorbed with each other. They were laughing and talking together, and this fast-developing relationship was fascinating me. I had invited Danny to spend the weekend with me, but Abby was now getting all of his attention.

Saturday morning Danny and I returned to the Maas Center at Hope College for the Dutch Breakfast Buffet and, somewhat to my surprise, Abby was there and joined us. After breakfast Abby invited us to her home on Lake Macatawa, and Danny agreed to go even though we had already made other plans for the day. We followed Abby's car to the Zondervine home on the shore of Lake Macatawa, a big lake on the west side of Holland that opens up to Lake Michigan. We entered what turned out to be the Zondervine estate through a security gate, which Abby opened and closed behind us using a device in her car. We then followed Abby's car up a long drive to her home. Danny and I looked at each other but didn't say a word, as we each knew what the other was thinking. We certainly had not expected this. The Zondervines were obviously very affluent. I thought "My gosh, Abby's not only beautiful but also rich. What a lucky girl."

We parked behind the Zondervine home, next to a four-car garage, as the front of the house faced Lake Macatawa. As soon as we got out of Danny's car, Abby called to us, "Come on guys, I want you to see the view of the lake from the front of the house."

As the three of us walked around to the front I noticed how beautifully landscaped the grounds were. The place obviously required a lot of maintenance. And they really did have an impressive view of beautiful Lake Macatawa. Immediately in front of their house was a swimming pool, and stretching all along the lake in front of their property was a wide boardwalk. Docked in a boat slip extending out from the boardwalk was a big boat, which towered above me when I stood next to it. Abby explained that the boat was her dad's pride and joy. He loved to cruise the Great Lakes whenever he could take time away from his business. The boat had just come out of winter storage, and Abby said they were planning to take it out tomorrow for the first time that year.

After standing out on the dock for awhile looking around Lake Macatawa, Abby led us into her home where we met her mother, Sarah, and her sister Becky, which was short for Rebecca. Abby's mother and Becky couldn't have been nicer. They made us feel welcome, and after we had talked for a while they insisted that we stay for lunch. Lunch sounded especially good to me as I was starting to feel hungry because I didn't eat much breakfast. I wasn't hungry then, but I sure was now.

When Mrs. Zondervine and Becky had lunch all prepared, we went out on the patio next to the pool. They served tuna sandwiches, garnished with pickles and potato chips, iced tea and a fruit cocktail for dessert. It was delicious and the five of us had a really pleasant, relaxed conversation enjoying lunch alfresco sitting around a picnic table on a delightful spring day. My intuition told me that both Mrs. Zondervine and Becky were becoming aware that Danny and Abby were quite attracted to each other, because they started asking a lot of questions about us, and our family. More so than what you would expect at a first meeting.

During lunch, Danny and I learned that the Zondervines owned Zon's Thrifty Marts, a chain of lumberyards that also sold building materials, hardware, tools, paint and all kinds of products for home improvements. It was a very successful chain with stores not only in Michigan, but Indiana as well. Over the years I had been in several of their stores in and around Grand Rapids, but had no idea who owned them. Each store was huge, and did a big volume of business because their prices were very competitive with the national chains. Mrs. Zondervine explained that Abby's grandfather, Joshua Zondervine, started the business in the early 1930's, but the impressive growth of Zon's Thrifty Marts took place when her husband, Andrew Zondervine, took over management in the 1960's. We also found out that Andrew Zondervine was a graduate of Hope College and had an MBA from the University of Michigan. Not surprisingly, he was an enthusiastic supporter of the U of M football team. I thought to myself, "I wonder what he's going to think when he learns that Danny is on the MSU football team?"

I would soon get the answer to that question because shortly after we finished lunch Abby's father showed up. He seemed genuinely pleased to meet us...especially Danny...and he insisted we call him Andy. "Everybody does," he claimed.

As it turned out, Andy knew a lot about Danny. Probably Abby had provided some information, but he said he was an avid reader of the sports pages and that he was disappointed several years ago when he read that Danny had decided to play football at MSU, rather than the University of Michigan. Apparently he was aware of Danny's achievements playing football when he was in high school. I noticed that Danny was smiling, but seemed to be a little embarrassed by all the praise being heaped on him by Andy Zondervine. I also noticed that Abby had an admiring look on her face and wondered to myself if and when just the two of them would ever go on a date together. So far Abby and Danny had not spent any time by themselves.

While Andy was talking, I noticed that he and Danny were about the same height. He was a tall, trim man with shoulders not quite as broad as Danny's, and he was very nice-looking and personable. I guessed he was about a foot taller than his wife. I liked his smile and was impressed that he had really white teeth. After Andy and Danny had talked for a while, he explained that he had left his office in Grand Rapids early so that he could work on his boat to make sure everything was shipshape. "We're taking the first cruise of the season tomorrow and I could use two more deck hands. How about the two of you joining us?"

I was the first one to respond and said, "I don't know anything about boats. The biggest thing I've ever been in is a canoe. So I wouldn't be much help as a deck hand."

Andy laughed and said, "I'm just kidding. I don't expect to put you to work. Just come along and enjoy yourselves. I think Abby would especially like to have you join us. We'll leave around 10:00, and we'll only be out on Lake Michigan for a few hours. I expect to return to our dock by 4:00 in the afternoon at the latest."

I knew that Danny had planned to return to East Lansing early Sunday afternoon, so I chimed in and said, "It's really up to Danny. I know he has to get back to school tomorrow, so he has to decide."

Danny looked at Abby who was vigorously nodding her head up and down indicating that he should accept the invitation, so I wasn't surprised when he replied, "Sounds like a lot of fun. Thank you for inviting us. Can we bring anything?"

"We don't drink alcoholic beverages," answered Andy Zondervine, "so if you want some beer, you'll have to pick some up. But we'll have pop, tea and coffee on board if that suits you."

"That sounds great," Danny answered. "but can't we bring some food, maybe some snacks?"

Mrs. Zondervine then took charge, saying; "You don't need to bring anything. There will be plenty of food and snacks. You two just show up here around 9:30 tomorrow morning to help us carry everything on board. Wear soft-soled shoes and bring along a light windbreaker or a sweater. It will be cool when we get out on the lake."

Late that afternoon, Danny and I departed after expressing our appreciation for the lunch and for the warm hospitality that Mrs. Zondervine, Becky and Abby had shown us. They really did make us feel welcome, and I had a strong intuition that we were going to see much more of them, not only tomorrow, but also in the future.

We drove to the senior residence in Holland where Papa John lived, as the three of us planned to have dinner together. Papa was waiting for us and during dinner we told him all about our visit with the Zondervines. He listened intently and found our reports fascinating.

I could hardly wait for the next day to arrive. A cruise on Lake Michigan on a yacht was going to be a totally new experience, and one that I had never even anticipated before. Danny and I arrived at the Zondervines promptly at 9:30 Sunday morning, so that we could help carry the food and beverages on board the boat. You would have thought we were going to be gone for several days, rather than a few hours, with all the supplies we put on the boat. Mrs. Zondervine must have guessed what I was thinking as she commented, "I've never understood why people eat so much when they're out in a boat. Must be all the fresh air!"

Shortly before it was time to shove off, another guy showed up. Turned out he was Becky's friend, Terry, and he apologized for being late. I didn't pay any attention to his excuses for being late, as I was intrigued with the boat's interior and the furnishings.

Danny and I stood on each side of Andy, who was sitting in the captain's seat, so that we could watch him operate the boat. He seemed really pleased to have us along and standing next to him so that he could talk with us…especially to Danny. He explained the controls to us, and described various features that he especially liked about his boat. He told us it was Hatteras motor yacht but he preferred calling it a family cruiser. "It's only 40 feet long," he said, "with twin 300-horsepower Cummins engines. It's a great boat for cruising with family and friends. And occasionally, I fish for lake trout or salmon. Mostly though, I just enjoy getting away. Especially to Mackinac Island and Georgian Bay. Usually I take two weeks in August to do that."

When we cast off, Abby and Becky impressed me as experienced deck hands as I watched them untie the mooring lines and pull up the big white bumpers that hung over the sides of the boat. As soon as we were out of their boat slip, Andy slowly cruised across Lake Macatawa, and then increased the boat's speed once we were out on Lake Michigan. The big lake was unusually calm with hardly any "chop" so I felt quite relaxed. I had secretly worried that I might get seasick.

In addition to all the mechanical features of his boat, Andy also explained to Danny and I that the bow was forward, aft was the stern or tail of the boat, starboard was the right side facing forward, and port the left side facing forward. He also told us that if we had any questions to please ask, as he was determined to make us both sailors.

After a while I joined Sarah, who was sitting by herself at the breakfast bar in the galley having a cup of coffee. Becky and Terry were sitting on the deck near the bow, cuddled up next to each other and Abby and Danny were talking together sitting on a couch in the cabin area. While visiting with Sarah, I noticed that Andy would occasionally make notes on a clipboard. I suppose the notes were about things he wanted to have checked on his boat.

Around 1:00 p.m. everybody was ready to eat, and I helped Sarah put the food out for a picnic lunch. And what a lunch it was! It started with mugs of hot chicken noodle soup. Soup was followed with big, thick ham sandwiches, potato salad, all kinds of veggies and dips, various fruits and hot chocolate, coffee, tea and a variety of canned beverages. Danny and Terry each polished off two sandwiches and Sarah was right…you really do have a big appetite when you're out for several hours in the fresh air on a boat.

Following lunch we cruised for about an hour, and I went out and sat on the deck in the warm sunshine. I enjoyed the day, and was fascinated by all the seagulls circling overhead. As soon as the boat arrived back at the Zondervine's dock, Andy insisted that Danny should be on his way to East Lansing, as he knew that Danny needed to get back to college. So Danny and I sincerely and enthusiastically thanked Sarah and Andy for including us in their first cruise of the year and for the delicious lunch. We definitely enjoyed ourselves.

Abby walked around the house with Danny and I to see us off, and I got into the car first. After a few seconds, I looked around to see where Danny was, and I saw him and Abby standing in back of the car, arms around each other and locked in a passionate kiss. I reached for my purse and pretended to be looking for something, as I didn't know what else to do.

When Danny finally was in the car, I didn't look at him nor did I say a word, as I was curious as to what he was going to say about Abby. As we drove down the driveway he finally spoke up and said, "I've got a date with Abby next Saturday. Papa John won't mind if I stay with him again. I'm really glad you insisted that I come to the Tulip Festival, Colleen, and introduced me to Abby. I think she's pretty terrific."

Danny dropped me off at my dorm, and on the way there we discussed the things we had done together the past several days, how much fun we had, and how impressed we were with the Zondervine family.

When I got to my dorm room there was a note taped to the door from Ukadean, saying, "Where have you been? Call me as soon as you return!"

I called Ukadean and she rushed to my room, as she was eager to find out what was going on. I proceeded to tell her in detail about Danny and Abby's relationship, which was getting quite warm, how nice the Zondervine family treated us, and what a thrill it was to take a cruise on a big yacht. I laid it on pretty heavy.

Ukadean responded by saying, "Sounds to me like Abby and Danny might be a match made in heaven."

"I don't know if it's a match made in heaven," I replied, "because it was me that introduced them. Right here on earth in Holland, Michigan!"

CHAPTER 3

Two Love Affairs

Danny and Abby did get together the following weekend, because Danny called me from Papa Johns, just to say, "Hi" and to let me know that he was back in town.

A week after that, we were both home for the summer, as Danny had finished his junior year at MSU and I had completed my freshman year at Hope College. That summer I got a job at a veterinary clinic, but I also helped Mom with the meals and the housework as well as some of the brush cleanup in the orchard. Danny spent the few weeks he was home helping Dad with the orchard, pruning trees, cleaning up the brush left from the pruning, mowing the orchard, spraying the trees, repairing apple crates and helping maintain all the equipment and machinery needed for a large apple orchard operation.

Abby was working as a sales associate at a Zon's Thrifty Mart on the north side of Grand Rapids, so she would often show up at our home when she finished her shift. Mom and Dad, as well as Papa John, who was frequently around to help with orchard chores, were very impressed with Abby. All of us tried to make her feel truly welcome. We must have succeeded, as Abby told me more than once that she loved to come to our house. And I never heard Dad complain when Danny took a day off to spend it with Abby or with the Zondervines when he was invited to join them for a cruise on Lake Michigan. It was a busy, unusually interesting summer.

In late August of 1984, Danny returned to East Lansing to start his senior year at MSU, where he had already informed the coaching staff that he was giving up football. A few weeks later, I moved to Holland to begin my sophomore year at Hope College. Ukadean and I were back in the same dorm, and this year we were roommates.

That fall almost all my time was dedicated to attending classes, doing homework and taking tests. Ukadean and I, along with several other classmates, chummed around together on the weekends. I dated different guys and felt considerably more comfortable with college life. Ukadean, however, was involved in a pretty serious relationship with a student named Bill Heilmeier. Bill, like Ukadean, planned to teach school after graduating from Hope College.

The Zondervines were invited to have Thanksgiving dinner at out home, and they accepted. Mom is a whiz when it comes to preparing food, and she outdid herself…preparing a scrumptious meal consisting of all the traditional things served for a Thanksgiving dinner, and then some. No wine was served though, as the Zondervines were members of the Dutch Reformed Church, which discourages the consumption of alcoholic beverages. Everyone got along fine, and the dinner was a success so far as I was concerned. Becky and I got to know each other better as we were able to spend some time talking together. The Danny and Abby relationship was now really serious, and we were all aware that Danny was going to give Abby an engagement ring at Christmas.

Abby accepted Danny's ring at Christmas, and the Zondervines hosted an engagement party at their home between Christmas and New Year's. Their home was beautifully decorated for the holidays, and they used a caterer to prepare and serve the food and beverages for the party. Mom, Dad and Papa John were there, along with about a hundred other guests. It was quite a party! During the party Abby and Danny announced that they planned to be married in June, shortly after Danny's graduation from MSU. For their honeymoon, they were going to Hawaii for two weeks, where they would be spending time on several of the islands. It was really exciting hearing all these plans, and I was thrilled and happy for my brother because he was so happy. It wasn't announced at the engagement party, but I also knew that Danny was going to join Zon's Thrifty Marts, as Andy had offered him a management training position with his business.

In the spring of 1985, Danny graduated from Michigan State and I finished my sophomore year at Hope College. It was an especially exciting time with the wedding plans underway, plus the construction of the golf course and a number of houses close to our home. The traffic and the noise around our place was really something. With so much happening in and around our home, I was glad to be employed at the Cunningham Veterinary Clinic again for the summer, because going to work there was a welcome diversion.

More than that, though, I was really learning a lot about how to care for and treat cats, dogs, horses and other animals for a variety of ailments and diseases. The possibility of becoming a veterinarian crossed my mind frequently. I liked animals and the people who brought their pets or livestock to the clinic for treatment were usually very grateful and sincerely appreciative of the care the clinic provided.

The main focus at home, however, was on Abby and Danny's upcoming wedding. My mother was especially excited, and it took her a week of shopping to find the right dress to wear. Dad and Papa John opted for new suits rather than renting tuxedos. Since I would be a bridesmaid, I had to be fitted for the dress that I would wear. Becky, Abby's sister, was going to be the Maid of Honor.

Danny and Abby's marriage on Saturday, June 22, 1985 turned out to be a major news event in Southwest Michigan. I guess I should have anticipated that, but I was surprised at the amount of attention it received. When the beautiful daughter of one of the most successful and respected business owners in the area marries a handsome young man who is an outstanding athlete and the fifth generation of a family well known in the state's apple industry, you know there's going to be some media coverage. There certainly was. Even local television stations covered the event. One newspaper reported Danny and Abby's marriage as the merger of the Dutch with the Irish. Since my mother is of German descent and Sarah Zondervine's genealogy is English and Welch, that observation was true in name only, and I thought it was a pretty dumb way to report their marriage.

There were just under 500 people invited to the wedding and the reception and dinner that followed. I could only speculate as to what the marriage cost the Zondervines. There were enough wedding presents to stock a store, and more than enough to fill the small house that Danny and Abby had rented in Holland, near Hope College. Abby was going to finish her college education while Danny would start his management training at the headquarters of Zon's Thrifty Marts in Grand Rapids. Danny had told us that, after six months or so at the main office, he would become an assistant manager at one of Zon's big lumberyards.

After Abby and Danny returned from their honeymoon in Hawaii, I only saw them twice that summer, not nearly as often as I had expected. When I returned to Hope College for the fall term though, Abby and Danny invited me to their home for dinner nearly every week. I enjoyed and looked forward to those occasions.

I celebrated my 21st birthday at Abby and Danny's home. Mom and Dad, Papa John and Ukadean were there, and Abby decorated their house with streamers, balloons and silly signs. Dinner was pizza, salad and a beautifully decorated double-chocolate birthday cake. Danny served champagne, and I was over-served. Every time my glass was low, Danny filled it again and regretfully I drank more than I should have. Fortunately Ukadean served as my designated driver. Afterwards I told myself, "You're only 21 once!"

A month later I was home for Thanksgiving. Sarah, Andy, and Becky Zondervine were present along with Abby, Danny and Papa John. Mom prepared and served a fantastic dinner and everyone seemed to really enjoy themselves. It was a warm, happy and pleasant day...one that would be remembered for a long time.

Between Christmas and New Year's we were all invited to the Zondervines for dinner. When dinner was finished, Danny tapped on his water glass for attention and said that he and Abby had an important announcement. For a few seconds he paused, looked at Abby with a silly grin on his face, and to everyone's surprise announced that he and Abby were expecting a baby. This was the first that any of us were aware that Abby was pregnant, and there was an immediate outpouring of excited statements. "That's wonderful!" "Congratulations!" "That's great!" Even a few "Wows!" were heard.

I was so startled by this surprise announcement that I think I was probably the only one at the table that didn't make some impulsive comment. Instead, I got up and ran around the table to first hug Abby and then my brother. When I hugged Danny he looked at me with a big smile on his face and said, "I hope you'll like being an aunt, Colleen."

"I'm sure I will, Danny," I replied. "Looks like 1986 will be quite a year for you and Abby. I am so happy for you."

In the spring of 1986, I finished my junior year at Hope College. Fortunately, I was offered my summer job again at the veterinary clinic, and Dr. Robert Cunningham talked to me seriously about being a veterinarian. He said that, in his opinion, "I was well qualified compassionately, emotionally and intellectually to be one." It made me feel good when he told me this.

Jennifer Abigail Malone was born early in the morning on June 13, and she weighed in at eight pounds, four ounces. I met my new niece the next day, and I thought she was the most beautiful baby I had ever seen. Looking at Jennifer,

I realized that my brother now had his own family, and that another generation of Malones was underway.

It was late in the afternoon when I left the hospital and Danny arrived just as I was leaving. He suggested that the two of us have dinner together and I readily agreed, as there hadn't been an opportunity for just the two of us to talk for a long time. I especially wanted to tell him that I had decided to become a Doctor of Veterinary Medicine. We went to a restaurant near the hospital and Danny insisted that we each have a cocktail. I agreed to have a glass of wine but he had several cocktails. When I asked him if he was celebrating the birth of his daughter he said, "I sure am. I couldn't be happier. Everything's going so great, Colleen, that I practically have to pinch myself to believe it."

He then proceeded to tell me that he was still working at Zon's headquarters, actually for a much longer time than he had originally anticipated. He told me that he was learning a lot, as he was spending time in various departments—including human resources, accounting, purchasing and marketing. All were important parts of the operation, but he especially liked working in the marketing department. Danny also explained to me that Zon's Thrifty Marts were much more than just lumber yards. They were actually home centers, or mass merchandisers.

Danny was really upbeat, talking so fast that I couldn't get a word in edgewise. He proceeded to tell me that he had been offered what he thought was a special opportunity. There was a company in Grand Rapids that manufactured steel wheelbarrows. Danny went on to explain that this company produced all kinds of wheelbarrows. They made several different kinds that were used exclusively by contractors and landscapers, plus a line of well-designed wheelbarrows for homeowners. The models they manufactured for homeowners were very popular with people who enjoyed gardening. These wheelbarrows were distributed through all the major home centers and hardware chains, and Zon's Thrifty Marts sold several thousand of them every year. The president and owner of this company, ACE Stamping Inc., was Ben Cockrell, and Danny claimed that he had gotten to know him really well over the past six months. He had met Ben Cockrell when he called on Zon's marketing department to discuss a special promotion for his wheelbarrows. Following that meeting, Ben had invited Danny to have lunch with him. According to Danny, they really got along well together and become friends. I learned that Ben had entertained Danny at his golf club, he'd gone fishing on Ben's cruiser and he'd also been invited to participate in poker games several times at Ben's home.

Danny went on to explain that Ben was in his early 40's, and had inherited the company when his father died of a heart attack about four years ago. Danny said that Ben had showed him financial statements, which revealed that the company was doing quite well, and that Ben had invited him to become a director of the ACE Stamping Company. He told me that he was going to buy some stock in the company, as he thought it would be a good investment and he should have an equity position when he became a director. Being a director, Danny explained, would require him to attend three or four board meetings a year, for which he would be paid a Directors Fee. Ben had told Danny that he needed to get some new, young people on his board of directors because it presently consisted of Ben, the company treasurer, an attorney, and three very elderly men who had been friends of Ben's father.

It was obvious that Danny was quite enthusiastic about becoming a director and buying stock in Ben Cockrell's company, so I told him that this really did sound interesting and hoped that everything would turn out OK. I did ask him if he had discussed this with Andy Zondervine to see if he had any objection. Danny said "No. I immediately accepted Ben's offer to be a director of his company and I'll be elected to the board at their next meeting."

Then I told Danny the news that I was going to apply for admission to the College of Veterinary Medicine at Michigan State. If I was accepted, and if I could get through the four-year program, then I would become a veterinarian. At first Danny seemed a little surprised, and also somewhat concerned, when I told him this. He apparently thought, or maybe hoped, that I really would take over the operation of the family orchard and farm market some day. It wasn't something he wanted to do, but at various times he had encouraged me to carry on the family business. The fact was, however, that I didn't want to make it my life's work any more than he did.

The golf course and housing development built on the land that we had sold the Grand Rapids developer was well underway. The golf course was finished and in use, and a lot of the homes had been sold. I speculated that some day soon the developer was going to offer to buy the rest of our property in order to build more homes. "In my opinion," I told Danny, "That's the best thing that could happen. Mom and Dad could retire comfortably, but it will be the end of an era for the Malone family as farmers."

Late in the summer, I returned to Holland to start my senior year at Hope. It was hard to believe that that I'd already finished three years of college, and now had just one more to go before possibly starting another four years in order to become a veterinarian. That was my hope, because I had made up my mind that I really wanted to be a veterinarian.

My senior year at Hope College went by uneventfully. I pushed myself to do better in all my courses in order to try and raise my grade point average. I thought this would improve the possibility of being accepted when I applied for admission to MSU'S College of Veterinary Medicine, as I had learned that enrollment was limited to about 100 students each year. My dedicated effort paid off, as I did get better grades in all my courses. I didn't have the distraction of a boyfriend—which was the case with my good friend Ukadean. She had found her future husband at Hope College, and was in love. She and Bill Heilmeier were going to be married in June, shortly after our graduation, and Ukadean asked me to be her Maid of Honor. Of course I said "yes." Bill and Ukadean both hoped to find positions teaching in the Grand Rapids school system after they graduated.

Ukadean and Bill were married in the Rockford Methodist Church. It was, as expected, a beautiful wedding with about 80 guests attending the reception and dinner that followed the ceremony. At the reception I met Ukadean's mother. It was the first time that I had ever seen her and I was surprised at how attractive she was. Later, after the dinner, I had an opportunity to talk with Ukadean and I commented that it was really nice of her mother to come to her wedding.

Ukadean said, "I'm surprised she came. I've heard from her occasionally over the years and she's been to see me a few times. But she abandoned me when I was five years old. My dad and my two brothers, and now Bill, are really my family."

"Your mother has certainly taken good care of herself," I observed. "I don't believe she has an ounce of fat on her body. She obviously works out a lot."

"She probably has a lot of exercise videos," Ukadean speculated. "As far as I'm concerned she's an extremely selfish, self-centered woman and a *real piece of work*. She's the one responsible for my name, which I think is kind of weird."

"Your name isn't weird at all," I responded, "You're a special person with a unique name. I've always liked your name."

We both laughed.

Shortly before Ukadean's wedding, I had been notified that my application to enter the MSU College of Veterinary Medicine was approved for the fall term of 1987. I learned that only 100 students are accepted each year out of more than 2800 that apply. I was simply elated to find out that *I made it*. During the summer, I was employed again at the clinic, and Doctor Cunningham told me that he would like to hire me to work with him full time as an associate when I graduated. That was reassuring, and I told him that I truly appreciated his offer and his confidence in me.

Late in August, I left for East Lansing and got settled in the apartment that I had rented near the veterinary college. I was determined to give it my best effort and avoid distractions. I did, and my grades were quite good that first term. One of my most difficult courses was gross anatomy. I had to memorize thousands of body parts for not just one, but several species. It's also dirty work, and the animals have an odor because Formaldehyde, pumped into dissection animals to prevent decay, doesn't always do its job.

In December, Abby and Danny had another baby. I knew that Abby was pregnant again, but I was so focused on my classes that I seldom thought about them. When my mother called me on December 13 to tell me that Julie Margaret Malone had been born, I realized that I hadn't thought about Abby and Danny hardly at all, and I felt a little guilty about it.

When I started the second term in January, 1988, I became better acquainted with Eugene Morris, who I sat next to or near in all my classes. Each class of 100 students takes the same class simultaneously. And the class continues to move as a group through the entire four years of their education. Gene, as everyone called him, was from Kalamazoo and a big basketball fan. He invited me to go to an MSU basketball game with him, and I accepted. The game turned out to be very close, with the lead changing many times. Michigan State ended up winning the game by one point, and I asked Gene if all the games were this exciting. He said he'd make sure they were if I'd go to more games with him.

That's how our relationship began. We went to quite a few basketball games and started dating regularly. I invited Gene to my apartment often for dinner, and we would study together and discuss the subjects we were taking in depth. Gene's father was a veterinarian and Gene's experience working with his father, plus mine from working summers at the clinic, gave us a lot of experience that we could share. It's required for admission to vet school that you have 250 hours of experience working with a veterinarian, but Gene and I each had many more hours of experience than that.

I tried not to be distracted by my relationship with Gene, but I found myself frequently thinking about him when we were not together. The more time that I spent with him, the more attracted I felt to him. While I never told Gene that I loved him, I was getting very close to doing so. In the spring, when we had finished our final exams, we had a date to celebrate. Gene and I both drank several beers at a popular local bar and when we got back to my apartment late in the evening we started necking. I had never felt so passionate in my life and Gene told me that he wanted to go to bed with me. I was really tempted, but I told him that when I was sixteen years old and started dating, that my father had explained to me that boys like to experiment. He asked me, "Do you want to be some boys experiment?" I told my father. "No, I absolutely do not want to be some boys experiment." So I decided then and there that I would wait until I was married so...that the first time that I ever have sex will be with my husband."

When I said this to Gene he seemed stunned, and I could tell by the expression on his face that he certainly didn't expect to hear what I had just told him. He drew back from me and acted hurt. But Gene had never said that he loved me, and I didn't want to end up being just his experiment. Even if he had said, "I love you, Colleen." I think I would still have resisted being intimate with him...even though emotionally I was hardly able to contain myself. I was concerned that our relationship might end, however, and I really didn't want that to happen. I was more than just fond of Gene. I really loved him, but I had never told him so.

A real meltdown followed, and after a while Gene said to me, "Let's see what happens over the summer. Maybe you'll be more agreeable in the fall."

This wasn't at all what I wanted to hear him say.

It was late, and Gene said he'd better go. In the morning we both had to pack the things that we needed to take home for the summer and he claimed that he planned to get up very early as he wanted to be on his way home before noon. Gene left. I went to bed, but I didn't sleep well.

After I was home about a week...a week that I really needed to kind of "veg-out"...I finally received a call from Gene. He wanted to know how I was doing, and if I had started working at the veterinary clinic yet.

I told him that I'd been very lazy since I got home, but that I planned to start working at the clinic again starting next Monday. I then invited him to our home for dinner on Sunday and he accepted.

For dinner that Sunday I helped Mom prepare a pot roast, which we cooked in a Dutch oven with potatoes, onions and carrots spread on top of the meat. I knew this kind of a meal was a man-pleaser and Gene's favorite. Gene had met my Mom and Dad on several occasions when they came to visit me in East Lansing, but he had never been to our home. When he arrived that Sunday, the house smelled wonderful with the aroma of a pot roast and a cake cooking in the kitchen. He wanted to take a peek at the pot roast so I lifted the lid and let him savor it. So it didn't surprise me when he said, "You obviously know that the way to a man's heart, Colleen, is through his stomach."

I gave him a playful punch and said, "I hope so."

The four of us…Mom, Dad, Gene and I…had a really enjoyable Sunday dinner talking and eating together. Afterwards Gene and I went for a walk—just wandering around through the orchard. We slowly walked along holding hands and I felt very close to Gene again. I told him that I had written him a letter, but that I hadn't mailed it. He stopped and faced me and asked, "What did you say in your letter?" I told him I'd give the letter to him when we got back to the house, which I did. Here's what I said in my letter…

Dear Gene,

I want you to know that I care for you very much. When I'm not with you, I think about you almost constantly, and can hardly wait until the next time we're together again. I've never said to you that I love you, but I want you to know that this is how I really feel about you. It's easier for me to write these words than to say them to you, because you've never expressed how you truly feel about me. I believe you like me a lot but how deep is your affection for me?

I'm sorry that the last time we were together I disappointed you. Please respect what I said to you, and trust that what I'm telling you is really true. I love you and sincerely want our relationship to continue, but I'm not willing to make going to bed with you a condition for that to happen. I hope you understand and will accept the decision that I have made to not have sex until I'm married. Where we go from here is up to you. But whatever happens between us, please understand that what I am telling you comes from my heart. I love you very, very much.

Colleen

After reading my letter several times Gene put his arms around me and we tightly clung to each other. I was elated when he whispered in my ear, "I love you, Colleen." How wonderful it was to hear him tell me that. And I knew from the way he said those words that they came from his heart.

Then Gene said he wanted to share something with me, which he hoped would help me understand him better. First of all he said, "Colleen, thank you for writing this letter. I am in love with you. It hasn't been easy for me to tell you how I really feel about you, and you deserve an explanation. When I was in high school I went steady with a girl in my class, and I really and truly believed that we loved each other so much that we would be married some day. We promised to be faithful to each other when we left to go to different colleges, and we made a commitment that neither of us would date anyone else. I committed myself to her and I didn't date anyone, but she didn't keep her promise to be true to me. She met another guy and I got a letter from her saying that she was moving on and that I should do the same. What a blow that was!"

"One year later," Gene explained, "I met another girl and we started going together and soon developed a close relationship. She was fun and exciting to be with, but she often drank too much, which concerned me. The first time that I met her parents she really took me by surprise when she introduced me to them as her future husband. I must have been awfully naïve, because her saying that convinced me that she cared for me a lot. That started me thinking seriously about the possibility of our getting married someday. However, during the summer break from college, she went to a party in her hometown where she met a guy visiting from California. When I called to talk with her I learned from her mother that she had gone to California to marry this guy. I couldn't believe it, and I felt like a damn fool. So you see I've been burned twice…pretty badly. As a result I have a hard time trusting girls, but I now realize and believe that you are different. I do love you, but I haven't told you that before because I didn't know how you really felt about me. Now maybe you understand why I didn't want to be disappointed or hurt again."

I responded by saying, "Gene, my life has been absolutely changed since I met and got to know you. I feel that you're as much a part of my life now as the air I breathe and, as I told you in my letter, I can't keep from thinking about you when we're not together. Believe me I would never do anything to hurt you. Your happiness means so much to me. When I look into your eyes I want to believe, and I hope that I see my future there."

After I said this we kissed each other passionately. Then Gene took my hands in his, looked into my eyes and asked, "Will you marry me, Colleen?"

"Yes," I replied.

We sat on the front porch of my home after our walk in the orchard. We sat together in the porch swing for a long time, discussing our plans to get married. After we had talked for quite a while, we agreed that we'd do it in August, a week or two before classes started, and possibly take a short cruise off the east coast for a honeymoon. I saw my Dad out by the barn and I shouted at him saying, "Please come to the house, Dad. I need to talk with you."

Dad, Mom, Gene and I gathered in the kitchen where Mom was putting some dishes away and I announced that I had something really important to tell them. I blurted out, "Gene and I are going to be married." Mom and Dad beamed with delight when they heard my words, as they were quite aware that I was really fond of Gene.

Gene then spoke up and said, "I hope this meets with your approval, and I now officially ask for the hand of your daughter in marriage."

First Mom and then Dad gave Gene a warm hug. Dad answered Gene saying, "Margaret and I couldn't be happier. Yes, you do have our consent to marry our daughter."

The four of us then sat down at the kitchen table to talk about our wedding plans. Gene and I explained to Mom and Dad that we wanted to have a small wedding in August. We wanted to be back in East Lansing at least a week before classes started in order to get settled in one apartment, and sublet the other one. We weren't sure if we would live in my apartment or Gene's. We wanted to go somewhere, possibly the east coast, on a honeymoon if there was time. I would ask Ukadean to be the Maid of Honor, and Gene planned to ask a close friend of his to be his Best Man. That would be the extent of the wedding party. After we had talked for a while, I said I wanted to call Danny and tell him the news.

When I talked with Danny and told him that I was going to marry Gene, he said he was happy for me and he and Abby offered their congratulations. After the wedding news had been discussed for a while, Danny said he had some big news too. He and Abby were going to move to Elkhart, Indiana soon. That was where the regional headquarters for the eight Zon's Thrifty Marts serving various cities in northern Indiana was located. Danny was going to head up this region, and he said he was "pumped" and ready take on the assignment. He told me that recently he had been taking speech lessons and learning how to make presentation. He had also taken a Dale Carnegie motivation course. He said he had a big challenge to meet in his new position, as he was expected to increase sales volume by at least 15% at every Zon's in his region.

Gene stayed at my home Sunday night, sleeping in Danny's old room, as I wanted him to meet Doctor Cunningham when I reported for work Monday morning. Gene and I met with him early the next morning, arriving before the clinic officially opened for business, so that we could tell Bob about our marriage plans. I also wanted to tell him that I planned to stop working at the clinic in early August. I knew that Doctor Cunningham was well acquainted with Gene's father, Doctor George Morris, who was also a veterinarian, so he was quite pleased to learn that Gene was going to be my husband. As soon as our meeting ended, I said goodbye to Gene and he left for his home in Kalamazoo. I then started my summer job at the clinic assisting Doctor Cunningham.

The following weekend I went to Kalamazoo to spend some time with Gene's mother and father. I had already met them in the spring when they came to visit Gene one weekend, and I had joined them for dinner. So I wasn't a total surprise package. All the anticipated hugs and kisses took place when I arrived, and I felt warmly welcomed and accepted. Gene had no brothers or sisters, so I believe I received far more attention and flattery than I should have gotten…but it certainly made me feel good.

In the weeks that followed, arrangements for our marriage started falling into place. The date was set, the church reserved, and the invitations to the wedding and the reception printed. Originally, Gene and I wanted to keep the number of invitations to no more than fifty, but the list grew and grew and grew. I had to include the "dirty dozen", as well as some new friends I'd made in college. When our relatives, plus Gene's family and his parents close friends were included, the number of invitations added up to 105. I had really wanted to have the reception in our home, but that would no longer be practical. There would be upwards of 200 people coming to the reception with all the spouses and children, so we decided to rent a large tent which would be placed in our yard and have everything catered. Mom took charge of making all the arrangements for this.

Late in July the wedding invitations were mailed and everything seemed to be under control. I felt like I was floating on a cloud drifting over a wonderful world. The second weekend in August…one week before our marriage…everything came to a horrible, unbelievable end.

Gene spent the weekend at my home and he left for his home in Kalamazoo late Sunday evening. Mom, Dad and I went to bed shortly after he left, but in the early morning hours our phone rang and Dad answered it. It was Gene's father calling to tell us that Gene had been in a very bad automobile accident on his way home. Doctor Morris and his wife were at a Kalamazoo hospital, and they thought I should come there as quickly as possible. As soon as my Dad hung up the phone, he woke me up and told me that Gene was in the hospital and we should go there right away. He said, "I'm sure everything is going to be OK, so let's just try to stay calm." Mom, Dad and I dressed quickly and drove to the hospital, which was about an hour's drive away.

We found Gene's parents in a waiting room adjacent to the surgical area, and their anguish was obvious. Gene's mother started sobbing the moment she saw me, and I immediately realized that Gene's accident must be much worse than I had imagined.

Doctor Morris told us that when they arrived at the hospital a state highway patrol officer met them and explained that Gene hit a deer that ran across the highway, causing him to lose control of his car. The car ran off the side of the highway and went down an embankment...rolling over several times. He had his seat belt on, and the air bag deployed, but driving a convertible with the top down did nothing to protect his head. People in other cars saw the accident happen and someone called 911 right away on their cell phone. Help arrived quickly, but they had a difficult time getting Gene out from under his car. When the ambulance arrived at the hospital, he was rushed to surgery and now we had to wait to find out whether he was going to live or die.

When I fully understood what had happened and how critical Gene was, I suddenly felt a wave of white light wash over me and I fainted. When I came to, I was stretched out on a gurney with a blanket over me. A nurse was standing beside me. She had used smelling salts to revive me and I heard her say, "I want you to lay here quietly for a while. When you feel better you can sit up, but don't try to walk unless there's someone to help you."

I did what the nurse told me, and when I felt like I could stand up, Dad took my arm to support me and we returned to the waiting room. It was close to noon before a doctor finally met with us and he reported that the surgical team had done everything they could possibly do for Gene. The doctor did not give us much hope, explaining that Gene lay suspended between life and death. All we could do now was wait and pray that he would come out of it.

Later in the day Gene went into cardiac arrest and a CT scan showed that his brain had ceased to function. The same surgeon that met with us in the morning was the one who gave us this terrible news and he then suggested to Gene's parents that they consider donating their son's organs. They agreed, telling the doctor that they wanted something more for Gene's life, and they were sure that he would have wanted this done too. And so Gene's heart, lungs and liver were harvested to give others the gift of life.

I can hardly remember the next four days. Visitation at the funeral home in Kalamazoo was scheduled for Wednesday evening and Thursday afternoon and evening. The funeral service was scheduled for Friday morning. Somehow I managed to get through all this, but I felt like a numb puppet with some unknown person pulling my strings. The shock of Gene's death had made it impossible for me to function normally. I heard essentially the same expressions of sorrow over and over from the people who came to the funeral home, and I responded with words that must have tumbled out of my frozen brain. I frequently stared at the closed casket at one end of the room, and I knew Gene was there because I could feel his presence.

I knew that I had to go to the funeral service Friday morning, but I wasn't sure I could handle it. Somehow I did. The worst part was the internment service at the cemetery. Next to the grave there was a green carpet on which there were two rows of folding chairs. I was directed to sit in the front row with my mother and father, Papa John and Gene's parents. Danny, Abby, and some relatives of Gene's family sat in the row in back of us. I have no idea what was said as I stared at the pile of dirt that I knew would soon be covering Gene's casket.

At the end of the service at the cemetery, the funeral director announced that everyone was invited to a lunch at the church that the Morris' attended. Some of the ladies at their church had prepared a meal, which was served in the meeting hall. When we arrived there, my mother suggested that I should try to go around the room and talk with people…but I couldn't. I sat down at one of the tables. My legs were trembling. After a while some nice woman put a plate of food in front of me. I glanced down at the plate and saw a slice of ham, what looked like scalloped potatoes and some applesauce. My stomach felt so queasy that I knew I couldn't eat any of it. So I took my fork, pushed the food around on my plate and picked at the food pretending to eat.

I was distracted for a while watching three little boys. They had made a paper ball by crunching a newspaper into a round wad and were taking turns trying to throw it and kick it. Their makeshift paper ball couldn't be thrown or kicked very far, but that didn't stop them from trying, and they were amusing themselves. I thought how fortunate they are. All they had to be concerned about was just entertaining themselves. They didn't have any real problems, no tragedy to deal with, and no responsibilities. For some silly reason I remembered my high school sophomore class float and its theme…"Don't Worry, Be Happy"…and I wondered if I would ever know real happiness again. I started to cry and I couldn't stop. The rest of that day is just a blur and the next day…the day that Gene and I were to be married…had to be the worst day of my life.

The rest of August and into early September I tried to pull myself together. I was registered to start my second year at the veterinary college, but emotionally and physically I just didn't have the will or the strength to go to my apartment in East Lansing and start classes. I simply wanted to stay at home as long as it took me to recover…taking it one day at a time. It was really hard for me to sleep, probably because I wasn't getting any exercise. I got a prescription for sleeping pills, but they didn't help much.

The apple harvest was underway, and taking a lot of Dad's and Papa Johns time. Mom was very busy with our farm market, but each of them took time during the day to check on me. Part of the time I sat in our den staring at the TV tube, sometimes I sat on the porch or just walked around the yard or out into the orchard. There was lots of activity going on all around me. We had a record apple crop, one of the biggest and best in years. The migrant workers who were picking the apples, most of whom I was acquainted with because they were our regulars, would wave or smile whenever they saw me.

Dad had a hard time talking to me, but he knew how terrible I felt. He'd put his arms around me, hug me, kiss me on the cheek and every time he did this I noticed that there were tears in his eyes. He loved me, and even though he didn't say it in words, it was obvious that he was sharing some of my grief. My mother brought me hot tea and glasses of cold fresh cider and kept asking if I needed anything. She shocked me once though when she asked me if I thought that the wedding presents I'd received should be returned. I hadn't even thought about it and I answered her by saying, "I really don't care what happens to the wedding presents. You decide what to do with them."

The minister at our church came several times to talk with me, and I appreciated his kindness and support. Ukadean came to visit me on a warm Saturday afternoon in early September. We sat in the swing on the front porch talking and drinking cider. She cheered me up with some funny stories about the kids in her third grade class, as well as several updates on the antics of her crazy mother. Ukadean and her husband Bill now lived in an apartment in Grand Rapids and both had jobs as schoolteachers.

I believe Papa John was the person who helped me the most. He would come to the house at different times of the day and just sit in a chair near me. Sometimes we talked a little and sometimes we didn't talk at all. He was there to keep me company, but he was apparently also waiting for the right time to say something to me that would help me through this period of grief and despair. That time came one afternoon when I was sitting in a chair on our front porch. Papa John came round the house and joined me. After a while he said to me, "Colleen, I really know how discouraged, lost and forlorn you feel. You may not believe this, but when your grandmother Mary died, I thought that my world had ended. I didn't care if I lived or died. It took a while for me to heal, but I can assure you that time will make a difference. You'll never forget Gene as he'll always have a special place in your heart. But I'm sure he would expect you to go on with your life and become the veterinarian that you've dreamed of becoming. Before your grandmother died, she told me that she knew her days with me were coming to an end. She told me that she wanted me to carry on, and if I didn't she would be very disappointed. She said you have a son, a daughter and grandchildren that need you and your love. Your son Ed particularly needs your support because you're not only his father, but also his best friend. After I'm gone, I expect you to do what you have to do every day…working in the orchard and on the farm and I'll be right there with you. Whenever you feel a soft breeze on your cheek, I want you to think that it might be me. We've had a wonderful life together, and you owe it to me to carry on the way I'm telling you. Colleen, whenever I start feeling down I remember her words. I just wish I could find the right words or do something that would help you through this terrible time. I hope what I've just shared with you will help do that."

I looked at Papa John for a while without saying a word. For the first time I was really aware how distraught he was when my grandmother passed away. He had grieved far more than I realized at the time. I was sad of course when my grandmother died, but I now realized that my sorrow didn't begin to compare with my grandfather's. I was a young girl then, and like most children, I was soon concerned about other things going on in my life. Not so for Papa John.

Papa John took my hand and pulled me up out of the chair I was sitting in. He said, "Come on, let's go for a walk. I think it would do you good."

We went around the house and out into the orchard. As we walked along, I became aware of the sweet smell created by the trees loaded with ripe apples. It's a pleasant aroma that exists only until all the apples are harvested, and it was very familiar to me. Papa John picked two Macintosh apples, rubbed them with his handkerchief and handed one to me to eat. For the first time in weeks I actually enjoyed eating something. I didn't realize how hungry I was, and the simple act of eating a juicy, sweet apple made me feel better.

After a while Papa John said, "Let's pick some apples." He went and got each of us a canvas bag used for picking apples. I slipped one over my shoulders and found a tree with lots of apples that I could reach by standing on the ground. I went around the tree filling the bag hanging on the front of my chest. When it was full, I took it to an empty crate, unsnapped the flap on the bottom of the bag, and released the apples gently into the crate. It felt good to be doing something and so I kept at it…filling crate after crate with apples. After I had been picking for several hours, Dad went by on a tractor. He was pulling a flat-bed trailer loaded with large wooden bins filled with apples. Dad smiled when he saw me, and waved and gave me a "thumbs-up" as he passed by.

I stopped picking apples and just stood watching my father as he drove through the orchard towards the storage barn. I suddenly had a manifestation of reality. It had to be an epiphany, as I said to myself, "Colleen, what are you doing picking apples? You should be at MSU going to your classes. You're registered for the fall term. You've paid all the tuition fees. You're paying rent for a furnished apartment. And here you are standing in an orchard with a picking bag hanging on your chest half full of apples."

It was at that very moment that I decided I must get on with my life.

I went to our house, packed what I needed to take to college and put everything in my Chevy. Then I went looking for Mom, Dad and Papa John to tell them that I was leaving for East Lansing, and that I'd call that evening to let them know how I was doing. They were surprised and concerned about my sudden decision, but there were no objections. My mother offered to go with me and stay through the weekend, but I assured her that it wouldn't be necessary.

As I drove to East Lansing, I began to have second thoughts about leaving home, particularly about how I would feel living in the apartment that Gene and I had planned to live in together. I tried putting that concern out of my mind, telling myself that it really wasn't that big a deal. It was, though, because I had a really good cry after I unloaded the car and got things put away. After washing my face with cold water, I felt better and I went to the grocery store to shop for the food I needed for the apartment. I kept telling myself, "I can do this. I've got to go on with my life. I know I can do this. I have to really try."

My biggest concern was catching up with my courses, as I had missed the first three weeks of the fall term classes. After I called home that evening, I also called several classmates. They were glad to hear from me, and offered to help me with my classes by sharing their notes and reviewing what had been covered in the textbooks. This was really encouraging, and I went to bed that night feeling better than I had in weeks.

The next day I started attending classes, and I explained to each professor why I had been absent for three weeks. They all knew about Gene's fatal automobile accident, but were unaware that Gene and I had planned to be married in August.

I didn't know what to expect from my professors, but fortunately my high grade point average my first year in the College of Veterinary Medicine saved the day. I think that was the deciding factor, as all the professors offered to let me stay in their class if I could get my classmates to help me get current. I told each professor that all I wanted was the opportunity to continue my education. I assured them that I could catch up.

And I did! That fall I totally dedicated myself to my courses in nutrition, environment, behavior, immunology, biochemistry and cell biology and passed them all with flying colors. Several classmates helped me by reviewing what the professors had covered in the classes I missed. My only break was the Thanksgiving weekend. I went home for the weekend, but even then I had my nose in a book most of the time. There was time, though, to visit with Mom, Dad, Papa John and even my friend Ukadean.

The Christmas break from college was truly welcome. I had really pushed myself to the limit to pass the finals for the fall term. I felt proud of what I had achieved. Not only for making up the missed classes, but for passing all my courses again with high grades. Now I really needed some time to unwind, chill out and just plain rest before starting the next term.

During the Christmas break, I spent a day in Kalamazoo with Gene's mother and father. I still thought about Gene frequently, but I had reached the point where I didn't cry or get teary-eyed every time I thought about him. Time, apparently, was helping to heal my emotions…but 1988 was a year that I'd certainly never forget.

Between Christmas and New Year's, Danny and Abby, along with their daughters stayed with the Zondervines for three days. Danny wasn't able to take any more time off than that, as his position supervising the eight Zon's Thrifty Marts was very demanding at yearend. The four of them came to our home one afternoon to exchange gifts. It was truly a delightful time. After all the gift wrapping paper was cleaned up, we had a delicious dinner prepared as only my German Mom can do it. I enjoyed getting acquainted again with my nieces, as I had not seen them since last summer. Jennifer was now almost two years old, and Julie was one.

While I was home from college and between terms, nothing else of any consequence happened, but I frequently wondered what the coming year 1989 would bring. Surely, I thought, it had to be a kinder, gentler year than 1988. But who knows?

As it turned out, the first half of the year went by uneventfully. I finished my second year in the veterinary college at MSU in the spring of 1989. Again that summer I worked at the Cunningham Veterinary Clinic, but in early August took a week off to go to Elkhart, Indiana. Danny and Abby invited me to spend a week with them. They needed a baby sitter for three days while they attended the National Hardware Show in Chicago, and I was glad they asked me to help them out. I got to their home in Elkhart two days before they planned to leave for Chicago because Jennifer and Julie needed to get comfortable with me as their caretaker and I needed to learn their routine. All went well the first two days, but my intuition antenna told me that something was not quite right. I didn't say anything or ask any questions, but I sensed a tension between Abby and Danny that concerned me.

The three days taking care of Jennifer and Julie passed quickly and all went well. We got along great. Danny and Abby arrived home from Chicago late at night, so we didn't have an opportunity to talk until the next morning. After breakfast Danny said he had something important he wanted to discuss with me. What he had to say to me was incredible.

Danny asked if he could borrow $40,000.00 from me from my trust fund.

His request surprised me and I asked him "Why do you want to borrow money from me, when you have a trust fund of your own?"

He answered, "Because my trust fund is gone."

"You can't be serious," I said, "You couldn't have spent more than $600,000.00. My fund is now close to $700,000.00 because of accumulated earnings, and we both started with $600,000.00 in our individual trusts."

"Some of the money went to buy and furnish this house and some went for expensive vacation trips Abby and I took. A lot of it though, I'm sorry to say, I lost gambling," Danny explained.

"Gambling?"

"Yes, I've been a fool, Colleen. Sometimes I won, of course, but obviously other times I lost. Then I became desperate trying to recoup my losses and I took chances I shouldn't have taken. Now I owe $40,000.00 to three men in Chicago that I lost money to betting on sports. I've got to pay these guys, and I really don't want to go to Mom or Dad or to Abby's parents for the money. You'll do me a great favor if you'll help me out of this jam. Believe me, I've learned my lesson. I'm not going to do any more gambling. I fully intend to pay the money back. I'm not asking you to give me the money. I'm asking you to loan me the money."

"Well, sure," I said a little hesitantly, "I'll call the Old Kent Bank Trust Department and ask George Gaehle to withdraw $40,000.00 from my trust. And, I won't say anything to Mom or Dad about this. I'll write you a check now, and I'll call you when I've deposited the $40,000.00 from my trust into my checking account."

Danny and I talked for a while longer and he seemed full of remorse. He told me several times how much he appreciated my help and support, and assured me that he was going to control his gambling. After he left to go to work, I called our Mr. Gaehle at Old Kent Bank to request that he sell $40,000.00 worth of investments, as I needed to withdraw that amount of money from my trust. There was an unexpected pause before Mr. Gaehle answered. I didn't expect him to question my withdrawal request, but he finally asked, "Colleen, I need to ask you if this money is for your brother?"

"Yes it is. But it's a loan," I explained.

"Colleen, I learned about Danny's gambling losses some months ago, and I tried to get him to seek help," Mr. Gaehle replied. "I'm convinced that he's addicted to gambling. If you are withdrawing this money for Danny, then you're just enabling him and he'll waste your trust fund just as he's wasted his. Please don't do this if that's what you're going to do with the $40,000.00."

I explained to Mr. Gaehle, "I've got to help Danny this time, but I assure you there will not be a next time. I won't withdraw any more money for Danny to pay any more gambling debts. He doesn't want our mother and father to know about this, but if I learn that he is still gambling, then I will make them aware of it. They'll make sure he gets professional help if this continues to be a problem. However, Danny assures me that he has learned his lesson and I have to believe him."

"All right, Colleen," Mr. Gaehle replied, "I'll have your check ready for you to pick up tomorrow afternoon. But I couldn't say nothing after I belatedly found out that most of the money Danny was taking from his trust was being used to pay for his gambling debts. Danny better get himself under control, as there will be serious consequences if he doesn't do so. If Andy Zondervine were to learn about this gambling problem, I know he would take it very seriously…and I have no doubt that it would affect Danny's career with Zon's Thrifty Marts. I sincerely hope that Danny has learned his lesson, because I've always thought very highly of him. But he's not alone. There are thousands of people in this country addicted to gambling, and I have personally witnessed several who have made a horrible mess of their lives because they couldn't control their urge to gamble"

I thanked Mr. Gaehle for what he had to say, and told him that I appreciated his concern and advice. I emphatically requested…in fact begged him…to please keep Danny's problem to himself. I especially didn't want this to hurt Danny's career. However, I knew that Mom and Dad were going to find out eventually that his trust was gone. When that happened, they were going to be terribly upset—particularly when they leaned that most of his trust fund had been squandered gambling.

After I finished the phone call with Mr. Gaehle, Abby and I talked for a long time about Danny's gambling problem. She was really distressed about it, and she unloaded all her pent-up frustration, telling me how upsetting it was. I'm sure it helped her to finally have someone she could talk with, as she had kept everything bottled up inside. She explained that whenever she urged Danny to seek help he refused to talk about it. I was surprised and I became angry when she said that Danny even threatened to leave her if she kept nagging him. Abby told me that Danny insisted that he didn't need any help because he could handle his gambling. "It isn't that big a deal," is what she said he kept telling her.

I asked Abby, "How did this gambling for high stakes get started? I know Danny enjoyed playing poker when he was in high school and college, but it was just for small nickel and dime stakes. He told me he usually won a few dollars. Come to think of it, I don't recall his ever telling me that he lost a few dollars. However, that's not even remotely close to what has happened in the past several years."

Abby told me that three years ago Danny went to the National Hardware Show in Chicago. He was there for several days and late one afternoon he stopped in the lounge in the hotel where he was staying to have a drink before going to dinner. There was a man sitting near him at the bar and he struck up a conversation with Danny. He asked Danny if he ever played poker. Danny told him that he was a pretty good poker player, but only played for small stakes. This man claimed he didn't know what the stakes were, but that there was an opening for another player for a poker game that night at a suite in the hotel. Danny was led to believe that the players were all men who were in Chicago for the Hardware Show, just like himself. Danny, unfortunately, went that night, and he won more than $2,000.00. The stakes were much, much higher than he had ever played for before, and he was very excited when he called me the next day to tell me how much he had won. The next night, though, he went back again…and this time he lost more than $23,000.00. He thinks some professional gamblers took advantage of him."

"You would have thought that would have been enough," Abby explained, "and that he had learned an expensive lesson. But no! It turned out to be just the beginning. He gets a thrill out of high-stakes gambling. I think Danny is so used to winning at sports that he can't understand how he can lose gambling. I believe he is so convinced that he will win that he plays a hand when he should probably drop out. I hate to say it, and I wouldn't say this to Danny, but that doesn't make him a good poker player. He told me one time he drew to an inside straight and got it but another player had a better hand. Sometimes when I pleaded with him to please stop his gambling he would say to me, "*If everything in life was a sure thing, what fun would it be?*"

"Danny plays poker at least once a week at our Country Club, and he's gone to Las Vegas several times to gamble. He bets on Monday night football games, and he lost a lot of money last spring betting on basketball games during 'March Madness'. It seems like nearly every team he bet on either lost or failed to cover the point spread. The more he bet, the more he lost, and then he bet even more trying to double up and get even. He just got deeper and deeper into debt because he made so many bad bets. That's why Danny had to take all the money that was left in his trust to pay for his losses. Mr. Gaehle was suspicious that something was amiss, and after some questions Danny finally told him in confidence that he had gambling debts that had to be paid. Danny was sorry afterwards that he explained to Mr. Gaehle what he needed the money for, because now he's scared that he might call one or both of our parents. He personally knows them. That wouldn't be good, of course, but I think the fear of that happening is making Danny think twice about placing any more bets on sports. At least I hope so." Abby said.

I assured Abby that, when I picked up the check the next day, that I'd again urge Mr. Gaehle to keep this problem confidential.

"The other thing, Colleen," Abby went on. "we're living beyond our means. Danny's well paid, and I have income from my Zon's stock. Some of the money from Danny's trust was used to buy and furnish this home. But we've re-mortgaged it to pay gambling debts, and we now have a huge monthly mortgage payment. We drive two expensive cars and belong to the Country Club because Danny wants to maintain a good image. I'd like to drop the Country Club membership, but Danny refuses because that's where he plays poker. His gambling has caused a lot of stress in our marriage. I still love Danny in spite of the problems and the trouble he's created with his gambling. I think about my marriage vows, especially the words '*For better or for worse.*' This has to be the worst of times. I'm reluctant to leave Danny, either with a trial separation or, as horrible as it sounds, to divorce him, as it would really start a firestorm of problems. If I went to my parents home, they'd soon learn the reason, and daddy would never promote Danny. The man that now heads the marketing department at Zon's will retire next June, and Danny hopes to be promoted into that position. We'd move back to Grand Rapids, and I'd love that. I just hope and pray this will happen. It would then be very difficult for Danny to continue his gambling, working in the company headquarters and living close to both our parents. Best of all, it would improve our marriage because, in spite of this gambling mess, I still love my husband very much."

I agreed with Abby that it would be good for them if they moved back to the Grand Rapids area, and I was glad to learn there was a real possibility of this happening. Their lifestyle would become far more involved with our families, and that would be the best thing that could happen, not only for Abby and Danny, but also for their children. Although they didn't live a long way from Grand Rapids, there wasn't much personal contact…it was mostly phone calls. In the past two years I could count on my fingers the number of times that I had been with Danny and his family.

I left Elkhart the next morning, stopping to pick up the $40,000.00 check at Old Kent Bank and deposit it in my checking account. That evening I called Danny to let him know that he could now deposit my check in order to pay the money he owed to the men in Chicago. However, I told him that in order for him to deposit the check he had to promise to do one thing for me. I said, "Danny, as a special favor to me, and for Abby too, I'm asking you to please drop your membership in the Country Club."

He replied, "Yes, I promise I will. I think it's a good idea. If I stop going to the club, then I won't be tempted to play poker when I go there. I've got to convince myself, as well as Abby and you, that I can get my urge to gamble under control."

I called Abby a week later and was happy to learn that they had resigned their Country Club membership. She told me that, as far as she knew, Danny hadn't placed any more bets with the Chicago bookies, and that he had paid them what he owed them. I thought to myself, "What a horrible waste of money."

In late summer and fall of 1989, I completed the first half of my third year in the Veterinary Medicine College. I was now more than half way through, and I felt that I had really accomplished something. During that term I called and talked with Abby and Danny once or twice a week, and so far as I could determine everything seemed to be going OK. Apparently Danny had his gambling under control now, and I hoped and prayed that it would stay that way. I was sure Abby would have told me if there was still a problem. I also sensed that there was an improvement in their relationship, which I mainly learned when I talked just with Abby. And, although she never admitted it to me, I think she was putting a lot of pressure on her father to promote Danny to the marketing position. Not just for Danny's benefit, but for hers as well. She informed me several times in our phone conversations that she was determined to move back to the Grand Rapids area. She had been away from there long enough.

The Christmas and holiday season of 1989 was really memorable. Abby, Danny and their two daughters spent two days at our house as well as several days with the Zondervines. *There was lots of good news.* Abby announced she was pregnant and the baby was due in May. Danny got the marketing position with Zon's Thrifty Marts effective July 1, 1990, and would start phasing into his new responsibilities in March. They had listed their home in Elkhart with a Realtor, and were looking for a home to buy either in Grand Rapids or in the surrounding area.

In January and February of 1990, Abby and Danny looked at a number of homes, and they decided to make an offer on a large turn-of-the-century home in Grand Rapids. It was a distinctive home that had been well maintained and extensively remodeled. However, it had been on the market for several years and the owners had not received a single offer. As a result, Danny and Abby were able to purchase this home at a bargain price. They made an offer considerably under the asking price, and the sellers accepted. Abby was really excited about the house and especially liked all the bedrooms. There were six of them. A huge master bedroom for Abby and Danny, one for each of their children, a guest bedroom and a sixth one that they planned to use for a den and game room. Quite a house!

There was another interesting development that winter. My mother and father bought a three-bedroom condo in a fifteen-story condominium building located right on the Gulf in Orange Beach, Alabama. In January they were invited to visit friends who owned a condo in this building, and Mom and Dad liked it so much that they bought a unit for themselves. I was really surprised when Mom called to tell me what they had done. She told me, "I can't wait to have you see our condo. You're going to love it, Colleen. There's a beautiful sugar-white sand beach that stretches for miles along the Gulf right in front of our condo. Ed and I take a long walk every morning on the beach. There are so many things to do here…all kinds of activities are available for the people who live in the building. We're going to spend January and February there from now on. We've had enough of winter."

It wasn't at all like my mother and father to do anything impetuously, so I was really and truly surprised and somewhat shocked when my mother told me that they'd bought a condo in Alabama. I knew they could afford it, of course, but when she told me "they'd had enough of winter" that was something of a surprise. I wasn't aware that they had come to feel this way, and I thought about Mom's statement a lot. Mom and Dad both liked to ski and ride snowmobiles, and on mild winter days Dad was usually out in the orchard doing some pruning…which he had always said he enjoyed. I'd heard my mother say a number of times over the years that, to really appreciate spring, you have to experience the freezing cold and snow of winter. "Nothing welcomes spring like the trees in an apple orchard when they're in full bloom shouting to the world spring is here," she liked to say. Apparently Mom and Dad's attitudes about winter were changing, and I thought maybe it was due to their growing older. Perhaps I'll feel the same way someday.

In the spring of 1990, Abby and Danny moved to their new home, and it didn't take them long to get settled. It wasn't an easy move for Abby, as she was seven months pregnant, but they got a lot of help with the packing and moving from friends and family.

John Andrew Malone was born on May 19, weighing in at a little over seven pounds. With the initials JAM I wondered if "JAM" or "JAMI" would become John Andrews nickname. I also couldn't help wondering if my nephew might someday be as good as, or maybe even a better, athlete than his father Danny was in high school and college. That was a long time in the future so I soon dismissed the thought. It was easy to tell that Danny was thrilled to have a son, and he was also very upbeat and looking forward to becoming the marketing director for Zon's Thrifty Marts. He told me that the phase-in process was going quite well, and that he was confident that he could handle the job with no problem.

As far as I knew or could tell, neither Andy Zondervine nor Mom and Dad knew that Danny had lost a lot of money the past few years gambling. Since Danny and I each had complete control of our trusts, there was no reason for the bank to inform our parents that Danny's trust no longer existed. I knew, however, that it would only be a matter of time before our folks found out. I knew, and so did Danny, that there would come a day when either Mom or Dad would ask how much money was still in his trust and Danny would have to answer truthfully. I didn't want to be present when that happened. I just hoped that Abby's parents would never learn about it, because that would affect not only their relationship with Danny, but also his future with Zon's.

Nearly every day I couldn't help but think for a minute or two about Danny's financial losses due to his gambling, and the bad choices he had made. It was hard for me to understand how he had gotten himself into such a mess, but I kept hoping and praying that his fortune was changing with the birth of his son, his new job responsibilities and his move back to Michigan.

I finished my third year in the MSU College of Veterinary Medicine in the spring of 1990. Just one more year to go, and I'd be Colleen Margaret Malone, DVM. That summer, for the fifth year in a row, I was employed at the Cunningham Veterinary Clinic...gaining more on the job experience treating cats, dogs, horses, cows, sheep, birds and even a monkey. I never had to take care of a pig, though, as very few are raised in Southwestern Michigan.

Late August was a difficult time for me because I frequently thought about what my life could have been like if only Gene and not died as result of that automobile accident. Gene and I should have been celebrating the second anniversary of our marriage. Instead I went to the cemetery and put flowers on his grave. I happened to read a newspaper article about the number of automobile accidents each year in Michigan that resulted from hitting a deer. I was astounded to learn there were more than 62,000 of them in 1988, and 13 people had died as a result of a deer being hit by a car. One of them unfortunately was Gene.

That summer, for the first time in several years, I was able to be with Abby and Danny frequently. They invited Mom, Dad, Papa John and me to their home almost every week and they were at Mom and Dad's for Sunday dinner once or twice a month. It was as if we were all making up for the time we didn't see each other when they lived in Indiana. Several times when they came to our home, Dad would take Jennifer and Julie for a ride through the orchard in a trailer that he pulled with a small tractor. They thought they were at Disneyland, but Dad would tell them it was really Appleland.

I also got together with Ukadean a few times during that summer. We never ran out of things to talk about. She was pregnant with her and Bill's second child. The baby was due in October. I couldn't help but be a little envious of her, because she and her husband Bill were so happy and were creating their own family. I wondered if they really and truly appreciated how fortunate they were.

Late in August, I returned to my apartment in East Lansing to start my fourth and final year in the vet school. My senior year went fine because I continued to dedicate myself to studying my courses, and I graduated in the spring of 1991. Mom, Dad and Papa John attended the graduation ceremony and soon after it was over we left for home. My dependable Chevy was already packed with everything I had brought with me to college, so we arrived home a little before dinnertime. I discovered, when I got home, that there were lots of cards, flowers and a few gifts from my family and some of my friends offering congratulations to Doctor Colleen M. Malone. Doctor Robert Cunningham sent me a large box of business cards printed with my name as a way of welcoming me to the practice as his associate. In anticipation of my joining his practice, Dr. Cunningham had expanded the clinic and added the latest in diagnostic and treatment equipment.

I had decided, however, that I wanted to take three weeks off to relax before starting to work full time. Two months before graduation, I withdrew $10,000.00 from my trust to pay for a two-week cruise in the Mediterranean. Mom and Dad offered to pay for the trip, but I insisted on paying for it myself. They had paid the entire cost of my college education, which had consisted of four years at Hope College and four years at MSU.

When I was home for Easter, I explained to my parents that I wanted to take a cruise of the Greek Isles as a kind of personal reward for achieving my goal of becoming a veterinarian. They thought it was a great idea and both decided they'd go with me. A few weeks later though, I learned that Papa John had not been feeling well, so Dad decided he'd better stay home to make sure the spraying of the apple trees would be done on schedule, as the spring sprays are the critical ones. So Mom and I shared this memorable vacation, which was also a great learning experience. While in Athens, the birthplace of Western civilization, we visited the Acropolis, walked around the Parthenon, and visited the major tourist attractions. We left Athens after several days to take a bus tour of the interior, including legendary Thebes and Delphi. We stayed overnight in the Hotel Amiklia near Delphi, where we had a fantastic view of the valley below filled with thousands of olive trees.

The next day we visited Mycenae and Nauplia. Our professional guide, Nikos, continually pointed out interesting things and explained what we were seeing. We crossed over to the Peloponnesus peninsula on a huge ferry and then traveled down the coastline to Corinth. We then went to Epidaurus, built in the 4th century BC, and from there to Mycenae, stopping to see the ancient sites of Tiryns and Argos. We proceeded to Nauplia, a beautiful town in an exquisite setting between twin fortresses, where we stayed overnight.

We were awakened the next morning by a rooster crowing. That day we boarded the cruise ship *Marco Polo* for a seven-day cruise to various Greek islands. First stop was tiny Delos Island where we were tendered ashore. Delos was once the religious and political center of the Aegean Sea, but today it is inhabited only by a wondrous assortment of ruins. We went back to the ship for lunch and then on to Mykonos, a ritzy, whitewashed town with nice beaches and boutiques. Next stop was Santorini, where we toured the ancient ruins at Akrotiri—which was buried by a volcanic eruption in 1500 BC. On the way to the ruins we passed many vineyards. On Santorini, Mom and I especially liked the town of Fira, perched high on the rim of a caldera, as there were many charming shops and spectacular views of the sea. We then sailed on to Crete, docking at Iraklion. We wandered all over town and bought some souvenirs. That evening we sailed for Rhodes, arriving there early the next morning. After breakfast we went ashore and took a bus tour of the city, ending up at a small village by the sea for lunch.

Our ship arrived at Kusadasi, Turkey early the next morning. We went ashore and boarded a tour bus, which took us to Selcut, successor to the great city of Ephesus. After our tour of Ephesus, we returned to Kusadasi, where we had a fascinating experience shopping for a Turkish carpet. Prices for goods are negotiated, but my German mother proved to be too tough a negotiator for the Turkish shop owner. So we left the shop without one. The next day we sailed all day without any stops, and it was pleasant to spend some time relaxing on the deck of our ship. The next morning we arrived at Canakkale, Turkey where we boarded a bus for Troy. The first thing we saw when we arrived in Troy was a replica of the famous Trojan horse. We were really impressed touring the remains of this legendary city. The next day the *Marco Polo* arrived in Istanbul and we left the ship and stayed in the Conrad Hilton Hotel the final two days of our vacation. While in Istanbul we toured the city, visiting many impressive mosques and the world famous Topkapi Palace. Then it was back to the U.S.A. and the end of an adventure that my Mom and I shared, and an experience that neither of us would ever forget.

It also marked the official end of my years in college, as this trip to Greece and Turkey was a celebration of my graduating from Michigan State University with a Doctor of Veterinary Medicine degree. It was now time for me to go to work.

CHAPTER 4

The Business World

In the spring of 1991, when I began my career as a veterinarian, Danny had already spent six years of his business career with Zon's Thrifty Marts. He was now Zon's Vice President in charge of Marketing. Whenever I saw Danny in person or talked with him on the phone he was upbeat, enthusiastic and seemed extremely happy with his job. He usually had something positive to say about whatever he was doing. He particularly liked to talk about, actually brag about, any special promotion that he had planned that resulted in more sales than they had anticipated.

It was quite obvious to me that Danny was working hard, loved what he was doing and putting in a lot of hours at Zon's. Farming and retailing have one thing in common. They both demand a big commitment of your time. Fortunately Abby understood that this was a necessary part of her husband's responsibilities. She accepted and never complained about the long hours that Danny worked, as she had grown up in the retailing business. To her credit, she ran their household efficiently...taking care of virtually everything for the house and the yard so that when Danny was home he could spend quality time with Abby and his children. Jennifer was now five, Julie was four and John was a year old.

As far as I knew, Danny's gambling was under control. I was sure that Abby would have called me if he started doing any gambling again. Mom and Dad had eventually learned about the money Danny lost gambling but *it was discussed only one time* with me. And it was obvious that it was a subject that *we were not going to talk about again*, because they both considered the large amount of money he wasted gambling a family disgrace. For Mom and Dad, it was an unfortunate episode in Danny's life that was best forgotten about, shut away, and kept confidential. So I respected their opinion, as well as their decision as to how they wanted to deal with Danny's gambling, and never brought the subject up.

But because I was personally involved, I couldn't help but think from time to time about all the money Danny wasted gambling. He had repaid $6,000.00 of the money he borrowed from me from my trust, and I told him it wasn't necessary to repay any more. As far as I was concerned, he could have the rest of the money, as my trust fund was growing unbelievably. It was well invested by the trust department of Old Kent Bank, and was now close to one million dollars. It was hard to believe that I had that much money in the bank.

Apparently, Abby's parents were still not aware that Danny had wasted a large part of the money in his trust by gambling it away. Hopefully, they'd never find out! Things, it seemed, had really turned out the way Abby and I believed and hoped they would when they moved back to Grand Rapids. Danny's new management responsibilities with Zon's, plus the close proximity to both parents, couldn't help but restrict or deter his opportunities to gamble. Also, I wanted to believe that Danny really had learned a bitter lesson and that he had, and would, resist the temptation to risk any more of his money gambling on sports or playing poker for high stakes.

As the weeks and months went by that summer and fall, I was so busy working as a veterinarian that I really had very little time or opportunity to think a lot about Danny, his family or much else for that matter. I found my work challenging, absorbing, interesting, rewarding and appreciated by our clientele…and I had absolutely no regrets about becoming a veterinarian.

I continued to live at home, and offered to pay my parents something for my "keep" but they wouldn't hear of it. They were glad to have me around, but after a few months, they also started hinting or suggesting that I should be doing more things socially with people my own age. Not sitting at home with them every evening watching television or playing Scrabble, Skip-Bo, dominoes or some other game.

My social life actually got started in an interesting way. The trustworthy Chevy that Papa John bought for me was now more than eight years old. It was showing some wear and tear, and it had suffered a few bumps and bruises. I got the urge to get a newer car and started visiting automobile dealerships trying to decide which make and what model car I wanted to buy. After visiting several dealerships, I decided to check out Buick, and to my surprise the salesman who greeted me at the dealership was Steve Hurley, my date for the high school senior prom. Hard to believe that event was a little over eight years ago. Steve gave me a big hug when I walked into the showroom, and we talked for at least a half hour before we started talking about cars. There was a lot of news to catch up on, although I was surprised to discover he knew quite a lot about my life. Steve knew that I had gone to Hope College and then to Michigan State, and that I had planned to be married but that my fiancé was killed in a car wreck. He was aware that I was a veterinarian, and asked me a lot of questions about my work, about Danny and his family and about my parents and Papa John. He had met and knew all of them when we were in high school, eight years ago.

Steve told me that he had gone to Grand Valley State College, where he got a business degree, and after graduating had worked for a furniture manufacturing company in Grand Rapids for two years before joining the Buick dealership. He liked the automobile business because it was a lot more challenging, and he claimed he had the best product on the market. "Someday," he said, "I want to own a Buick dealership."

I also learned that he was still single, with no special relationship with anyone, so I wondered if he might ask me out on a date sometime." I ended up buying a Buick Riviera from Steve, and after I'd signed all the sales agreement forms, he did ask me to have dinner with him and go to a movie. I accepted his invitation and that was the start of my social activities. Word soon got around that I was living at home and still single. Nearly all my high school girl friends were either already married or engaged to be married. It wasn't long before I received calls from several guys that I had dated in high school, and several others that I knew, but hadn't dated before.

Starting in the late summer and through that fall I enjoyed going on dates with Steve and quite a few other guys…mostly on the weekends. In addition to dates to go to dinner and a show or concert, I went horse back riding, and on dune buggy rides and canoe trips, and salmon fishing in Lake Michigan. My life was really pretty interesting, and I was enjoying myself. I loved my "Riv", as I called my Buick Riviera, and was very glad I bought it. It was fun to drive, smooth riding, classy-looking and had a lot of zip when I needed to put the pedal to the metal.

In late November I took a day off from work because I needed to take care of some personal things, but primarily because Abby had called and invited me to come to her house for lunch. She said it was important. While we were having lunch, Abby told me some very disturbing news. "She and Danny," she said, "were greatly concerned about a lawsuit that had been filed against a company called Ryan Chemicals in Dayton, Ohio."

"This company," Abby explained, "produced plating and rust-proofing chemicals that ACE Stamping used in the manufacture of their wheelbarrows. About two years ago, Ben Cockrell learned that this company was for sale, and he was successful in acquiring it. After the acquisition, Ryan Chemicals became a division of ACE Stamping.

Unfortunately, Ben had not done sufficient due diligence in negotiating to acquire the company, and soon after he bought Ryan Chemicals he learned that the company had been cited several times for polluting the land on which the plant was located.

"An ambitious prosecuting attorney in Dayton decided to go after Ryan Chemicals," Abby explained, "especially since it was no longer locally owned, and he was suing ACE Stamping for twenty-five million dollars. Ben Cockrell closed down Ryan Chemicals after this lawsuit was filed, and all the workers at the plant were laid off. There has been a lot of really bad publicity in Dayton about the pollution, and about the workers losing their jobs. The financial consequences for ACE Stamping were going to be absolutely dreadful. It might even force ACE Stamping to declare bankruptcy."

I had forgotten all about Danny's involvement with ACE Stamping, as it was years ago when he mentioned that he was going to become a director and a stockholder at Ben Cockrell's invitation. I said to Abby, "What a mess! I wish Danny had never, ever gotten involved in any business dealings with Ben Cockrell. What little income he must have received as a director or from dividends on the small amount of stock he bought in the company certainly wasn't worth all the aggravation and the expense that this lawsuit is going to involve."

Abby further explained that, "ACE Stamping has an Officers and Directors Liability Insurance policy but it's only for one million dollars. The legal expenses for defending this lawsuit, which is not only against both companies, but also names Ben Cockrell, Danny and all the other officers and directors as defendants, will cost far more than the one million dollars available through the insurance policy."

"Danny wanted to resign as a director," Abby went on to say, "but that wouldn't have removed him from the lawsuit, and if he did resign, then the officers and directors insurance might not be available to help pay his legal fees. We've asked our attorney, Doug Graham, to investigate the situation, and provide counsel until a Dayton law firm is hired to represent Danny and the other two directors at the trial. Doug Graham is trying to remove Danny from the lawsuit. Right now that doesn't look very promising."

This was really upsetting news. I told Abby that, and then added, "I certainly hope Danny will be able to get out of this lawsuit. It doesn't seem at all fair to me that he should even be a part of it. Danny was just an outside director and a small stockholder in ACE Stamping. I'm sure he didn't know about the pollution problem before this company was acquired and he certainly wasn't responsible for it occurring."

"Unfortunately, Colleen," Abby explained, "Danny had considerable involvement when ACE Stamping took over ownership of Ryan Chemicals. As director of ACE he voted for the acquisition at Ben Cockrell's urging. Then he signed all the acquisition papers and became a director of Ryan as well as of Ace. The owner of Ryan Chemicals said nothing about the pollution problems when he sold the company, and now he's claiming that it isn't as big a problem as the lawsuit claims it is. It's no wonder he was so eager to sell the company. It looked like a great bargain when Ben Cockrell bought it. Now it's turned out to be a disaster."

Abby went on to tell me that, "This is a horribly serious matter. It's going to be a really big distraction because Danny is going to have to take time off from his job to meet with the attorneys in Dayton who will be defending him and the two other directors, and attend hearings and prepare for the trial. We're both very worried about how much this is going to cost us. Danny made a terrible mistake getting involved with Ben Cockrell. He just never dreamed that something like this could ever happen."

"Does your father know about this lawsuit?" I asked.

"Yes, he's aware," Abby told me, "and he's very upset! Daddy told Danny he should never have gotten involved as a director of any company that sells products to Zon's Thrifty Marts. It's a conflict of interest and he was not happy to learn about it."

Just when I thought that Danny's life was really going well, this lawsuit had to come along and create a lot of anxiety and turmoil. Several days later I happened to come across a magazine article that included the line, *"Life's what happens to you when you're making other plans."* I thought, *"How right that is!"*

Months went by before we heard anything more about the lawsuit. Finally, in September, we learned that a pretrial hearing had been held and the date was set for the actual trial. It was scheduled to start March 22, 1993 in Dayton, Ohio.

In the meantime, my life Monday through Friday and some Saturday mornings was taken up with my career. I enjoyed going on dates with Steve and several other guys...but mainly on weekends. Ukadean and I got together at least once a month for dinner. Papa John came for dinner several times a month, and there were numerous other things happening in my life that distracted me from thinking about Danny's problem. There were always plenty of things going on at the orchard...particularly in the fall. All during the fall of that year, I helped whenever I had time by assisting Mom in the farm market. I actually enjoyed helping Mom now because I did so as a volunteer. When I was a high school teenager I had no choice. I was expected to help, and I did! As a result of all this, I seldom thought about Danny's lawsuit until we learned that the trial date had been set. However, once we knew the trial was really going to happen, and that Danny was going to be included in it, we did discuss it a lot...especially when Mom, Dad and I were together for dinner.

Midway through November of 1992, I arrived home one evening from the clinic to find Mom and Dad sitting at the kitchen table with a bottle of Dewar's Scotch on the table. They were both having a drink. *This was really unusual.* They seldom ever had an alcoholic drink during the week, and if they did it was either a beer or a glass of wine. Occasionally, on the weekend, they might have something stronger, but even that didn't happen very often. A number of thoughts flashed through my mind when I saw this, but the only thing I could think to say was, "Are we going out somewhere for dinner tonight?"

Once or twice a week Mom, Dad and I did go to a restaurant for dinner, but this was almost always discussed the night before while we were having dinner at home. I thought maybe we had decided to go somewhere for dinner this particular night and I had either missed hearing about it or had forgotten about it.

Mom answered me saying, "Yes, we're going to go somewhere for dinner. But first fix yourself a drink if you'd like one. There's something that's happened that you need to know about."

I sat down at the kitchen table and poured a light amount of scotch in a glass and added a lot of water. As I did this I asked, "Has something happened to Papa John?"

"Papa Johns OK," Dad reassured me, "This has to do with Danny and ACE Stamping."

Dad then proceeded to explain that Danny had called him about an hour ago to tell him that he had resigned as a director of ACE Stamping. There was a board meeting at noon today at which Ben Cockrell informed the board that two of their largest customers had cancelled their orders for wheelbarrows and had notified them that they would no longer do business with ACE Stamping. Earlier this year, Ben decided that a way to cut costs was to reduce the thickness of the steel used in manufacturing the wheelbarrows. He didn't immediately notify their customers of this slight reduction in the thickness of the steel tray of the wheelbarrows, nor were corrected specification sheets included in the boxes in which the wheelbarrows were shipped. These two big customers discovered that the metal was not as thick as the specifications claimed and this was reported to the Federal Trade Commission. Now ACE Stamping was faced with having to recall a lot of wheelbarrows, as well as pay a substantial fine. Ben told the board that corrected specification sheets and a little folder used as a store handout were ordered and printed, but they had not been distributed because they first wanted to use up the ones they had on hand. Apparently Ben thought he could get by with this because it was a very slight reduction in the thickness of the steel used to form the tray of the wheelbarrow. "However," Dad said, "he got caught and it's going to cost him dearly."

"Does Danny think this will have any affect on the Ryan Chemicals Lawsuit?" I wondered aloud.

"I don't think he knows that," Dad responded. "but Danny felt that, because of these circumstances, he had no other choice but to resign and try to distance himself from this mess. He told me that Ben pleaded with him not to resign as a director because he desperately needed his support. Danny also believes that ACE Stamping will have to file for Chapter Eleven bankruptcy protection. He wanted out before this happened and the ship went under."

That evening Mom, Dad and I had dinner at our favorite restaurant in downtown Rockford. During dinner we continued discussing this situation, particularly the terrible decisions that Ben Cockrell had made affecting ACE Stamping. First by acquiring the company in Dayton with the soil pollution problem. Now it was very likely that ACE Stamping would end up declaring bankruptcy because the jerk tried to get by without informing buyers that there had been a reduction in the thickness of the steel tray used in his wheelbarrows. Mom, Dad and I had never met Ben Cockrell, but we mutually agreed that he was not a good businessman. There were also a few stronger words that Mom and Dad used to describe Danny's buddy Ben. Most of all, though, we were just glad that Danny was no longer a director of Ben's company, and hoped that his involvement with ACE Stamping would not damage his reputation or his career.

Three weeks later, when ACE Stamping filed for chapter eleven bankruptcy, the entire situation erupted into front-page news. All the area newspapers, as well as the news programs on the radio and television stations, reported the bankruptcy and the reasons for it happening…including the pollution lawsuit in Dayton and of course the Federal Trade Commission fine for misrepresenting the wheelbarrows metal specifications. Danny unfortunately was either mentioned or, in some cases featured, in the stories as a former director of ACE Stamping. I felt that his name as well as our family name was unnecessarily dragged through the mud. Some of the news stories were really brutal…stating that ACE Stamping had cheated customers and that this was another example of corporate fraud. Statements like this really hurt.

Two television stations interviewed Danny in reporting this news story, and I thought he handled the interviews especially well. "It was his understanding," Danny said in the interviews, "that ACE Stamping did not immediately notify the buyers with the chain stores and with the wholesalers that the thickness of the metal in the tray of the wheelbarrows had been reduced slightly. This slight reduction did not affect the integrity or the durability of the wheelbarrows because ACE manufactured a strong, durable product. ACE Stamping had produced a quality product for many years, and if anything they were over-built. However, buyers should have been notified that there was going to be a change in the metal specifications at the time this decision was made. This was not done and it was a critical mistake. Another huge mistake was to continue putting the old specification sheets in the cartons that contain the wheelbarrows. This was really wrong and now they have to recall a lot of units and pay a substantial fine. It's a shame this happened and a great disappointment to me personally. Consequently, when I learned of this I resigned as a director."

In the interviews, Danny did not mention Ben Cockrell's name nor did he say anything negative about him. He reported the facts as he knew them, and said that serious mistakes were made that simply should have never have happened. I don't think I would have been quite as kind to Ben Cockrell had I been the one that was interviewed.

ACE Stamping was news for a couple of days, but was quickly replaced by other breaking news stories. Also the upcoming holiday season was the main focus of everybody's lives, and it was good to have that and other things to think about and talk about.

We had a warm, wonderful and happy Christmas celebration, which I especially enjoyed. There was the usual big family dinner at our home late in the afternoon on Christmas day, following a brunch at Abby and Danny's that morning. The week between Christmas and New Year's there was either a party or an open house every day for me to attend. Steve took me to a formal dinner dance at a Country Club on New Year's Eve, and that was great fun. There were a number of couples there that we both knew, and it was far and away the best New Year's Eve celebration that I had ever experienced. That last week of December was a great way for me to end the year.

In early January 1993, Mom and Dad packed and left for Orange Beach, Alabama. They planned to stay in the condo they owned there until the end of February. As they had for the past two years, they drove their car down south…taking three days to travel from our home to the condo. Papa John came to stay at the house in Danny's old room while mom and dad were away. During the days, if the weather was decent, Papa John pruned apple trees. If it was too cold or snowing, he stayed inside watching television or reading a book. I was delighted to have him around to visit with, and to keep me company in the evenings and on the weekends.

Papa John was very interested in my work, and asked me many good questions about how I treated various animals when they were injured or sick. He often surprised me as to how much he knew about the care of pets and livestock, and I realized that he could have been a very good veterinarian. One evening, when I told him about treating a horse that day with sore legs, he described a solution he used to make for that purpose. He said it really worked. I was so intrigued that I told Papa I wanted him to prepare some as I wanted to try it the next time I had that same problem to treat.

In mid-February, I flew to Pensacola, Florida, which is less than an hour's drive from Orange Beach. Dad picked me up at the airport and I spent a week with them at the condo. This was actually the second time that I had visited them at the condo, and it was a welcome break from the winter weather in Michigan. Of course we talked some about the trial scheduled to start in March, and it was our mutual hope and prayer that it would go well for Danny. It seemed so unfair to us that he was being subjected to this, as it was entirely due to the poor decisions or choices that Ben Cockrell had made. Ben was the responsible party. It was Ben Cockrell's decision to acquire the company in Dayton, and he was the one who decided to reduce the thickness of the metal tray part of the wheelbarrows. He chose not to notify customers of this change and, to make matters worse, in order to save a few lousy dollars he continued putting the old specification sheets in the boxes in which the wheelbarrows were shipped. I thought this whole stupid mess which Ben Cockrell had created could best be summed up or described in one word, "YUCK."

Mom and Dad returned from Alabama in early March, but Papa John stayed around for several more weeks to help with the pruning and with the early sprays of the apple trees. It always impressed me how much Dad and Papa John enjoyed working together, because their relationship seemed to be more like brothers than father and son. They explained that they approached each apple tree as if they were barbers giving a tree a haircut. When they finished pruning their trees they then compared their workmanship to decide which one had done the best job of pruning. This competition between the two of them obviously made their work far more interesting.

On Wednesday, March 17—St. Patrick's Day—I received a call from Danny shortly after I arrived at the clinic. He was very upset. He told me that Ben Cockrell had committed suicide. His wife had discovered his body in their garage early that morning. Ben had told his wife the night before that he was going to meet with his attorney that evening and would be getting home late. He left right after dinner and she assumed he had gone to his meeting. Instead he sat in his car in the garage with the motor running. The garage door was closed and he died of carbon monoxide poisoning. His wife had no reason to go to the garage, and went to bed believing he'd be home when the meeting with his attorney ended. In the morning, though, she discovered Ben wasn't in his bed and went to the garage to see if his car was there. That's when she found him and called 911. It was too late. He was dead.

Danny went on to say that Ben's wife told him that her husband has been extremely depressed for the past several months. She told Danny that Ben frequently said to her that he had destroyed in two years the business that his father had worked so hard for so many years to build. It was apparently more than he could handle, so he took his own life. Danny told me at the end of our conversation that, in spite of the problems that Ben created, he really liked the guy. "It's too bad," Danny said, "that Ben tried to expand ACE Stamping by getting into areas that he knew virtually nothing about. If he had only concentrated on manufacturing wheelbarrows and had possibly added a compatible line of products in order to grow the company...like garden tools...then I believe that none of this would have ever happened."

The trial was delayed for several weeks due to Ben's committing suicide. All of us hoped and prayed that it would go away now that Ben Cockrell would no longer be a party to the lawsuit. No such luck! It was rescheduled for Monday, April 12, 1993.

I didn't go to Dayton for the trial, but Mom and Dad did. Of course Abby was there while Jennifer, Julie and John stayed with her mother and father. The remaining three members of the board of directors of ACE Stamping were also defendants, as they had been named parties to the lawsuit in addition to Ben Cockrell. This included Danny, as outside director. The other two were William York, who was the Treasurer of Ace Stamping, and Martin Vanderman, the company attorney. Vanderman also served as the Secretary of the board and was responsible for preparing the minutes of the board meetings. The three elderly men who were directors when Danny first joined the board were not re-elected when their terms ended. Thus the members of the board of directors for ACE Stamping consisted of just these three men, plus the late Ben Cockrell, who had been the board chairman.

The trial lasted only four and a half days and the jury took just two hours to reach its decision. *They decided that the directors were guilty.* The three of them were each sentenced to two years in prison and fined $20,000.00. Danny and the other two directors were handcuffed, and taken from the court to the low-security level Federal Correctional Institution at Elkton, Ohio. This was just unbelievable to me. It was so incredibly unfair. Danny was in prison, and he would be there apparently for the next two years. *It was such a shock. We were absolutely stunned by the verdict!*

Mom and Dad explained to me that the prosecutor had made the case that when ACE Stamping bought Ryan Chemicals they acquired both the assets and the liabilities of the company. He strongly emphasized that the liabilities also included the soil pollution of the plant's property, and that ACE Stamping was responsible for correcting the problem. Instead of accepting this responsibility, he claimed the officers and directors took the coward's way out. They fired all the dedicated employees of Ryan Chemicals…a number of whom had worked there for more than twenty years…and shut down the business. No effort had been made by the new owner to determine what it would cost to clean up the pollution. It was easier to run away to Michigan where they could write off the loss for the company they had acquired, instead of taking care of the problem and keeping the business going. The prosecutor described Danny, Bill York and Martin Vanderman as selfish, evil businessmen and he did a much better job of prosecuting than the defendants attorneys did of defending.

I asked, "Why wasn't the previous owner of Ryan Chemicals included in this lawsuit? The soil pollution took place when he owned the company."

Dad explained that he had asked the same question, and Danny told him that a separate lawsuit had been filed against this man. Danny told Dad that, "Before the lawsuit came to trial, his attorney plea-bargained a settlement. He was fined $450,000.00. However, he was never put on trial and didn't serve any time in prison."

My brother was in prison. PRISON! I just couldn't believe this was really happening to him and to our family. I strongly felt that Danny didn't deserve this punishment for the small investment he made in ACE Stamping and for his limited involvement as a director. It occurred to me one day that guilt must be like pregnancy. There's no such thing as being a little pregnant. You're either pregnant or you're not. Is there a difference between being just a little guilty, or a whole lot guilty? Apparently, not! You're still guilty!

Those first few weeks after the trial my emotions ranged from anger to sadness.

I also felt embarrassed that my brother was in prison. But most of all, I was really disappointed that Danny hadn't used better judgment. I couldn't fathom why he had ever gotten involved with Ben Cockrell. It was, as Abby pointed out, a conflict of interest because ACE Stamping was one of Zon's suppliers. Why didn't he realize that? Did he so eagerly agree to Ben's invitation to make him a director that he didn't stop and think about this, or the time it would take away from his job? Did it "stroke his ego" when he became a director of a sizable manufacturing company? What could a young man like Danny, fresh out of college with limited business experience, offer to a company as a director? Not much in my estimation. The whole matter seemed ludicrous when I really thought about it. Danny certainly gained little financially, as I found out that he invested just $2,000.00 in ACE Stamping stock. That money, of course, was down the drain. Wasted!

And Danny received only a $250.00 directors fee for each board meeting he attended. There were usually four meetings a year but, according to Abby, he managed to attend only one or two a year when they were living in Indiana. What a terrible price to pay for this limited involvement. A two-year sentence in a federal prison and a big fine. I loved my brother, but at this particular time I had a pretty low opinion of his ability to make good choices. I thought he made wise choices marrying Abby and going to work for Zon's Thrifty Marts. However, some of the things he did in high school, in college, and during his business career didn't show much good judgment.

In fact, I wondered what kind of a business career Danny would have after he got out of prison. Would he be able to rejoin Zon's Thrifty Marts? They would have to hire someone to replace him while he served his prison term, so his former position might never be available again. There were lots of questions. No clear answers.

Never once did I shed any tears during this awful ordeal. Mom, however, cried a lot. I saw Dad put his arms around her and comfort her many times, and sometimes I did the same. There was no doubt in Mom's mind that Danny had been unfairly treated. She was absolutely positive that her son hadn't committed any crime. Danny had been sent to prison as a result of a terrible miscarriage of justice. She was heartbroken. If my father ever cried, I never saw him do so. It would not have surprised me, as I knew he was hurt very, very deeply and felt quite strongly that Danny didn't deserve the extreme punishment he received as a result of the jury's decision. "A small fine yes," I heard him say many times, "but prison for Danny's limited involvement? No way."

For as long as I can remember, my mother had subscribed to the "Daily Word'…a small booklet with a daily inspirational message. A copy came every month, and it was always on the kitchen table for anyone to read if they wanted to. These daily messages were brief and took only seconds to read. One morning I opened the little "Daily Word" booklet to the message for that particular day and it was headed, "Let Go, Let God." The message explained that, if there's a problem in your life that you're ready to relinquish control over, then the best thing you could do was to let go and let God take care of it. By letting God handle it, you would accept the best possible solution to a problem because you would be relying on God for the answer. You wouldn't be wasting your time and energy trying to control the outcome of a situation where you really had no control. That was pretty profound!

That message made a big impression on me. I thought about it while I was eating breakfast, and decided right then and there that this was exactly what I must do…let go and let God handle it. I couldn't live Danny's life. I couldn't change what had been done. I couldn't get him out of prison. I had to stop letting what happened to him affect my life. The disillusionment, the disappointment and the embarrassment that I was feeling was only hurting me. So the best thing that I could possibly do was to, "Let go and let God handle it."

That very day I started living my life the way I wanted to live it. Every time Danny's situation crossed my mind I immediately said to myself, "Colleen, forget about it. Let God Handle It." This perspective really changed my attitude when it came to dealing not only with my brother's status, and also with other situations where I had no control over the outcome.

For the past two years there had been lots of attention given to Danny by his family and of course by me, because of the trial and its consequences. This was only natural because of the great concern and love that those close to Danny felt for him. Consequently, I hadn't taken any significant amount of time to really think seriously about my own life, my lifestyle, my career and my prospects of ever getting married. But late one afternoon at the clinic I was sitting at my desk and I said to myself, "What about you girl? How is your life going? Are you happy with your status? Should you start making a real effort to find a husband? Should you move out of the family home to a place of your own? What does your future look like?"

It was not a particularly busy day at the clinic, and I had already taken care of my last case for the day. So I closed the door to my office and told our receptionist that I didn't want to be disturbed for a little while. I leaned back in my chair and spent about an hour reviewing and thinking about my life...starting with my career. Going to work at the Veterinary Clinic was something that I looked forward to every day. No question about that! Bob Cunningham was a good, solid, nice man and an excellent veterinarian. The clinic's staff was well-trained and highly competent, and I liked each one of them personally.

Financially, I was exceptionally well off. I had a sizable, well-invested trust that was steadily growing, and I was earning a good income as a veterinarian. Living at home kept my expenses at a minimum, providing me with a substantial amount of money to invest every two or three months in the stock market. The stocks in my portfolio were doing fantastic—paying dividends and increasing in value faster and far beyond what I ever expected. In order to learn more about investing and to stay abreast of the financial markets, I read the *Wall Street Journal* nearly every day while eating my lunch at the clinic. If I moved away from home I would not be able to invest as much in the stock market, and I'd have to prepare my own meals, shop for food and clean the place. That option didn't have a lot of appeal. Maybe I was a little spoiled, but I decided that there was a nice order to my life, and that was good.

My prospects for getting married were currently not very good. I had dated at least a dozen guys since returning to Rockford and starting my career as a veterinarian two years ago. The only one that I felt might make a possible husband was Steve Hurley, but I knew I wasn't in love with him, nor was he really in love with me. Perhaps I would never meet someone that I'd feel the same way about as I did for Gene Morris. I liked Steve and enjoyed his company. Maybe if I told him that I had a trust with assets of more than a million dollars, he might get more serious about our relationship. I quickly dismissed that idea, however, and decided that I was not that eager to get married. Besides, it was better that I keep my financial status confidential, so that I didn't discover later that some guy had married me for my money. My little review of my life ended with a knock on my office door by our receptionist. It was time to close up shop for the day. But I decided that this had been some time well spent, and that I must do this now and then to seriously consider how I was living my life. I made a vow to do that because I didn't want to wake up one day and discover that my life's path had become a rut!

On the fourth of July, Papa John was at the house having dinner with us and while we were eating the four of us discussed what we should do to help Abby while Danny was in prison. I decided to withdraw $20,000.00 from my trust and write Abby a check for that amount, which would cover the cost of the fine the court had ruled that Danny had to pay. That would be my contribution. Mom and Dad decided to take enough money from their trust to pay off the mortgage on Abby and Danny's home. That way all Abby would basically have to pay out in order to stay in her home would be the real estate taxes, home owners insurance and the utilities. Papa John said he would give her a check for $5,000.00 to help her with living expenses.

Abby was very appreciative when we did this. She told us she loved her home and their neighborhood. Her neighbors had been very supportive, and all agreed that Danny had been dealt a great injustice. Jennifer and Julie both liked the school they attended and they had lots of friends to play with in the neighborhood. She didn't want to move and now, with this help, she wouldn't have to. Papa John told her that anytime she needed anything fixed around the house she should call him and he'd take care of it. "Papa John will come to the rescue," he told her. I was pleased when Abby gave him big hug and a kiss on his cheek after he said that, and I noticed she had tears in her eyes. This was the kind of support she truly needed, and the Malones had certainly stepped up to do their part.

Abby was sincerely grateful and she expressed her appreciation to each of us saying, "I just can't begin to find the right words to tell you how much I appreciate what you're doing. Thank you from the bottom of my heart. I love each of you so very much." With that Abby gave each of us another loving hug. She was sincerely grateful. That was for sure!

Abby's parents were going to help her as well, so it was a matter of going forward as best everyone could under the circumstances. Abby, Jennifer, Julie and John would be able to continue living quite comfortably, but they would have to get along without a husband and a father for many months.

In early July we learned that Danny and the two other directors of Ace Stamping who had received prison terms had hired a new attorney to appeal the jury's verdict. However the appeal process was going to take time and, even with time off for good behavior, it was likely that Danny and the two other directors would be in prison for at least eighteen months.

In mid-July, we were informed that we could now visit Danny. Mom, Dad, Abby and I left Friday morning, July 16 for Elkton, Ohio, a small town on the far-east side of the state, south of Youngstown and close to Pennsylvania. It was an all-day drive to get to the prison and we checked into a motel in Canton, Ohio late in the afternoon. Early Saturday morning we drove to nearby Elkton and spent most of the day with Danny. It was a tearful family reunion when we first arrived and the whole situation seemed absolutely surreal. During the day I asked myself several times, "How can this be happening?" It just seemed to be so unbelievable. Horribly unfair as far as Danny's family and friends were concerned.

Late that afternoon we all returned to the motel in Canton where we had stayed the night before. Sunday morning we checked out of the motel and went back to Elkton. We wanted to spend a little more time with Danny before starting our long drive home.

Dad, Abby and I took turns driving back to Michigan and all the way home we discussed the lawsuit, Danny's situation and all its ramifications. As a result the time passed quickly. We dropped Abby off at her home in Grand Rapids late in the day, and arrived at our home just as it was getting dark. This was one weekend that I figured I'd remember for a long time, as I would never in my wildest dreams have ever thought that someday I would be visiting my brother in prison.

Several weeks later, in early August, Aunt Amy and Uncle Joe arrived with two of their four children and they stayed a week with us. Uncle Joe was on his vacation and they drove to Rockford from Baltimore. On the way to visit us they had stopped to see Danny at the Elton Correctional Institution, which in reality was a prison so far as I was concerned. They were able to spend several hours with him and they reported that Danny was actually in much better spirits than they had expected. Uncle Joe and Aunt Amy told us that Danny was quite optimistic that the new attorney, Ralph Thomas, who he and the other two directors had hired would be successful in getting the jury's verdict overturned. Their new attorney was with the Tyler, Moss & Thomas law firm in Cleveland, and they specialized in environmental legal issues and particularly soil pollution. As soon as Ralph Thomas was appointed to represent them in the appeal process, he had immediately hired a company to determine the actual extent of the soil pollution around the Ryan Chemicals plant. Danny had just learned that the soil tests conducted by this company revealed that the soil pollution was far, far less than the twenty-five million dollars the government had claimed in its lawsuit. In fact, the problem could be corrected for just over $600,000.00, which included removing all the contaminated soil and replacing it with clean fill dirt. This was really encouraging news.

Danny told Aunt Amy and Uncle Joe that it was really too bad that Ralph Thomas had not represented him and the other two directors at the trial in Dayton. He was absolutely sure the outcome of the trial would have been completely different.

The Dayton legal firm that defended Danny and the other two directors in the lawsuit had accepted the prosecution's claim that there was extensive soil pollution around the Ryan Chemical plant, and that it was going to cost twenty five million dollars to clean up. They should have hired an environmental impact company like Ralph Thomas did in order to determine whether or not this was true.

They didn't do that. And what a crucial mistake that turned out to be!

In the meantime, there was an interesting new development in my life as a veterinarian. Earlier in the year, Papa John told me about a solution that he mixed and used to relieve pain and stiffness of horses' muscles and tendons in their legs, knees, shoulders and hindquarters. I was intrigued, and had asked him to prepare some of this solution so that I could try it. He mixed several gallons for me to test, and I discovered that it really did produce outstanding results. It was an exceptionally good product!

I asked him how he had come up with this solution, and he explained that, in the late 1930s, he had a good friend who was a pharmacist. This man had a drug store in Rockford and also owned horses. Papa John and his pharmacist friend worked together to develop a solution that would relieve pain and stiffness in horse muscles, joints and tendons. After a lot of experimentation, they had settled on one solution that seemed to work the best. The pharmacist actually sold some in his drug store but, during World War II, it was difficult to get all the ingredients so they stopped making it. Papa John explained that he and the pharmacist had talked about starting a company to produce and market this solution but never did. Shortly after the war, the pharmacist who helped Papa John develop the solution passed away. Papa John, though, had the complete list of ingredients and the exact proportions needed for the solution. From time to time, he prepared some for treating his horses when they had pain or stiffness in their muscles.

I became so convinced that this was a good product that early in the spring I did some research and located a company in Kalamazoo that could produce, package and ship liquid products of this kind. Papa John gave me the list of the ingredients, including the right proportions for each ingredient. I invested $4,000.00 to have the company in Kalamazoo prepare sixty gallons of it. I then had them ship the sixty gallons to a list of veterinarians that I provided who I knew had a significant equine practice. A cover letter enclosed in the box containing each gallon of the solution explained why I was sending it, and asked them to please test the product.

My letter also explained how simple it was to use the product. One cup of the solution was mixed with three cups of warm water. This mixture was then applied to the horse's affected muscles or joints with a sponge. Then, for best results, you gently rubbed or massaged the area by hand.

The results of the test were really exciting. There was unanimous praise for Papa John's solution. I decided to call my friend, Joyce Kallman, who had been a classmate for many years, and had been part of the so-called "dirty dozen" when we were in high school. Joyce had been the valedictorian of our senior class and was now an account executive with an advertising agency in Grand Rapids.

I called Joyce and invited her to meet me for dinner at a Grand Rapids restaurant. We met, and I shared with her my desire to market the product that Papa John and his pharmacist friend had developed. Joyce listened patiently, asking pertinent questions, but I did not sense much enthusiasm until she read the letters from the veterinarians who had tried the product. I had also paid a laboratory to test the product to make sure there were no harmful side effects. There were none.

One letter in particular was quite impressive. It was from Kathryn Davis, a veterinarian that I knew quite well, as we were classmates for four years at MSU's College of Veterinarian Medicine. Kit, as every one called Kathryn, lived and practiced in Metamora, an area that easily qualified as the horse capitol of Michigan. There were thousands of horses in and around Metamora, and Kit was an equine specialist. I had sent Kit two gallons of the solution to test, and she wrote a very descriptive and enthusiastic letter describing her results. She said that performance animals often have soreness as a result of training and exercise. According to Kit, it was a great product to use on performance horses, and she wanted to order more. In fact, Kit thought the clinic where she worked could sell several hundred gallons of it every year to their clientele, over and above the amount they would use when they were called to treat horses suffering with sore muscles or tendons.

After reading the letters from the veterinarians who had tested the product, Joyce offered to write a marketing plan. She said she would suggest names for the product and also prepare some label designs for the packages. I had already determined that the best way to package the product was in plastic quart and gallon containers.

Following my meeting with Joyce in early July, I met with our family attorney, Doug Graham, and asked him to set up a company for me and file all the necessary forms and papers to start a business. I told him that the name of the company would be C.M. Malone, Inc. By using my initials no one would know which gender the name represented. Mr. Graham recommended that C.M. Malone, Inc. be organized as a Sub-Chapter S corporation, as this would reduce the taxes I'd have to pay if and when there were any profits.

C.M. Malone, Inc. was initially incorporated with 100,000 shares of stock with a par value of $1.00 per share. I intended to put $50,000.00 into the company to start, and Papa John said he wanted to invest $5,000.00. Fortunately I was in a position to add more capitol as needed. My annual gross income at the Cunningham Clinic was $90,000.00, and I had minimal living expenses. I was living at home, which cost me next to nothing. After taxes and my personal expenses, I was saving close to $50,000.00 a year, which I had been investing in the stock market. Now I was going to invest some of my income into a company to market a product to treat horses. Would it be a good investment? Only time and effort would tell.

When the incorporation papers were received, I opened a bank account for C.M. Malone, Inc. and deposited the $55,000.00. My attorney then issued a stock certificate for me for 50,000 shares and a certificate for Papa John for 5,000 shares.

It only took Joyce Kallman a few weeks to write the marketing plan, and I found it to be not only interesting but also quite impressive. She had used information from the last census, as well as from an agricultural statistics service as the basis for the plan. She defined the potential market with a breakdown of the number of horses by state. There were just over five million horses in the country. That was a big market.

The marketing plan recommended that sample packs containing one cup of the solution be used to introduce the product. These samples would be mailed in a plastic pouch to veterinarians with an equine practice in the twenty states with the highest population of horses. If they liked the product and wanted more they would have a choice of five basic ways to order the product. That was because five different shipping containers were available and carried in stock by the Kalamazoo company that would be producing the solution. These shipping cartons would accommodate orders for either two quarts, four quarts, one gallon, two gallons or four gallons...and all orders would be shipped by UPS. I thought this was a sensible, practical way to handle orders, but at this point I really didn't know what to expect. Maybe there would be so few orders that my little venture would turn out to be a huge flop.

The marketing plan that Joyce recommended went into additional phases following step one. The first step, consisting of mailing the samples of the product to the twenty states with the highest population of horses, was critical as this would really determine whether or not there actually was a market for the product. The target date for this mailing was September, 1993.

The name Joyce suggested for the product was not a word but initials...FPR. The FPR stood for Fast Pain Relief. This really made sense when I saw the label design. FPR was in large letters and below that was a bold subhead that read..."Fast Pain Relief for horse knees, joints and muscles." I told Joyce that the name and the label design were perfect.

I had already arranged with a secretarial service in Grand Rapids to use their address as the business address for C.M. Malone, Inc., rather that renting office space of my own. I negotiated an arrangement whereby all orders for FPR would go to this secretarial service. As part of their service they would process all orders. This involved typing a list of the orders as they were received, specifying the quantity ordered, and supplying a shipping label for each order. They would also provide a telephone answering service in case there were any questions. Those I would handle. I gave Joyce the address, FAX number and phone number that I was going to use for C.M. Malone, Inc. and requested that she prepare the artwork and key lines needed to print stationery, labels, and all the materials needed for the sample mailing as quickly as possible. I was really anxious to get going.

All of the activity involved in starting a business and launching a new product took a considerable amount of time away from the clinic during May, June, July and August. I had told Doctor Cunningham about my decision to start a company to market Papa John's solution for treating horses with painful muscles and tendons. However, he became somewhat concerned and confronted me one day in late August. He was not concerned about the time I had been away from the clinic, as I had not taken much vacation time. But he wondered if I was planning to leave the clinic to run the business I was starting. He had assumed when I became his associate that I would purchase the practice when he retired. He owned the practice and the building, but we had never discussed when or how much I would have to invest to buy the practice, along with the equipment and the building.

I was glad he brought the subject up, because it helped to clear the air. I told Bob that I had no intention of leaving the Cunningham Veterinary Clinic as I really enjoyed working there. And yes, I would like to purchase the practice and we should start talking about it now rather than later.

I told him in confidence something that I had not told anyone else. He knew that my brother Danny was in prison. I explained to Doctor Cunningham that I hoped C.M. Malone, Inc. would be a successful venture so that Danny could take over and manage it when he got out of prison. I knew that he was not going to be able to return to Zon's Thrifty Marts. Abby had told us that this was not going to happen, but she hadn't explained the reason why. Maybe Danny wouldn't be interested in managing my company, but it would at least be an option for him to consider.

After I explained all this to Bob Cunningham, he felt quite relieved, and so did I. Our discussion brought a number of significant things into focus. I now knew that he was definitely planning on having me take over the clinic when he retired, and the lines of communication were now open to discuss the time table and what the financial investment would be for me.

Joyce Kallman and I met for dinner a number of times that summer to review the progress of the marketing plan. Joyce was still single, but she was engaged. Her fiancé, Jim Cooper, held a marketing position with a large company and he joined us several times for dinner. Jim made some helpful suggestions, and also told me about a retired sales and marketing executive he knew who was looking for something to do part time. His name was Clay Taylor, and Jim recommended that I meet with this man to see if he would manage the business once orders started coming in. Processing orders, and watching and maintaining inventories would be time consuming. I knew that I could not do it all, and still have time to fulfill my responsibilities at the clinic.

Clay Taylor turned out to be an ideal solution, as he was intrigued with the challenge of getting a new business up and running. Clay had an outstanding resume and excellent references. I was fortunate to find him. Thanks to Jim Cooper. Clay agreed to a one-year contract at a very reasonable salary to operate and manage my company.

The operation of the business would require Clay Taylor to go to the office of the secretarial service three days a week...on Monday, Wednesday and Friday. It would be his responsibility to review the typed list of orders and proofread to make sure that this list and the address labels were correct. He would also have to deposit all the checks received at the bank where I had opened the company's account. Then, one or two days a week, depending on how many orders there were, he would drive to Kalamazoo to turn over the address labels for each order received, along with the list that specified the quantity of product to be shipped by our supplier. Clay's duties also included monitoring the number of quarts and gallons of FPR that we had in stock at the Kalamazoo supplier, and reordering quantities as needed so that we could fill all orders promptly. All in all, I thought that I had the business pretty well organized. I couldn't help but feel kind of proud that I had managed to set up my business with a very low operating overhead. First, by arranging to use the offices of a secretarial service as the business address for C. M. Malone, Inc., and then by hiring at a low salary a very capable retired executive to operate my company. In terms of marketing expertise, I was fortunate to have the counsel of Joyce Kallman.

I was really grateful for the assistance that Joyce provided. She gave me confidence to move forward at times when I was having doubts or questioning whether or not this was really a worthwhile venture. I was sure we had a good product, but would it sell? Joyce had written the marketing plan on her own time and had charged only $7,000.00 for her counsel and services. I offered to give Joyce 7000 shares of stock in C.M. Malone, Inc. rather than pay her with a check. She readily accepted the stock as payment for her services, as she believed there was a market for FPR based on the tests that I had carried out both with veterinarians and with a laboratory. Besides, I felt that Joyce deserved to share in whatever success the company achieved as she had contributed so much to the marketing strategy of FPR.

The mailing of the samples of FPR to veterinarians with an equine practice in the twenty states with the largest number of horses went out mid-September. In the last three months of 1993, orders for FPR totaled $31,460.00. Joyce and I were absolutely delighted with the results.

Based on this response, I decided to invest more money in my company in 1994. This would be necessary in order to expand the mailing of samples of FPR to another twenty states with the next sizable population of horses. In the forty states that would be covered by the two mailings of samples, there were well over four million horses. We would then have the bulk of the market introduced to FPR. I also planned to start advertising FPR in the leading trade magazine serving the veterinary field. Unless something unexpected happened, I was starting to feel somewhat confident that the marketing of the solution that Papa John and his pharmacist friend had developed for treating horses with sore muscles and tendons would be a success.

In December, as Christmas drew near, there was a lot of discussion about how it would be celebrated without Danny being present. Ever since Danny and Abby had moved back to Michigan from Indiana, Christmas had been celebrated both at our home and at Danny and Abby's. On Christmas morning, Abby had served a delicious brunch which Mom, Dad, Papa John and the Zondervines and I enjoyed as we got to see what Santa Claus brought Jennifer, Julie and John. There were many presents for my nieces and nephew to unwrap, and their joy and excitement made Christmas the happy, wonderful and special time that it is. Late in the afternoon on Christmas day, all the Malones then gathered at Mom and Dad's home for a big dinner. That was when the adults exchanged gifts.

Jennifer, Julie and John had not seen their father since last spring, as Danny did not want them to visit him in prison. He missed seeing them so much though, that it was decided that we would all go to the Elkton Correctional Facility, including the three children, and include Danny in our celebration of Christmas. In 1993, Christmas Eve was a Friday. On Saturday morning, we all participated in the usual brunch at Abby's home, but there was no dinner at our home that afternoon. Instead, Mom cooked her heart out all afternoon, and I assisted. She baked a fresh ham, made hot German potato salad, deviled eggs and a variety of side dishes, homemade bread, two apple pies and two streuselkuchens.

Bright and early Sunday morning, Mom and I packed all the food prepared the day before into picnic hampers. Dad helped us load everything in the van, and we drove to Elkton. Papa John went with us, while Abby and her three children rode with her mother and father in their car. Abby's sister Becky did not go with us, as she opted to return to her home in Glen Ellyn, a suburb of Chicago, where she had a boutique. Becky joined Marshall Field's in Chicago when she graduated from college, but several years ago she resigned her position with the department store and opened a boutique. According to Abby, her business was doing exceptionally well.

Late Sunday afternoon, we checked into the same motel in Canton where we had stayed last July. That evening after dinner, the ten of us gathered in Abby's room at the motel to discuss plans for the next day, when we wanted to visit Danny. We were not sure if we could all be with him at the same time. Usually, the Correctional Institution allowed only two people at a time to be with a prisoner. However, since it was a low-security facility, and it was Christmas, perhaps they would be more accommodating and allow all of us to have dinner together. Anyway, that was our hope!

On Monday morning, December 27, we drove to Elkton. We assembled and waited in a visitor's room for about ten minutes until Danny joined us. Finally the door from the prison area opened and Danny entered. He took only a few steps before dropping to his knees and holding out his arms for his three children. They screamed and ran to their daddy. Danny wrapped his arms around the three of them pulling them tight against his chest. I could hear Julie loudly shouting, "Daddy I want you to come home," but I couldn't quite understand what Jennifer and John were saying.

I think it was the most joyous scene I had ever witnessed in my life. Then Abby joined Danny. She too got down on her knees and stretched her arms around Jennifer, Julie and John so that the three children were enfolded in the arms of their mother and father…the five of them tightly clustered together.

I looked around the room. My mother was crying and my Dad was holding her close to him. The same was true of the Zondervines. Sarah was wiping the tears from her eyes with a hankie and Andy had his right arm around her. Andy, I noticed, was slowly swinging his head from side to side, which was his reaction in expressing how moving his scene was to him. Papa John was sitting in a chair off to the side of the room. He had his hands cupped over his eyes, as you would do in order to keep the sun out of your eyes. There was no bright sunlight. He was doing this to hide his tears. I observed that even the guard who escorted Danny to the room was a little teary eyed. Tears were flowing down my cheeks too, but at least I wasn't crying like my mother.

It took a few minutes for all of us to pull ourselves together, but we did manage to calm down. We visited with Danny for several hours before having our Christmas dinner together. After dinner, Danny opened his presents, which included books, toothpaste, socks, underwear, writing paper and current photos of his family. He made each gift seem like it was the best thing he had ever received in his life.

As the day wore on, it became apparent to me that Danny had become quite bitter. When I last saw him in July, it seemed to me that he had resigned himself to serving his sentence, much as you would resign yourself to recuperate from a broken leg. You just accepted the misfortune and did the best you could under the circumstances. Mom, Dad and Abby had visited Danny every month since July. I had not, so I believe this change in his attitude was much more obvious to me. Or, if they were aware of this bitterness they had never mentioned it to me. I knew my brother pretty darn well. *He was really bitter!*

Listening to Danny talk during the day, he was blaming everyone else for what had happened to him. He was bitter that Ben Cockrell had not invested some money to find out how extensive the soil pollution really was around the Ryan Chemicals plant. Danny told us that Ryan Chemicals was first offered for sale for fifteen million dollars. The price gradually came down to eleven million dollars when potential buyers learned about the soil pollution. So when Ben offered nine and a half million, the owner accepted the offer. However, there was more than four million dollars of retained earnings in the company. When the lawsuit was filed, Ben closed down the plant and used the retained earnings to pay off most of a six million dollar bank loan he had gotten to buy Ryan. He also sold off some of the company's assets to further reduce his loss. Danny was angry and disgusted that Ben hadn't used some of Ryan's retained earning to determine what it would have cost to have the soil pollution problem corrected. I didn't say anything, but I thought to myself, "Danny, you were a director of the company. Why didn't you urge or insist that Ben do what you're now telling us?"

Danny blamed Martin Vanderman, the attorney for ACE Stamping for the mistake he made in selecting the Dayton legal firm that defended them at the trial. He said he learned, too late, that this firm had absolutely no experience in environmental issues. Danny was disgusted with their representation and the fact that the trial turned out to be a "slam-dunk" for a guilty verdict for the prosecution.

According to Danny, the jury that convicted him was made up of "rednecks" and union members who were prejudiced when it came to businessmen, and the judge, an alumnus of Ohio State, disliked anyone who attended or graduated from Michigan State. I wondered to myself if this was really true.

Danny's bitterness was quite obvious to me. I became concerned about it as I thought this attitude would only hurt him…not the people he was blaming for his being in prison. On the positive side, I noticed that he had lost some weight and looked very trim and fit. He told us that he worked out every day in the gym during his open or free time. Last summer and fall, he had been assigned to the crew that mowed the lawns, pruned the trees and shrubs and took care of the gardens. He was grateful that he got this assignment, as he was able to spend a lot of his time outdoors.

The Elkton Correctional Institution was a strange place for us to have our family Christmas dinner, but we made the best of it. Danny praised mother's cooking and said this day and the meal were the best things that had happened to him in a long, long time. He appreciated seeing, holding and talking with his children so much that day. I didn't know what Abby and Danny had explained to Jennifer, Julie and John as to the reason why their father was not able to live at home. Early on, I knew that Danny had decided that he did not want to have his children visit him while he was in prison. However, he had reached the point where he simply couldn't wait any longer to see them.

In my opinion, having them stay away and not visit him at Elkton was not a good decision on Danny's part. His family, friends and everyone that I knew who were familiar with his sentence thought that my brother was an unfortunate victim paying the price for bad decisions that he did not make. It was only natural, though, that Danny would feel humiliated and embarrassed to have his children see him at a place like Elkton…but he was no axe murderer. Jennifer, Julie and John needed and missed their father and I surmised that Abby would start taking them with her each time she went to visit Danny now that the ice had been broken.

We left the Canton motel early Tuesday morning, and arrived home that evening. Abby, however, wanted to see Danny again, so Andy Zondervine drove her back to Elkton before they started their long drive home. There was one thing that I did feel quite confident about—and that was the love that Danny and Abby shared for each other. They missed being together so much that I felt sorry for them. Shortly after Danny was sent to Elkton, Abby told me that she would never again take Danny's presence in her life for granted. She said to me, "When he returns home I'm going to start every day by saying to Danny…*I love you!*"

The few remaining days in December slid quickly by, and Steve Hurley invited me to celebrate New Year's Eve with him. Steve hadn't called me in several months, so I was a little surprised when he asked me to go to the dinner dance at the Country Club we had gone to a year ago. I accepted his invitation and was glad I did because I really enjoyed the dinner, the dancing and the interesting people we met and talked with during the evening.

1994 started off with big news about Zon's Thrifty Marts. In early January, it was announced that the large national chain Home World, with more than a thousand stores, had acquired Zon's Thrifty Marts. The ten Zon's in Michigan and the eight in Indiana were going to be converted to outlets for this national chain. The Zon's name would be no more. Under the new ownership, the former Zon's would be expanded to include Garden Centers as well as to offer a broader line of home appliances. This was front-page news and was reported extensively by the papers and radio and television stations in Southwest Michigan. According to the news reports, Andy Zondervine was now a major stockholder in Home World, which was a public company. He was also going to be on their board of directors. The Zondervines were already financially well off, but now, with the sale of their company to Home World, they were going to be a whole lot richer.

Abby told me shortly after Zon's was acquired that her father was setting up new trusts for her and her sister Becky as well as for Jennifer, Julie and John. "She and Danny," Abby said, "will be able to live very comfortably from the annual income from my trust." I was delighted at their good fortune, but also wondered what Danny would do with his life when he returned home again. He was too young to retire. I just couldn't picture my brother as a man of leisure. I knew he would need something to occupy his time, and he would want something challenging. I still planned to offer him the possibility of managing my company and decided that I would discuss this with him the next time I went to visit him at Elkton.

Later in January, I received a call at the clinic from Kathryn "Kit" Davis.

Kit called me from her clinic in Metamora to tell me about a conference scheduled to take place in early April at the Greenbriar Resort in West Virginia. This conference was specifically for veterinarians with an equine practice. Kit suggested we both attend, and I quickly agreed, as I thought it would be a special opportunity to spread the word about FPR. Word of mouth advertising is the best advertising there is according to my Dad. Kit offered to handle the registration for both of us, and I mailed her a check to cover my participation in the conference and for my share of the room and the meals at the Greenbriar. I put the conference on my calendar, and looked forward to attending.

Looking at a map of Ohio later that day I noticed that we would pass close to Elkton when we drove to West Virginia. I thought Kit would not mind this slight detour in order to give me an hour or so to spend with my brother when she understood the situation.

As things turned out, this would not be necessary...as Danny was released from the Correctional Institution on Friday, March 11, 1994. We were already aware that the court in Dayton had rejected an appeal for a new trial. However, this was expected and had been anticipated by their new attorney. He immediately appealed to a higher court in Cincinnati, which ruled, after reviewing the case, that the sentencing of Danny and the other two directors had been far too severe. First, they were not directly responsible for the soil pollution at the Ryan plant. Second, they had minimal opportunity to correct the problem, as the decision to close the Ryan plant had been made by the president of ACE Stamping without board approval. And third, the amount of soil pollution had been greatly exaggerated by the prosecution. Danny and the other two directors were not required to serve the rest of their sentences, and were free to go home immediately. Danny's last day in prison was March 11. When I heard that he was coming home I was thrilled and thought, "Thank God this nightmare is finally over."

Danny and the other two directors flew to Grand Rapids from the airport in Canton, Ohio. When their plane arrived Friday afternoon at the Grand Rapids airport, Abby and the three children, Mom and Dad, Papa John and I…as well as Sally and Andy Zondervine were all waiting at the arrival gate.

There was a homecoming party at Abby and Danny's home that night that turned out to be quite an event. Abby and the children had decorated the house with welcome home signs, streamers, and balloons…and the oak trees in the front yard had yellow ribbons with huge bows tied around them. You would have thought that my brother was a war hero returning from some overseas battle.

The welcome home party started as soon as we arrived at Danny and Abby's home. Some of their friends and neighbors were already there waiting to welcome Danny home. Word must have spread quickly, because within an hour their home was packed wall to wall with people. All the soft drinks, beer, wine and liquor they had in the house were soon consumed and Dad and I went to a store to buy more as well as plenty of snacks.

It was a wonderful, happy and exciting occasion and we were delighted to see so many people warmly welcoming Danny home. When Mom, Dad and I left the party it was well after midnight, but there were still a few stragglers left celebrating with Danny when we parted. Fortunately Mom was able to serve as our designated driver, as neither Dad nor I had any business driving a car.

When I fell into my bed that Saturday morning it was with a great sense of relief that my brother was out of prison and home with his family again. I was also especially grateful that I wasn't scheduled to work that Saturday. I would not have been able to function very well because I woke up with a terrible hangover. It was the first time this had ever happened to me. I tried to remember how many drinks of scotch I consumed. It must have been five or six, maybe seven? I decided that I had learned my lesson and made a commitment that in the future I would never have more than two drinks of anything containing alcohol at a party…or on any other occasion for that matter. I am proud to say that I have kept that vow. Danny's welcome home party was the last time that I ever drank more than two drinks. Two drinks, I decided, would always be my limit.

CHAPTER 5

The Aftermath

329 days! When Danny was released from the Elkton Correctional Institution on March 11, that's how many days he and the other two directors of ACE Stamping had served of their original two-year sentences. Were their sentences a miscarriage of justice? Or was it simply just plain rotten luck? After all, bad things do happen to good people. But it really didn't matter any more. It happened. It was now over. Done. Finished. It was time to move on, and I hoped that my brother would do that with his head held high.

The welcome home party for Danny turned out to be a blast. We didn't call him the week following the party, because we figured he needed some time at home with his wife and children. On Saturday afternoon of the following week, when I arrived home from the clinic, there was Danny and Dad sitting at the kitchen table having a beer together. I got a loving bear hug from my brother when I walked in, and I joyfully said to him, "It's so great to see you sitting here in the kitchen."

Danny told me that he had taken a long walk through the orchards earlier that afternoon to help reaffirm that he was really a free man. "Walking through the rows of apple trees made me feel good," he claimed, adding, "It was also kind of a 'back to my roots' experience. I definitely needed that!"

Danny stayed to have dinner with us, and while we were eating he told us some very interesting things. I was especially pleased when he told Dad that he was going to help him with the spraying of the apple trees this year. "I thought it was time," Danny said, "To give Papa John a break. Knowing Papa John, though," Danny speculated, "he'll probably show up to make sure we do it right...that every tree is covered."

Our apple trees were sprayed from fifteen to twenty times each year depending on weather. An oil spray was the first one applied in the early spring, and that was followed with different sprays using chemicals to control pests, mites and fungus. In years when there was a lot of rain, the trees got sprayed more often because a steady rain or a heavy downpour washed the chemicals off the trees.

Hearing Danny tell Dad that he was going to help him spray the trees I figured that we'd be seeing him frequently in the weeks and months ahead.

However, the next thing he told us was that he and Abby were going to Hawaii and staying on the island of Maui for a month...leaving as soon as school was out in early May. Jennifer, Julie and John were going with them, and they were not returning until early June. Danny explained, "This getaway should help bring my family close together again. And going to Maui will be like a second honeymoon for Abby and me."

It sounded like a good idea to me, but I thought to myself, "There's usually five or six sprays that have to be done during May and early June. Danny obviously won't be around to help Dad spray the trees then."

Danny also gave us an update on what had happened to ACE Stamping and Ryan Chemicals. He informed us that the bankruptcy court had auctioned the two companies separately. The highest bidder for ACE was a company in Massachusetts that was also a manufacturer of wheelbarrows. They acquired ACE Stamping at a bankruptcy auction for about 20% of the actual value of the plant and equipment. The company planed to reopen the plant and use it as a manufacturing and distribution center. "The mistakes that Ben made," Danny told us, "Resulted in a takeover of his plant by his major competitor. He'd probably turn over in his grave if he knew that this had happened."

"Ryan Chemicals," Danny further explained, "was acquired at its bankruptcy auction by a holding company headquartered in Philadelphia. The holding company owns nine different companies around the country producing products for a variety of markets. Most of them need the chemicals that Ryan produced in order to make their products made of metal. The holding company put in a bid of three million dollars for Ryan, and that was the best offer the bankruptcy court received. As a result, the holding company got a fantastic bargain. As soon as the soil pollution was cleaned up, they were going to reopen the plant and Ryan would become another division of the holding company. Not only would the holding companies manufacturing divisions become captive customers of Ryan, but they would also sell their rust-proofing and plating chemicals to other users as well. So Ryan Chemicals future success was virtually guaranteed. It's really incredible how all this has turned out."

When Danny finished telling us all the news that he had to report, I commented to him, "I see a big difference in your attitude since I saw you last Christmas. You seem to have made an adjustment now that you're home again, because the bitterness I noticed when I saw you then is not at all apparent. And that's a good thing!"

"Well," Danny replied, "I believe the ruling made by the appeals court in Cincinnati vindicated me and the other two directors. The three of us should never have been sentenced to serve any time in prison, but the government wanted to punish somebody for the soil pollution and we turned out to be the victims. Getting released when we did helped restore my faith in the judicial system. Then when I came home, I got a great welcome from my family, my neighbors and from many friends. The time that I spent separated from Abby made me realize more than ever before that I'm married to a woman that I love very deeply. Absence really did make my heart grow fonder. My wife is not only a beautiful woman, but she's a wonderful mother and homemaker. I can't begin to tell you how much I love and appreciate her. On top of all that, she now has a lot of money because of the trust her father set up for her. As soon as I arrived home Abby insisted that I stop feeling sorry for myself. She told me that carrying on with my bitterness was like hauling around a heavy bag of stones. So Abby is mainly responsible for helping me change my attitude. She's been very supportive, and this past week we have talked a lot about how fortunate we really are. As a result of our talks I've been making a concerted effort to be cheerful and positive…to just try to smile more. I must be making progress because you noticed a difference in my attitude, Colleen."

When Danny stopped talking there was a long silence as Mom, Dad and I sat quietly thinking and absorbing what he had just said to us. I hadn't expected this kind of response from my brother when I made the comment about his attitude adjustment. Such a personal confession of his feelings was something quite unusual for Danny. I noticed that Mom and Dad were both smiling, and they were obviously delighted to hear what Danny had just revealed about himself.

Dad spoke up first. "My mother," he said, "Liked to quote Ralph Waldo Emerson. Whenever I got mad about something she's usually say to me, '*For every minute you are angry you lose sixty seconds of happiness.*' She credited that wisdom to Ralph. I'm glad that you have decided to put the time you spent at

Elkton behind you Danny. Looking forward to the future with a positive attitude is a good thing. From now on everything is going to be a lot better for you. I just know it will be."

Not to be outdone, Mom reinforced Dad's response telling Danny, "I believe it was Martin Luther who said, *'Change your thinking and you change your life.'* I just want you to be happy and Abby's right…bitterness is a heavy and unnecessary load to carry."

"You have such a wonderful smile, Danny," I added. "I've missed seeing it. You certainly haven't had much to smile about the past two years, but now you do."

"Hmmm!" Danny kind of murmured, looking at me with just a slight smile on his face.

"I mean it Danny," I insisted. "Your smile is one of your best assets. Whenever I see you with that big smile of yours it brightens my day. It's kind of like seeing a sunrise on a beautiful spring morning. I'm sure your friends have the same reaction when they see that special smile of yours…it's got to make them feel good too."

Then I decided that this was the opportune time to offer Danny the management of C.M. Malone, so I started by saying, "There's something I've been wanting to discuss with you, and this seems like an ideal time to do it."

"Lay it on me," Danny answered.

I began by telling him how well the sales of FPR were going. "In January," I proudly reported, "we had sales of just over $21,000.00…and for February sales exceeded $19,000.00. The marketing program started last September, when samples of FPR were mailed to veterinarians that included the care of horses in their practice. I started with the twenty states with the most horses. I asked the vets in these states to test FPR, and got such an enthusiastic response that I decided to produce and market it. I'm shipping a lot more FPR than I ever anticipated. Close to 90% of what we now ship goes to just five states…Texas, Florida, California, Tennessee and Kentucky. There are a lot of horses in those five states. And Texas is not only a big state, but has more horses than any other state…would you believe more than 500,000?"

"A second mailing of samples," I continued, "will be going out this month to the next twenty states with a significant number of horses. Hopefully, this mailing will result in a further increase in sales. Veterinarians with a practice that includes the care of horses have really accepted FPR."

"Clay Taylor," I told Danny, "is now responsible for managing the business, and he's doing a super job. My contract with him ends next September and he may or may not want to continue. He recently told me that he sees his involvement turning into a full time job if sales keep increasing, and that's a problem as Clay only wants a part-time job. The position is open for you if you want to consider it, regardless of what Clay decides to do. I'd be delighted to have you take over and run the company. Think about it, and if you're interested, we can talk about the specifics and I'll be glad to answer any questions you might have."

My proposal came as quite a surprise to Danny. He looked at me for a few seconds, apparently thinking about and absorbing what I had just presented. After a long pause he finally said, "Gosh, that's quite an offer. You obviously don't need an answer right away and I need time to sort things out. I can tell you though that I am really impressed, Colleen, with what you have accomplished marketing FPR...and I sincerely appreciate your offer. Right now I don't know what options are available to me, but before I make a decision we'll thoroughly discuss your offer. I want to find something challenging, and the salary is secondary. Fortunately, I'm not under any financial pressure with the income we're receiving from Abby's trust, so I don't have to rush to find something."

The dinner which we shared, and particularly the discussion during and after the meal would be remembered for a long time. The family closeness that existed when Danny and I were children and teenagers living under the same roof and sharing virtually every meal was restored that Saturday evening. It was a good feeling.

A few weeks later, in early April, I drove to Metamora, Michigan to pick up Kit Davis. The Greenbriar Resort is in White Sulphur Springs, West Virginia, and that was our destination. We were registered to attend the conference for veterinarians with an equine practice. From Kit's home we drove to Marietta, Ohio, where we stayed overnight at a Holiday Inn. The next morning, after breakfast, we resumed our drive to the Greenbriar. Leaving Marietta, we crossed the Ohio River into West Virginia, taking I-77 to Parkersburg, then on down through Charleston to Beckley. The drive was absolutely spectacular. The mountainsides were ablaze in shades of pink, red and purple flowering trees accented by a background of the striking white blossoms of thousands of dogwood trees. Spring had arrived in the Allegany Mountains, and it was glorious. It was hard for me to keep my eyes fixed on the expressway because the scenery was so beautiful and distracting.

At Beckley we turned onto I-64, and the mountains were higher and even more colorful and impressive as we drove east. We regretted that we hadn't stopped to have lunch in Beckley because we soon realized that we were both very hungry. It was nearing 2:00 p.m. so we decided to get off at the next exit in order to find someplace to eat. The next exit off I-64 took us to Green Sulphur Springs, which we discovered was a tiny mountain village with a general store, a farm elevator, a church and a few houses. No restaurant.

Kit and I were famished, so I parked my "Riv" and we entered the general store, which could only be described as major league rustic. A woman and three elderly men were sitting around a pot-bellied stove. The day was slightly chilly so these four people and a fat cat that was sprawled on the well-worn wood floor were sharing the warmth of a fire in the pot-bellied stove. The woman greeted us and asked, "Can I help you?"

When Kit and I explained that we were starving and needed something to eat she said, "No problem. I'll make you each a sandwich. Come on over here and sit down while I make your sandwiches."

One of the men pulled two more chairs up beside the pot-bellied stove. We sat down and introduced ourselves and explained that we were both veterinarians going to a conference at the Greenbriar. The men's first names were Charley, Sam and Ted and the lady's name was Phyllis.

Not only did Kit and I have a delicious lunch, but we also had a really interesting experience. Our lunch consisted of sandwiches of stacked ham and cheese on soft white bread with mayonnaise, lettuce and sliced tomatoes. The lettuce, bread and tomatoes couldn't have been fresher, while the ham and cheese were sliced especially for our sandwiches. Kit and I shared a big bag of Lay's potato chips. She drank a Pepsi with her sandwich, and I had a chocolate soda. Then we topped off our lunch with Eskimo Pie ice cream. We ate our lunch off little TV tables sitting around the pot-bellied stove talking with the three men and Phyllis who owned the store. They seemed delighted to have some new people to talk with, and while we ate our lunch we learned about various old cures used to treat animals.

Charley told us that, "They used to take old wasps nests and burn 'em and hold them under a horse's nose to cure distemper, I've heard. If you can't find any old wasp nests, you can also take a bucketful of chicken feathers and burn 'em and have the horse inhale the fumes. Whether it cured 'em or not I don't know."

Kit responded with a smile stating, "Thank goodness we now have antibiotics to treat distemper. I'd hate to have to rely on finding some old wasp nests."

Sam informed us that, "When a horse or mule gets stung by a wasp or bumble bee, if you put lard or bacon grease on the sting it'll keep the hair from coming out white. Treating the sore place with lard or bacon grease will make the horse's hair come back the same color. If you don't do that then the bee sting will make the hair come back in white."

Ted contributed to the discussion, telling us that, "When a horse gets sweeny, which is fallen shoulder muscles, the best remedy is soak a thick cloth in vinegar. Then you put that cloth on the horses shoulder and take a hot flat-iron and iron over it. You need to get the horse's shoulder good and hot. If you don't have a flat iron you can use an electric heating pad. That will work just as well."

I said to Ted, "That's really interesting. I'd never heard of that before."

While we were enjoying our lunch, they told us about a number of other old Southern cures or treatments for ailments such as cows with a caked bag and horses with sore tendons and muscles. When they stared talking about caring for horses with sore muscles Kit proceeded to tell them all about FPR, how it was used and that I was the person who was producing and selling the product. I then had to explain that it was actually a solution developed by my grandfather. That really impressed them and they asked a lot of questions about Papa John. Sam made the most telling statement when he said, "Your grandpa is one smart feller." I agreed!

When Kit and I finished eating, we somewhat reluctantly said goodbye to our new friends and continued on our way to the Greenbriar, arriving a little after 5:00 p.m. When we arrived, I was really impressed. The Greenbriar was far and away the most incredible place that I had ever seen. The grounds, the buildings and the interior décor were so attractive that my reaction to it all was, "WOW! What a place."

Kit and I shared a large, beautifully decorated room, and after we unpacked our things we went to the conference registration desk. There we picked up a packet of materials about the conference including our nametags, the daily meeting program and information about the various sessions. Attached to my packet was a note from the conference chairman, Henry Danforth. The note said that he would like to have me chair one of the breakout sessions. When I contacted Henry, I learned that when Kit registered us for this conference she had included the fact that I was the person responsible for producing and marketing FPR. Consequently Henry assumed that I was an equine specialist. When I told him I was not, he was quite surprised. I then proceeded to tell him how FPR was created, and why I decided to produce and sell it. When I finished my explanation, I suggested that he ask Kit to chair the breakout session as her practice in Metamora was primarily dedicated to caring for horses. I passed the buck and Kit accepted when Henry approached her about chairing this particular session.

That evening, Kit and I had dinner in the Greenbriar's magnificent dining room. The ambience, the dinner and the service were beyond anything either of us had ever experienced. We couldn't help but reflect upon the incredible difference between our lunch in Green Sulphur Springs and the meal we were enjoying that evening. However, we both agreed that the food we had for lunch at the country store tasted wonderful. We were both absolutely famished when we stopped for lunch and Phyllis, Sam, Charley and Ted were such interesting people that we would remember them for a long time. Attending this conference was turning out to be quite an experience.

The conference started the next morning with a general session. Henry Danforth, the conference chairman, welcomed the 445 veterinarians in attendance and reviewed the program for the three days of the conference. When he finished, I was totally taken by surprise when he asked me to stand. He then introduced me and informed the audience that I was the C. M. Malone behind the popular new product FPR. I was so taken off guard that I felt a little embarrassed by the recognition and the polite applause. I nodded to the audience, looked at Henry, mouthed an inaudible 'thank you' and sat down. Kit looked at me and commented, "Wasn't that nice!"

There were interesting and informative presentations made in the morning session by different speakers. Mid morning, there was a coffee break and while Kit and I were standing in line for coffee, Paul Ross, a very good looking man in his mid to late thirties came over and introduced himself. Paul explained that he was the executive vice president of the Upson-Ross Company. Kit and I were both very familiar with this company, as they supplied a number of pharmaceuticals as well as other supplies used by all veterinarians.

Paul congratulated me on the successful introduction of FPR, and said he was quite impressed with how well my product had been accepted by veterinarians. As usual, I had to give him a brief and quick explanation as to how the product was conceived and why I decided to make and sell it.

When the coffee break ended, Paul asked if Kit and I would join him for lunch. He said he'd like to learn more about FPR and what my plans were for the future for the product. I turned to Kit to get her response and she kind of shrugged her shoulders and said, "That's fine with me."

When we returned to our seats Kit leaned towards me and in a low voice said, "That Paul's a handsome dude. A real hunk! Wonder if he's married? I didn't see a wedding ring on his left hand."

I quietly said to Kit, "You're engaged to be married. What on earth are you thinking?"

Kit then turned to me and whispered, "He's not for me, silly girl...for you."

We were getting glances from people sitting near us so we stopped our whispering and I tried to concentrate on what the speaker was saying. My mind, though, was distracted as I thought about the brief meeting with Paul Ross. I thought to myself, "He is handsome, has a pleasant smile and nice teeth. Why am I so impressed with teeth? Maybe I should have been a dentist. Come on, Colleen, enough already. Pay attention to the speaker."

When the morning session ended, Paul was waiting for us at the back of the meeting room. The three of us then went to the dining room, and while we were having lunch, Paul told us that it was his grandfather who had started the Upson-Ross Company. His father was deceased and his uncle was now the president of the company. We also learned that Paul had flown to the conference in their corporate plane, which he said was a lot easier and faster than driving from Chicago to the Greenbriar. He also reminded us that Upson-Ross had a hospitality suite. Kit and I had noticed in our packet of materials for the conference that there was an invitation to visit this suite. We promised Paul we'd stop by later in the day before we went to dinner.

The afternoon meeting consisted of breakout sessions with a choice of subjects. Kit and I stayed together, attending the same sessions, including the one she chaired. When they ended late in the afternoon, the two of us went to the Upson-Ross hospitality suite. Upon entering we were both really impressed with the large beautifully decorated suite, which Upson-Ross was using to host veterinarians. It was called the State Suite, and it had an impressive foyer with a floor of black and white marble. From the foyer we walked through huge twin doors into an enormous parlor. Kit and I each got a glass of wine and walked around introducing ourselves and talking about the conference with other veterinarians in this grand suite. When we walked into an adjoining room, we saw Paul engaged in conversation with several people. He smiled and waved when he saw us, and after a few minutes came over to where Kit and I were standing.

"Thank you for coming to our hospitality suite," Paul said. "there's plenty of hors d'oeuvres, so please help yourselves. This is our way of thanking you for using our pharmaceuticals and other supplies, so please don't be bashful about helping yourselves."

"We won't," I replied. "but we're also looking forward to enjoying another delicious dinner in the dining room tonight. Gotta' save room for that."

"During lunch today I monopolized the conversation telling you about the Upson-Ross Company," Paul answered. "I don't want to make a pest of myself, but I would really like to join the two of you for dinner. You can tell me about yourselves, and we didn't really get around to talking about FPR during lunch. Besides I'm not keen on eating alone, and would enjoy your company."

I glanced at Kit to get her reaction before responding to Paul, and was glad to hear her say, "Fine with me. You're welcome to join us for dinner."

"Great! What time should I meet you in the dining room?" Paul asked.

"Let's meet there at 7:30," I suggested.

Paul said he'd see us at 7:30 and then excused himself, as two men were waiting nearby to talk with him. Kit and I stayed a little longer sampling some of the hors d'oeuvres before going to our room. After we got to our room we decided we needed fresh air and some exercise. So we changed our clothes, put on our tennis shoes and took a brisk walk. Neither of us were used to sitting in meetings all day, so the walk around the historic grounds at the Greenbriar was a welcome and delightful release from being held captive all day.

That evening during dinner, I told Paul quite a lot about myself. "I'm a farm girl," I explained. "My father is the fourth generation of the family in agribusiness. We raise a lot of apples, and my mother operates a farm market four months of the year. We had a much larger farm where we raised various crops, but several years ago we sold 580 acres to a big developer. Now there's lots of homes and a golf course next to our orchards. Sometime in the near future I expect that this developer will make an offer to buy the orchards as well, in order to build more homes. My brother Danny and I broke the mold. Neither of us wanted to take over the farm and the orchards. I decided that I wanted to be a veterinarian and my brother wanted a business career." (I did not reveal that my brother Danny had recently been released from prison. I didn't want to have to explain all the circumstances and felt it would have been a little embarrassing, as I hardly knew Paul.)

I did tell Paul about my fiancé, Gene Morris, and how he tragically died a few days before we were to be married. Paul showed sincere sympathy when I told him about the accident and he commented, "What an unbelievably horrible thing to happen, Colleen. First for your fiancé to lose his life in such a bizarre way…as a result of hitting a deer. Then what grief and sadness you and his family must have suffered to have him die so suddenly. What you went through must have been terribly difficult. Even though this happened a few years ago, I'm sure you still feel your loss." After saying this he took my hand, squeezed it and said, "I'm sorry."

Kit was not overlooked in our discussion, as Paul asked her to give us her resume when I finished talking. Kit provided a brief oral biography, which I found interesting as I learned some things about her that I wasn't aware of. "My father," Kit told us, "is also a veterinarian. His practice is in Metamora and he only takes care of horses. It was my dad who encouraged and convinced me to become a veterinarian. However, we don't agree on a number of things, so I didn't join his practice when I graduated from the vet school at MSU. I work at a large clinic in Metamora and we take care of a lot of horses, but we have a small animal practice as well. I didn't want to be in a practice totally dedicated to horses, even though I love horses, and have one of own. I also have a black lab named Charlie. I have an older sister and two older brothers. They're all married and have children. I'm engaged to be married, but we haven't set the date as yet. I'm quite happy with my life doing what I do. Maybe I've been a little too satisfied. Richard Dixon, the man I'm going to marry, has been urging me to set a date because he wants to start having children right away. I'm the one that's not been ready to commit to a date. I think it was good for me to get away for a while and attend this conference, as I've thought a lot about my situation the past several days. I've decided that when I get home I'm going to tell Richard that this coming September would be a good time for us to be married. You two are the first people that I've told about my decision."

"That's wonderful!" I responded. "I hope that date works out, and that you are blessed with many, many happy years married to Richard. Maybe I'll get to meet him sometime."

Paul then added his best wishes, and said he hoped that Kit's marriage would turn out to be much better than his did. He then explained that he was divorced and had a ten-year-old daughter Alicia. "My ex-wife," Paul explained, "is now married to a man who was once my best friend. I travel a lot in my job with Upson-Ross, and often have to be away from home a week at a time attending conferences such as this one at the Greenbriar. I also have to spend time meeting with our sales reps across the country, and going to various business meetings. My wife apparently didn't like being alone so much, so she and my former good friend spent a lot of time having dinner together, taking in movies and going to concerts. As a result they decided they were in love with each other. so my wife divorced me and married my former best friend. Obviously, he and I are no longer buddies. I'm sure, Kit, that you'll have a much better experience than I did."

When Paul finished his candid exposure of what happened to his marriage, I didn't know quite what to say. I detected some bitterness in his voice and decided that it would be best to change the subject and talk about something else besides marriage.

"Tomorrow afternoon is open," I said, trying to turn the conversation in another direction, "There are no meetings scheduled after the morning session. Kit and I thought we'd go horseback riding." I was about to suggest to Paul that he might want to consider joining us, but before I could do so he interrupted me to tell us about his plans.

"Two veterinarians that I've known for some time," Paul explained, "who by the way are also pilots, have asked to go for a ride in our new corporate plane. One lives in Lexington, and the other one is from Knoxville. I've agreed to take them for a ride and I plan to fly them over their hometowns. The two of you are welcome to go with us. Our company plane is a new Beechcraft King Air, less than a year old. Our corporate pilot will be flying the plane and I'll be the copilot, as I'm also a licensed pilot. The King Air can carry five passengers, so there's room for the two of you. We'll be leaving right after lunch. I have a van reserved to take us to the Greenbriar Valley airport at Lewisburg, which is about fifteen minutes away from here. The weather forecast is for a beautiful day with just a few scattered clouds. So you'll be able to see a lot, and we'll be back in time for dinner. What do you think? Would you like to go?"

"I'd love to go," I quickly answered, not waiting for Kit's reaction. I was glad and also relieved when I heard her say, "Sure, I'd like to go too."

"You're on!" Paul said.

While we were having our dessert, I provided Paul with more details about FPR and described how I was handling production and distribution. I explained how I had test-marketed the product, and told him that sales were averaging a little over $20,000.00 a month. "I'm hoping sales will soon increase to more than $30,000.00 a month as a result of a recent mailing of samples of FPR to another twenty states. If this happens, I'll be able to recover my initial investment in about a year and a half. This venture has turned out to be far, far more successful than I ever anticipated."

Paul asked, "Have you received any complaints about the product?"

"None so far," I replied, "and there have been no delivery problems...which kind of surprises me. Frankly, it amazes me that everything has gone so smoothly. The credit for that really goes to Clay Taylor, the man who runs the business for me."

That evening after dinner, Kit and I went to the room we shared and jabbered away for several hours. The TV set was on but we paid very little attention to it. Kit told me a lot about her fiancé, Richard Dixon. She said he lived in

Lapeer, a town in Michigan's thumb area, that he was a building contractor and was really a great guy. Dick, she explained, had built several "spec" homes and made a good profit on them. After they were married they would live in Lapeer, which is about a twenty-minute drive from Metamora. She also told me some interesting stories about her nieces and nephews, whom she frequently baby sat for. Mostly I listened, because Kit has a delightful sense of humor and the stories she told about her family and some of things that had happened to her at the clinic where she worked were simply hilarious. I hadn't laughed so much in a long time.

The next day Kit and I attended the morning session of the conference, had a fast lunch, and met Paul and the other two veterinarians promptly at 1:30 p.m. at the front entrance of the Greenbriar. Paul introduced the four of us. Dr. Jim McKelvey was from Lexington, and Dr. Frank Walters was from Knoxville. We boarded the waiting van and went to the airport. I knew nothing about airplanes, but as we walked to where the King Air was parked, I thought it was a sleek-looking plane and that the four-blade propellers on the twin engines gave it a powerful look. The pilot was already on board…apparently going through his preflight review. Paul joined him as copilot, and the four of us who were passengers took our seats in the cabin. I was a little nervous and was doing my best to appear calm, but I don't think I completely hid my anxiety, as I had never been up in a small plane before. Kit, I know, shared my preflight jitters and we kept glancing across at each other—checking to see how the other one was doing.

We were soon airborne and gazing down at the earth. It looked peaceful, clean and beautiful. Spring had arrived…turning the trees and grass many and various shades of green, and the flowering trees provided splashes of color as far as my eyes could see. The Allegany Mountains were awesome, and the rugged terrain we were flying over made me a little anxious, as there was no place that I could see where a plane would be able to land in case there was an emergency.

When I looked straight down at the earth the landscape flashed past, confirming that we were flying very fast. When I looked off in the distance though, objects moved past slower, so that became my sightseeing preference. It was intriguing to look out at houses, barns and sheds scattered here and there and to see a village or small town tucked in a mountain valley. Smoke rose from the chimneys of many houses as the day was a little on the cool side, and I pictured women going about their daily tasks in their warm, cozy homes. Streams snaked through the valleys and on the roads and highways there were cars, trucks, school buses and other vehicles moving in what looked like slow motion from my vantage point in the sky. My jitters gradually melted away, and I soon realized that flying in a corporate plane like this King Air was just an absolutely awesome experience.

After leaving Lewisburg, our first destination was Lexington, Kentucky. As we flew west the Allegany Mountains gradually turned into foothills followed by a rolling, somewhat leveler terrain. Looking out from my window, I now could see farms stretching to the horizon. Towns became larger and traffic on the highways heavier. It was fascinating to observe the world below, which changed minute by minute as we flew west at a high rate of speed.

Circling Lexington, I observed a patchwork of fences, mostly white, enclosing fields which contained grazing horses. There were lots of stately homes with fancy porches and barns of all sizes and descriptions. Dr. McKelvey pointed out his home and he called his wife on his cell phone to tell her he was in a plane circling their home. She came out in the front yard and waved at us.

From Lexington we headed south and soon circled Knoxville. Dr. Walters pointed out both his home and his clinic. I thought he would call his wife as Dr. McKelvey had done, but he didn't. From Knoxville we went a little further south and flew over the Great Smokey Mountain National Park. It was incredible to see this huge park from the air. We checked out Gatlinburg at the entrance to the park. It looked very crowded, with solid traffic on the main street moving slowly through the town.

Next it was Ashville, where we saw the famous Biltmore home and estate. From Ashville we flew north, following the Blue Ridge Parkway to Roanoke. From Roanoke we turned to the northwest, heading for the airport at Lewisburg. Before landing we circled the 6500 acres that make up the Greenbriar resort, and looking down at all the impressive buildings, golf courses, cottages and other facilities gave me an even greater appreciation of this elegant one-of-a kind place where I was staying.

After we landed at the Lewisburg airport Kit and I, as well as the other two vets, enthusiastically thanked Paul for taking us for a ride in the King Air. It was a memorable afternoon and an experience I'd long remember. When we arrived back at the Greenbriar, Paul asked if he could talk privately with me for a few minutes specifically about FPR.

I accompanied Paul to the State Suite where he proceeded to tell me that the Upson-Ross Company had considered producing a product like FPR for a long time, but had never made it a priority. Paul said that, from everything he had heard about FPR, it was an exceptional formula and his company would like to make an offer to acquire it if I would consider a buyout. He explained that he had discussed this with the President of Upson-Ross last night, and he had approved approaching me about the possibility.

His proposal didn't come as a total surprise. I had a hunch that his company might possibly be interested in acquiring FPR because of the unusual interest he had shown in the product, and all the questions he had asked. However, I had kind of a mixed reaction. On the one hand, I had been flattered by the attention he had shown me, and my friend Kit. But now I realized that his primary interest was obviously to see if his company might be able to acquire FPR. I listened as he presented various ways a purchase could be structured—everything from an outright buy-out, to a deal where I received royalties for a number of years. Paul told me that his company had grown through acquisitions and had a history of being fair and generous in their business dealings.

When Paul finished talking, I told him his offer was something I hadn't expected, but that I would be open to the possibly of selling FPR to Upson-Ross. I explained that the launching of the product had taken considerably more time than I had originally expected. He wanted to know what my plans were for the future for FPR, and I told him that I had made a commitment to buy the Cunningham Veterinary Clinic. That was going to be my life's work, and I had no intention of leaving the clinic to manage C. M. Malone, Inc. "The man who now manages the business," I told Paul, "is doing an outstanding job." However, I did not reveal what my financial arrangement with Clay Taylor was, nor the fact that I had offered the management of C. M. Malone, Inc. to Danny. I did tell him that my company was a Sub-chapter S corporation, and that there were three stockholders. I owned 100,000 shares, my grandfather held 5000 shares and Joyce Kallman had 7000 shares. Paul wanted to know more about Joyce, and I explained the key role she had played in the marketing of FPR. Our meeting ended with an invitation from Paul for me to come to Chicago to tour their plant in Northbrook, and to consider a buyout proposal. I agreed to do that, and we parted with a handshake.

That evening, Kit and I enjoyed another great dinner in the Greenbriar's dining room. After dinner we went for a walk then turned in, as it had been a full, exciting day. The conference ended the next morning at 11:30, and the morning session was not well attended. Kit and I surmised that a lot of the veterinarians had skipped the session in order to play golf or to enjoy some of the other amenities at the Greenbriar.

Kit and I left in the afternoon, and started the long drive back to Metamora and Rockford. As we drove along, Kit and I discussed Paul's interest in acquiring FPR and she asked me what I thought I might do. I explained, just as I had with Paul, that launching the product had taken a lot more time than I thought it would, and there was ongoing monitoring that had to be done. I told Kit that I had offered my brother the opportunity to manage my business, and that if he accepted this position, then I wouldn't consider selling FPR to Upson-Ross. If Danny decided he didn't want this responsibility, then I would very seriously consider an offer from Upson-Ross.

I further explained to Kit, "I've made a firm commitment to Bob Cunningham to buy the clinic when he retires. That's going to happen not too many years in the future. Working as a veterinarian, managing the clinic and the staff and having another business on the side…even with a good manager…would be very time consuming and a lot of responsibility. How much time will I have to call my own? Not much, I'm afraid!"

"Do you think your brother will accept your offer?" Kit asked.

"I doubt it," I replied, "I think he'd prefer to do something far more challenging. It's an option that's available for him to consider and it would solve a problem for me, as I don't expect the man now managing the business will want to continue after his contract ends at the end of September."

"Paul told me," I informed Kit, "that he was confident that Upson-Ross could produce FPR in their plant at a much lower cost than what I'm paying the Kalamazoo Company that produces it for me, and they would be able to ship it more efficiently as they process thousands of orders to veterinarians every day. I'm really not in a position to negotiate a lower manufacturing cost basis with a single product. In fact, my supplier has already notified me that they will have to charge more to manufacture and to handle the shipping of FPR when my contract comes up for renewal this fall."

Late in the afternoon, we decided to stay overnight at a motel in Canton, Ohio and finish the drive to our homes in the morning. We were up and on our way early the next morning and arrived at Kit's home in Metamora at noon. I stayed just long enough to have lunch there with Kit. When I finished eating we said out goodbyes. The two of us had quite an experience as a result of attending the conference at the Greenbriar, and we had shared an adventure that had resulted in a close friendship.

When I got home late in the afternoon, I told Mom and Dad all about the conference, the plane ride in the King Air, and what a fabulous resort the Greenbriar is. I explained that a major supplier of pharmaceuticals for veterinarians was very interested in acquiring FPR so a lot had happened the past week. I must have sounded enthusiastic describing everything that had happened as Mom commented, "I haven't seen you this up-beat in a long time, Colleen. Attending this conference was good for you, and it's going to be interesting to see what the future brings. Sounds to me like you might have an opportunity to make a lot of money if you decide to sell FPR to this Chicago company."

Almost two weeks went by before I heard from Paul. He called me at noon on a Wednesday to ask if I had any plans for the upcoming weekend. He explained that he had been traveling all over the country ever since the Greenbriar conference, and said he had been thinking about me a lot. This latter statement I took with some skepticism, as I thought to myself that if he'd really been thinking about me as much as he claimed that he had then he would have surely called me before now. But I was still flattered.

I told Paul, "I haven't made any plans for the weekend. Just what do you have in mind?"

Paul said he could drive to Rockford Saturday morning and find a place to stay. He'd like to meet my family and I could show him around the area. We could have dinner Saturday night at some nice Grand Rapids restaurant and maybe go to a movie.

"You're welcome to stay at my home," I told Paul, "No need for you to stay at a motel." Paul accepted my invitation. He also informed me that he thought that the President of Upson-Ross and their Chief Financial Officer would be ready to meet with me in the near future. They had been discussing ways that FPR could be acquired, and their goal was to make it a mutually beneficial arrangement. I was pleased to get this update, and to learn that they were still serious about making an offer. We then talked about the Greenbriar meeting, and he asked what I'd been doing since returning home. He asked if I had heard from Kit and I said I had not, but suspected that she had been quite busy…just as I had been…since returning for the conference. Our telephone conversation concluded with Paul telling me, "I'll see you around noon on Saturday, Colleen. I'm really looking forward to this weekend."

In spite of my skepticism about how sincere Paul's interest was in me personally, I found myself thinking about him a lot after his call, and was pleased and kind of excited that he was coming to Rockford for the weekend.

Weather wise, Saturday was a gorgeous day. Paul arrived at my home around 11:00 a.m. I introduced him to Mom and Dad, and the four of us sat around the long table in our kitchen drinking coffee while we visited. When it was time for lunch, Paul watched with considerable fascination as Mom made beef barley soup from scratch and grilled cheese sandwiches. He was really hungry, because he ate two bowls of soup and two grilled cheese sandwiches, and told Mom he hadn't enjoyed a lunch this much in a long time. Mom smiled in appreciation, and thanked Paul for his compliments.

After lunch Paul and I went for a walk. I showed him our barns where the tractors, spraying equipment, trucks and trailers were kept and the large refrigerated storage room, now empty of apples. We walked though the rows of apple trees in the orchard and he commented several times, "This is such a beautiful place. It would be a shame to see it all replaced with another housing development."

Paul was surprised when I told him that China now produces more apples than the United States. "Most of the apple juice in the grocery stores," I told him, "is made from concentrate of apples grown in China. The future for apple farmers in the United States is somewhat uncertain due to the low-cost competition that they face from growers in China. As a result, there aren't many prospective buyers when an apple orchard is put up for sale in Michigan...or in any other state, for that matter. Mom and Dad are actually fortunate that they have the possible option of selling our farm to a housing developer."

This revelation surprised Paul, as he had no idea that China was now producing more apples than the United States. "Some of the supplies that Upson-Ross sells to veterinarians," he commented, "are made in China. This dependence on China as the source for so many of the products we use in this country is a strange situation. You have to wonder what it's going to lead to a few years from now."

During our stroll through the orchards, Paul took my hand as we wandered about, and I enjoyed spending the day with him. I tried to convince myself that maybe he really was more interested in me personally than I first thought. We talked about a variety of things, laughed about some silly things...and got to know much more about each other. He told me about his ten-year-old daughter, Alicia. "She's usually with me every other weekend," he said, "and I try to do something special with her on those weekends so that she'll look forward to spending time with me." I also learned a few things about his mother and his two sisters. "My mother," Paul explained "lives in Lake Forest in the house that I grew up in. But my sisters live on opposite ends of the country. My sister Nancy lives in Annapolis, and Susan lives in Laguna Beach, California." I found out that Paul had graduated from Northwestern University, and had an MBA from Harvard. "That's quite impressive," I thought to myself.

As we walked along, I decided to tell Paul all about my brother Danny and that he had recently served time in a correctional facility because of a soil pollution situation at a plant in Ohio. After hearing all the crazy circumstances Paul's reaction was, "Sounds like he got a really bum rap to me."

When we returned to the house, Paul put his suitcase in Danny's old room, and we joined Mom and Dad who were sitting on the front porch. Dad served cocktails while we had a pleasant conversation relaxing and enjoying the beautiful spring weather. Paul invited Mom and Dad to join us for dinner, but they declined his invitation. That evening Paul and I saw a really entertaining movie and then had a late dinner together. It was a good day!

Our Sunday morning, breakfast included my Mom's wonderful streuselkuchen coffee cake, and Paul said he'd never tasted anything that good before in his life. After breakfast Paul and I went to see the Gerald R. Ford Presidential Library in downtown Grand Rapids, followed by lunch at the Amway Grand Plaza Hotel. Next we visited the Frederik Meijer Gardens and Sculpture Park, where Paul was quite impressed when he saw the three-story high sculpture of Leonardo Da Vinci's horse. Only two of these incredible bronze sculptures exist. One is in Milan, Italy and the other one is in the Frederik Meijer Garden. It was fun serving as the tour guide, especially when Paul told me how much he was enjoying the day.

Late in the afternoon, we drove to Holland and after a quick tour of the town, we had dinner at one of my favorite restaurants, which is in a marina on Lake Michigan. When Paul learned that the annual Holland Tulip Festival would take place in two weeks he said he would like to come back for it, and bring his daughter, Alicia. I invited them to stay at our home, explaining that he wouldn't be able to find a room in a motel or in a bed and breakfast within a hundred miles of Holland, as everything would be booked by now for this special event.

Paul stayed overnight and left for Chicago early Monday morning. He thanked Mom and Dad for their hospitality, hugged Mom and gave Dad a hearty handshake. I accompanied Paul to his car in the front drive and after he put his suitcase in his car he turned around and put his arms around me. We embraced and then we kissed for the first time. Then Paul looked at me with a big smile on his face and said, "I've had a wonderful time. Thank you for everything, Colleen. I hope the next two weeks go by quickly so that we can be together again."

The time did pass quickly, and Paul and his daughter arrived before noon on Friday, May 13. After lunch, Paul and I took Alicia on an orchard tour and I showed her everything that I had shown her Dad two weeks earlier. Later we played croquet, and in the evening we played the popular card game SkipBo, and Mom and Dad participated. Saturday morning Paul, Alicia and I drove to Holland and spent the day and the evening enjoying various events and shows that were part of the Tulip Festival. Alicia got some wooden shoes, which she clomped around in part of the time. Papa John joined us for dinner, and I was glad they got to meet my grandfather. Paul especially wanted to meet the man who helped create FPR.

For Sunday morning breakfast, as a special treat for Alicia, Mom baked a Streuselkuchen, which she served with scrambled eggs and crisp bacon. I was happy to see that Alicia was a good eater and she was obviously enjoying herself. We then went horseback riding, which I had arranged with Bill Stevenson, a man that I knew through the clinic. He had a beautiful farm with a large stable where he bred, raised and also boarded a lot of horses. While we were riding I told Alicia about my horse, Star, and how much I enjoyed riding him when I was a young girl. She quite wistfully said to me, "I wish I could have a horse of my own."

"Hopefully some day you will have your own horse," I answered.

The weekend went especially well, and I thought that my relationship with Paul was getting much closer. I really enjoyed being with him and I was becoming convinced that he actually did have an interest in me, not just in getting FPR for his company. When Paul and Alicia departed for Chicago late in the afternoon, Alicia said this was the best weekend she had ever had, and asked, "May I come back again sometime?"

Almost in unison Mom, Dad and I said, "Of course you can!"

Several days later, Paul called to see if I could arrange to come to Chicago on Thursday, May 26. He explained that I could tour the Upson-Ross plant on Friday morning and in the afternoon the acquisition of FPR could be discussed in a meeting with the President and their Chief Financial Officer. Then Paul invited me to stay in Chicago for the Memorial Day weekend. "There will be lots of things happening that weekend," he said, "and I'd like to share some of them with you. You'd be welcome to stay at my place or you could stay at my mother's home. Wherever you'd feel most comfortable."

"I'll arrange my schedule to come then," I told Paul, "but I think, all things considered, that it would be best if I stayed at your mothers…if you're sure she wouldn't mind."

"She'd love to meet you, and I know she'd make you feel very welcome," Paul assured me.

I informed Bob Cunningham that I needed to be away from Thursday, May 26 until Tuesday, May 31, and he agreed to cover for me on the days that I was scheduled to work at the clinic. I think he was somewhat relieved to learn that I was going to Chicago to seriously consider an offer from Upson-Ross to buy FPR. While I had assured him that this product would never change my commitment to take over the clinic from him when he retired, I suspect he wasn't totally convinced. And, while he never said anything to me specifically about the time I had invested in starting another business, I knew he felt that it had distracted me from my career as a veterinarian. "To really succeed at whatever you do in life," Bob mentioned to me one day, "you really need to give it 110% effort."

It wasn't hard to figure out what he meant by that statement.

Before going to Chicago for the meeting with Upson-Ross, I also talked with Papa John and Joyce Kallman to inform them that this company was going to make an offer to acquire FPR. Both told me that whatever I decided to do was OK with them. Danny and his family were in Hawaii, so I wasn't able to tell him about the upcoming meeting with Upson-Ross. However, Mom and Dad both thought that Danny was not going to accept my offer to manage C. M. Malone, and that I should seriously consider selling FPR to Upson-Ross.

I left for Chicago on Thursday morning, and arrived in the early afternoon at Paul's mother's home in Lake Forest. When I pulled my car into the driveway leading up to the house I was impressed with the manicured lawn, the attractive landscaping and the tall trees which provided a park-like setting for the property. I received a warm welcome from Constance, Paul's mother, and she insisted that I call her Connie. After a quick tour of Connie's beautifully decorated home, she said it was time for tea. We then went to the sunroom where we had the tea. Along with the tea, Connie served a plate of little sandwiches. Half of them were made with thin slices of a nutty brown bread spread with cream cheese mixed with chopped fresh watercress. The other sandwiches were made with soft white bread spread with cream cheese and thin slices of cucumber. No crust was on the bread and they were cut into either squares or diamonds. I was impressed.

In sharing the ritual of tea with Connie, I felt that there was a bonding taking place between the two of us that probably wouldn't have happened had we just sat and talked.

During the tea, I learned that Connie was a director of Upson-Ross, so I assumed that she was a large stockholder. She also informed me that she had great admiration and respect for veterinarians. "If I could live my life over,"

Connie said, "I would be a veterinarian." That comment made me feel espe-cially good because she said it like she really meant it. Paul arrived late in the afternoon and that evening the three of us had dinner at a private club of which Connie was a member.

On Friday morning, Paul joined us for breakfast then drove me to the Upson-Ross plant. Two things especially stood out when I took the plant tour. I was impressed at how clean the plant was, and I was intrigued by the compli-cated-looking machinery that produced the various products. In the afternoon I spent several hours with Harold Ross, the president and David Martin, the treasurer.

The acquisition proposal they presented was very attractive. They offered to pay $4.30 for each share of stock in C. M. Malone, Inc. The stock of Papa John and Joyce Kallman would be acquired for cash. However, I had several options that I could consider. I could accept an all-cash offer for my 100,000 shares of stock...payable over one, two or three years, or take half in cash and half in stock in Upson-Ross. This was a generous offer for a company that had been in business for just one year.

Before the meeting ended, I expressed my appreciation for their interest in FPR and for what I thought was a very fair offer. I told them that I needed to review the offer with my attorney and my accountant, and would give them an answer within two weeks. (I did not reveal that my decision actually hinged on whether or not Danny accepted my offer to manage C. M. Malone. Danny and his family would be returning from Hawaii on June 10, and I planned to talk with him the next day to get his decision. I could not accept a "maybe"...my brother either had to tell me "yes" or "no").

The next three days of the Memorial Day Weekend were truly delightful. I got along famously with Connie. On Saturday and Sunday the three of us...Paul, Connie and I...did a variety of interesting and enjoyable things. Monday, Memorial Day, though was somewhat more serious and traditional. Alicia was with us, and we all went to a cemetery, where flowers were placed on the graves of Paul's father and his grandparents, as well as on those of some other relatives. They did what Memorial Day is really all about. I kind of felt like I was an extension of their family by being included and sharing in the time they spent at the cemetery remembering departed loved ones.

After breakfast on Tuesday morning I left for home, and Mom and Dad learned all about my big weekend in Chicago that evening. They were both amazed that I had an offer of $4.30 for each share of stock in C. M. Malone, Inc. Dad wistfully said, "I wish I had put some money in your company." It was a generous offer, as my company had no physical assets beyond the existing inventory of FPR. There was $46,000.00 in the company checking account, but essentially Upson-Ross was buying an outstanding and proven formula for a product that had been well accepted by veterinarians. If Upson-Ross decided to develop and try to market a competing product it would cost them as much or more than what they were paying to acquire FPR. I was also convinced that, if I did not sell FPR to Upson-Ross, they would come out with a competing product, which would dilute the market. And they would be strong competition.

I did review the offer with both my attorney and accountant. They agreed that the offer was most attractive, and I told them I planned to accept it if Danny told me he did not want to manage my company. Papa John was pleased, and Joyce Kallman was thrilled when she learned about the windfall profit she was going to receive.

On Saturday, June 11, I called Danny to welcome him home from Hawaii, and I told him about my meeting in Chicago with Upson-Ross. After listening to everything I had to say, Danny expressed his appreciation for me offering him the management of C. M. Malone, but urged me to move ahead with the Upson-Ross deal. He told me that he was investigating the possibility of buying a golf course that had a beautiful clubhouse. It was for sale, but he needed to come up with a million dollars to swing the deal. He hoped that Mom and Dad would provide some of the money as an investment, and he was going to approach Abby's parents as well. "The land is very valuable and, if worse came to worse, the golf course could be sold for a housing development," Danny explained.

I told Danny that I would consider investing some of the money I received from the sale of FPR in this golf course if he succeeded in raising the rest of the money he needed. After I told Danny this, he responded by saying, "I'm so lucky to have you as a sister. You have helped me so much in so many ways. I love you, Colleen, and thank you for everything you've either done or tried to do for me. I owe you more than you know. I just hope that I can do something special for you in the future."

After I finished talking with Danny, I immediately called Paul to tell him that I had decided to accept the Upson-Ross offer to buy FPR. Paul was pleased and said he would notify the President and the Treasurer. The next step would be for their attorneys to prepare the necessary documents to finalize the acquisition. He thought this would take several weeks to accomplish, but they would try to move everything along so that Upson-Ross could start making FPR in their plant in late September. I also informed Paul that I wanted a cash buyout for my stock, payable over two years to reduce the tax payments.

The following weekend, Paul flew to the Kent County International Airport on the east side of Grand Rapids, and I met him there early Saturday morning. This airport is only twenty miles from my home. From the airport we went to a restaurant in Kentwood for lunch, then to Abby and Danny's home, as Paul had never met my brother and his family. We spent the afternoon visiting, and Mom and Dad showed up late in the afternoon because Abby had invited all of us for dinner. Paul stayed overnight at my home, and we hung out together on Sunday. Late that afternoon, I drove him back to the airport and he flew back to Chicago in the single engine plane that he had rented for the weekend.

Paul returned with his daughter, Alicia, for the Fourth of July weekend. We did some hiking, went horseback riding again, canoed on the Rogue River and went to a fireworks display. We did a lot of barbecuing…of hot dogs, hamburgers, German sausage and steaks…and Danny, Abby, and their children were present some of the time. It was a good old-fashioned Fourth of July celebration.

Two weeks later on Thursday, July 21, I went to Chicago and stayed through the weekend at Connie's home. On Friday morning, all the documents were signed transferring ownership of FPR to Upson-Ross. My attorney had reviewed all the papers before I signed them. A wire transfer of $215,000.00 was sent to my checking account, and I would receive another $215,000.00 in 1995. I received a check made out to Papa John in the amount of $21,500.00, and another check for $30,100.00 for Joyce Kallman. I was really looking forward to giving them their checks.

I didn't see Paul again until the last weekend in July. I spent the weekend in Chicago and was a guest at Connie's home again. Connie made me feel so welcome that I didn't feel like I was imposing. We got along famously. It seemed like my relationship with Paul, though, was going to consist of getting together one or two weekends a month…either in Chicago or in Rockford…with frequent phone calls in between.

When I received an invitation in early August to attend Kit's marriage to Richard Dixon, I called Kit to congratulate her and to tell her about everything that had happened to me since the Greenbriar conference. Kit was pleased to find out that Upson-Ross had purchased FPR and delighted to learn that Paul and I were dating. "How exciting," she said when I told her this, and she insisted that I invite Paul to come to her wedding as my "significant other." "Dick and I have already bought an eighty-acre farm near Lapeer with a four bedroom house and you both can stay there," Kit said. For emphasis, she added, "I won't take 'No' for an answer."

"I'll invite Paul," I replied, "but I don't know if he's already made plans for that weekend." Kit and I talked for a long time on the phone that day, and she described her wedding dress, the plans for the wedding, where they were going on their honeymoon and all about the home she and Richard had bought. After listening to everything she had to say, I told Kit, "You really have your act together."

Several days later. when I heard from Paul, I asked him if he'd liked to go to Kit's wedding with me in Metamora on the Labor Day weekend. He said, "You bet! I'd really like that. It should be a lot of fun, and I'd like to see Kit again. She's a neat gal, and I enjoyed the time I spent with her at the Greenbriar." Paul told me he would come to Rockford the third weekend in August, and we could shop for a wedding present. "If I'm going to the wedding," Paul stated, "then I should pay for the gift."

Also in early August, Mom, Dad and I had an important meeting with Danny. He came to the house one evening to tell us that he had signed a purchase agreement that afternoon to acquire the Castlewood Country Club Golf Course, contingent upon payment of one million dollars within sixty days. The best price Danny was able to negotiate for the place was $3,100,000.00. Castlewood was a private club and golf course with nearly 800 members. There were two classes of membership. A full membership included use of the golf course, clubhouse, swimming pool, tennis courts and exercise facilities. A social membership included everything except golf. However, neither the full membership nor the social membership included any equity interest in the Club.

The photos that Danny showed us of the golf course, tennis courts and swimming pool, as well as of the clubhouse and all its facilities, were impressive. He was quite businesslike in showing us the photos and he carefully, calmly and methodically presented information to assure us that this investment was an excellent business venture. But underneath his calm exterior, I knew he was really excited about the possibility of becoming the owner of the Castlewood Country Club. Danny explained that he had several ideas as to how he planned to add to the membership base, as well as increase the use of the dining room for events such as business meetings, receptions, social events and Christmas parties. "The club pro has agreed to stay on," Danny informed us, "to manage the golf operations and the pro shop, as well as give golf lessons. He's a big asset, because he's well liked and respected by the present members."

Andy Zondervine had committed to backing the deal, and was going to invest $700,000.00 according to Danny. I told Danny that I would invest $150,000.00 and Mom and Dad decided to divert $350,000.00 from their trust, and put that amount into this venture. Danny now had more than he needed for his one million dollar down payment. The Zondervines, my parents and I, would share in the ownership of the club, but Danny and Abby would be the majority stockholders. Danny had not finalized the financing of the balance of the money needed to purchase the club, but he said that was not going to be a problem. Several banks that he had met with had already agreed to finance the balance, but he planned to explore other financing options as well in order to come up with the best possible arrangement.

I was glad that Danny was going to get a business that he really wanted, and I thought this would be the ideal situation for him. He was a good golfer, and was known for his athletic ability. And with his great smile and personality, operating the Castlewood Country Club would be right down his alley. A perfect use of his talents! I considered the money I was investing a good financial decision on my part. Castlewood was for sale because the owner had died but, according to Danny, the club had provided him with a substantial income for many years. With Abby's trust, Danny would not have to depend on the club for any of his living expenses. As a result, he was not going to take a salary from the club for several years. He wanted to build the financial resources in order to make further improvements in the kitchen and the dining room. Everything sounded almost too good to be true, but if anybody deserved some good fortune it was Danny. After all he had gone through the past few years, it was time for his life to take a turn for the better. I just hoped and prayed that would now happen.

The last weekend in August, Paul and I were together again. He flew a single engine plane that he had rented for the weekend to the Grand Rapids airport, and I met him there early Saturday morning. Paul invited me to take a ride in the plane and I accepted. This was the first time that the two of us had gone flying together with Paul as the pilot, and it was a special experience for me. Just the two of us cruising around the area together in a small plane was thrilling, and I felt very confident with Paul as the pilot. We flew over Rockford and it was interesting looking down at my home, our orchards and the clinic where I worked. I felt much more relaxed than I did when I was in the Upson-Ross corporate plane. I said to Paul "I feel like the two of us are on top of the world."

We flew around for about an hour, then returned to the airport to have lunch. After a long, relaxed lunch together at a very nice restaurant, we shopped for a wedding present for Kit and Dick at a nearby department store. We decided to get all the bedding for a double bed, plus a down comforter, and had it all gift-wrapped in one package. It made quite a huge bundle. Paul carried the present to my car, and even though it wasn't heavy it was something of a struggle for him because it was such a big bulky package. I had to direct Paul where to walk because he couldn't see where he was going carrying the present. It was a funny situation and we were both laughing. When we finally got the gift in the back seat of my car I told Paul, "It's a good thing that we're taking this present to the wedding. We would have had to have a special crate made in order to have it shipped." Later, we went to see an early movie, then had dinner during which we talked about anything and everything that came to our minds. We were sharing many things about our lives, and I felt that our discussions during lunch and dinner were bringing us closer and closer together. Paul stayed overnight at my home and flew back to Chicago Sunday afternoon. We had a great weekend together.

The week before Kit and Dick's wedding, I really looked forward to seeing Paul again. He was on my mind a lot and my reservation that his attention to me had been based on helping Upson-Ross acquire FPR was a thing of the past. I had become very fond of Paul, and I now believed that he was quite interested in me as we were developing a close relationship. I truly relished the time that I spent with him, and every time we were together he told me how much he enjoyed my company. I really believed he was sincere whenever he said this to me. My hope was that we would get even more serious, as the possibility of becoming Paul's wife crossed my mind quite a few times.

On Friday morning, September 2, Paul arrived at the Grand Rapids airport in a rented plane. After lunch at my home, we left for Lapeer in my Buick "Riv." Late in the afternoon, we finally located the house Kit and Dick had purchased. It was out in the country on a gravel road south of town. Dick Dixon was at the house waiting to welcome us. Kit was at her parent's home in Metamora. She was staying there until after the wedding. After introductions and some "chit chat", Dick gave us a tour of their home, ending up in the den where he served us cocktails. While we were relaxing in the den, Dick explained that, as soon as they returned from their honeymoon, he planned to build a barn to house Kit's horse as well as for hay storage. He also informed us that the home they had bought included eighty acres, so Kit would be able to ride her horse on their property, or for miles on the gravel roads in the area. I found Kit's husband-to-be just as nice as she had described him to me, and I was especially impressed that his focus seemed to be on doing everything he could to provide Kit with a happy life as his wife. What a guy!

After the three of us had talked for about an hour, Dick showed Paul and I our bedrooms. We brought our suitcases and our wedding present into the house and then learned that, following a rehearsal at the church that evening, there would be a dinner for the wedding party. Dick and Kit's parents, a few close relatives and some friends, which included Paul and me, were also invited to attend. Paul and I already knew that the wedding would take place on Saturday at 2:00 pm. Their reception was scheduled to take place at 5:00 pm, followed by dinner at 6:00 pm. What we didn't know until Dick told us, was that he and Kit planned to leave the dinner around 10:00 that evening, as they had to drive to the Flint airport to catch a midnight flight to Miami. They were going on a cruise for their honeymoon, and the ship they were taking left Miami on Sunday morning.

Dick gave Paul a key to the front door and told him where to hide it when we left on Sunday. After that he said, "Make my home your home, and enjoy yourselves." I thought to myself, "This is going to be interesting, because it will be the first time that Paul and I have been alone overnight. Only the two of us would be in the house and I wondered what kind of move Paul was likely to make, and if he did make a move, what I would do?"

On Friday evening, Paul and I went to the rehearsal at the church where Kit and Dick would be married, and had a lot of laughs as the wedding party stumbled through the trial ceremony. Everybody was in a happy mood, and the minor gaffs or mistakes became hilarious. Later Paul and I really enjoyed ourselves at the dinner following the rehearsal. We met and talked with a number of interesting people who were either friends, or part of Kit and Dick's families. All of them were delighted that these two people, who were held in the highest regard by everyone we talked with, were finally getting married. Paul commented to me several times, "I've been to a number of weddings, but I've never seen so much fondness or love expressed by everyone involved for both the bride and the groom. Everybody apparently believes this is an ideal union, and I just hope that Kit and Dick live up to everyone's expectations."

Saturday morning was busy and somewhat hectic, with a few people popping in to leave a gift or just stopping by to see how Dick was doing. Paul helped me make some sandwiches for lunch, as the three ushers and the best man all came to accompany Dick to the church. Everybody virtually bolted down a sandwich due to the time pressure. A little before 1:00 p.m., we departed in five different cars for the church. It was a good half hour drive from the house. My car was the last one in the caravan, so finding our way to the church was easy as we simply followed the car in front of us.

The wedding, the reception and the dinner all went especially well. Paul and I stayed to dance for a while after Kit and Dick left for the airport to go on their honeymoon. It was a little after midnight when Paul and I arrived back at Kit and Dick's home. We'd had a delightful evening together, and had been especially amorous hugging and kissing each other more than we had ever done so before…probably due to, or influenced by, the occasion. We had participated in the celebration of Kit and Dick's wedding 100% and I just felt great. When we were in the house Paul asked, "How about a nightcap?"

I said, "Sounds like a good idea to me. Kit and Dick would certainly approve if they were here."

We went to the den and Paul poured each of us a scotch over some ice. I slowly sipped my drink while we talked about the wedding and the reception, but Paul soon finished his and poured himself another one. When he had finished his second drink I looked at my watch. It was almost 1:30 a.m. and I said to Paul, "We'd better get to bed or we won't be leaving for Rockford before noon." After I said that we both stood up and put our arms around each other. Paul held me very tight against his body for close to a minute and then we kissed…not with great passion, but with what I would consider warm affection. For me it was a goodnight kiss so I went to the bedroom that I was staying in, put on my pajamas, washed my face, brushed my teeth and crawled into bed. I switched off the light in the lamp next to the bed, and the next thing I heard was Paul getting into bed with me and asking me to move over and give him more room.

"Whoa," I said, as I reached over to turn the lamp next to the bed back on. "We need to talk before this goes any further."

"What's the problem?" Paul asked. "I thought our relationship had reached the point where you'd enjoy having me sleep with you."

"This is going to come as a big surprise," I told Paul, "and you'll probably find this hard to believe in our modern free living society, but I'm still a virgin."

"That is hard to believe." Paul replied. "Frankly, I don't know what to say."

I proceeded to tell Paul about my decision when I was in high school that I was not going to be some boy's sexual experiment. "Then when Gene and I fell in love," I explained, "It was a great temptation to make love to him. But when Gene learned that I was a virgin, he was the one who decided we should wait until our wedding night. I agreed…but after his death I was very sorry that we hadn't made love. However, I decided that remorse wasn't going to resolve any-thing. So I focused my life on other things besides sex. I made my career and my health my priorities. As you know I work out regularly, watch what I eat and, most days, it's early to bed and early to rise in order to do my best on the days that I work. I have decided that since I've waited this long to have sex with a man, I'll try to hold off until I get married so that our wedding night will be very special. He won't be a virgin I'm sure, but I will be…which will make the difference. It certainly will be a unique experience and a memorable occasion for me. But if it turns out that my destiny is to be an old maid, then so be it."

Paul intently listened to everything I had to say, and when I finally stopped talking he responded by telling me, "Colleen, I have tremendous respect for you. That respect is very important due to the circumstances of my marriage. My ex-wife, Evelyn, and I had a huge wedding. Several hundred people wit-nessed her swearing to love, honor and be faithful to me. However, just two years later she was cheating on me…with a man who I thought was my best friend. She finally confessed her adulterous relationship with my former friend when they decided they were in love and wanted to be married to each other. You have no idea how horribly shocked and hurt I felt. I don't hate Evelyn. In fact we're civil to each other…but I have absolutely no respect for her."

"If I had married you," Paul continued, "instead of Evelyn, I'm confident that something like that would never have happened. You are a person with high morals. You're absolutely trustworthy, and as a result I sincerely and deeply respect you. I apologize if I have offended you, Colleen, but you must realize that I find you very attractive and desirable."

"I don't want you to apologize Paul," I replied. "You don't need to. I like you very, very much. I enjoy your company, and look forward to being with you whenever possible. I just hope I haven't put a damper on our relationship. I want you too, but my decision to wait to have sex until my wedding night is a high hurdle for me to get over. Could we sleep together on that basis? I don't want you to leave."

"Of course," Paul said, "But I don't feel very sleepy. This is really the best communication that we've had so far, and I think this discussion has brought us even closer together. At least I think so. I just assumed you took birth con-trol pills, and obviously you don't. That's a surprise. I want you to know that there are a lot of reasons why I admire you, Colleen. I've told you several times how much I respect you for what you achieved marketing FPR. I don't think I could have done it any better, and launching new products is an important part of my job. I also respect your integrity, your intelligence, your confidence and your self-control. You're really something!"

This was quite a conversation between two people lying in bed next to each other. We talked for a long time, and mostly I listened, because Paul had a lot to say. He finally got around to telling me that he had thought a lot about the possibility of marrying me. When he made that statement he really got my attention. He went on to say that he had wondered if his constant traveling schedule would be a problem again? It concerned him very much. Then he reminded me that he expected to be the president of Upson-Ross in about ten years, which meant he had to live in Chicago while I was committed to taking over a veterinary clinic in Rockford.

Paul asked if I would ever consider moving to Chicago and I said, "Of course, but I would have to resolve the commitment I've made to Bob Cunningham to purchase the clinic. I'd have to find another veterinarian to buy the practice. That might take some time to accomplish, as it would have to be done with Bob Cunningham's approval."

Paul's frankness in expressing his concerns, and his desire to overcome them in order to marry, made me feel warm all over. I rolled into his arms and we kissed passionately. For the first time Paul said to me, "I love you, Colleen" and I honestly answered, "And I love you, Paul."

Following this confession of our feelings about each other Paul said to me, "I think we truly enjoy the time we spend together and we are good companions. And I believe we could make a marriage succeed by both of us making a real commitment to make sure it does. Even the time we are separated can bring us together if we tell each other about our experiences, our joys and our challenges when we are apart. Our love for each other can bridge the time when we are apart…and by sharing our thoughts and feelings, our relationship will become closer and closer. I think we have a lot in common and have similar attitudes about a lot of things, including how we interact with other people. I know from experience that a marriage without trust won't last, and I've never known anyone I'd trust more than you, Colleen. We might have to go through a difficult time for a while due to the miles between Rockford and Chicago, but I'm willing to accept that challenge if you are. *Will you marry me?*"

As soon as I heard the words, "Will you marry me?" I gasped and then exclaimed, "Yes! Yes! Yes! I love you! I'll marry you Paul, and I'll do everything in my power to make you a good wife. I know we can resolve this distance problem…maybe even sooner than we might think possible right now."

It was three o'clock in the morning when I turned off the light next to my bed. That night I slept with Paul's arms around me, and I hadn't felt that happy in a long time. Life was absolutely wonderful because I realized I was in love with the man next to me.

When we woke up Sunday morning, it was almost noon. We dressed, put our things in my car and I straightened up the house with Paul's help. Paul hid the key to the house where Dick had told him to put it, and we left for Rockford. On the way there, we stopped for brunch and arrived at my home around 5:00 p.m. All the way home I could hardly wait to get there, so that I could tell Mom and Dad that Paul and I were going to be married.

When I told them the news they were totally taken by surprise. They were well aware that I liked Paul and enjoyed being with him, but they had no idea that our relationship had become that serious. When they got over their initial shock they responded with real joy and wanted to know when we planned to be married.

Paul explained that the time and place was up to me, and then he added with a wink to me, "The sooner the better, as far as I'm concerned."

The four of us talked for about an hour, and it was a good discussion because Mom and Dad realized that Paul and I had obviously talked seriously about our careers and the commitment we had made to each other to make our marriage succeed. Paul told Mom and Dad a lot about himself, including some of the details about his unfortunate marriage to Evelyn. Mom and Dad were already acquainted with his daughter, and they had many nice things to say about her, which I knew they really meant. Paul said he appreciated what they said about his daughter…now Mom and Dad's future step grand-daughter…and thanked them for their compliments.

While Mom and I prepared dinner, Paul and Dad continued talking in the den. Dad was pouring the scotch, and from the way the two of them were laughing and talking, I figured dad was being quite generous in pouring. It was an especially happy and memorable day. I even wondered to myself if my mother and father were somewhat relieved to learn that their nearly thirty-year old daughter was finally getting married, because I hadn't seen them this excited in quite a while.

Paul stayed overnight. Monday of Labor Day weekend was a peaceful, relaxed day. We played some cards, went for a walk and in the afternoon Dad barbecued steaks. We also called Connie to tell her the news and she claimed she was, "Just delighted and totally in favor of our marriage." After dinner, I drove Paul to the Grand Rapids airport so he could fly back to Chicago in the plane he had rented. When we arrived at the airport, we sat in my car for a while and my emotionalism got the better of me. I really didn't want to say goodbye to Paul and I got all teary-eyed. I said, "I'm sorry. I just hate to think that I won't see you again for a week." Paul held me and said he'd call me every day. After I got my emotions under control we reluctantly parted. I saw his plane take off and watched it until it was out of sight.

CHAPTER 6

Marriage and Murder

On Tuesday morning, September 6, 1994 I arrived at the Cunningham Veterinary Clinic a good half hour before our workday officially started at 8:00 a.m. I wanted to meet with Bob Cunningham as soon as possible, to inform him that Paul Ross and I had decided to be married in October. But when I arrived at the clinic there were eight people already waiting with ailing or injured pets for the clinic to open. It was just one of those particularly hectic days, as more and more people arrived with dogs and cats that needed our attention. We were swamped. It was late in the day before I was able to meet with Bob. When I finally did have the opportunity to meet with him in his office, Bob looked at me and said, "From the jumpy way you've been acting today, and the look on your face, I can tell that something is up? What's happened?"

"I'm going to marry Paul sometime in October," I blurted out. Then added, "As soon as we have a confirmed date I'd like to be away the following week for our honeymoon. I know this is sudden and comes as a big surprise. And I'm sure you're already wondering if this will affect the agreement we have for me to take over the clinic when you retire. All I can tell you, Bob, is that Paul and I have discussed this extensively, but I can't give you a definite answer right now. As I said, Paul does a lot of traveling and that will continue for maybe another ten years. In about ten years, though, Paul expects to become the President of Upson/Ross. When that happens his responsibilities will change completely and he'll spend almost 100% of his time at the plant in Northbrook. We both hope that by then we will have resolved the distance problem so that we're together more than just on weekends."

Bob sat there speechless with a stunned look on his face.

"Our lives sometimes take an unexpected twist or turn," I continued, "And mine is about to take an exciting and wonderful turn in another direction when I marry Paul. Fortunately, it's not necessary to make any decision now as to who should be your successor here at the clinic. I see no need for me to move to Chicago anytime soon, and Paul agrees. If I moved there I'd only see him on weekends anyway. So for the time being we're planning to be together on the weekends either in Chicago or in Rockford."

As I was saying all this Bob Cunningham looked at me in a kind of astounded way. But then a big smile finally appeared on his face. He got up out of his desk chair and came around his desk to where I was sitting, and said, "Stand up." When I stood up he hugged me and I was truly relieved when I heard him say, "Congratulations, Colleen. I'm very happy for you, and I hope you and Paul have a long and happy life together."

Bob returned to the chair behind his desk and we continued talking. He wanted to know more about how and when Paul and I had decided to get married. Bob was aware that Paul and I had known each other for just five months. I explained that, especially over the past two months, Paul and I had recognized that we were very compatible. We enjoyed each other's company a lot, and looked forward to sharing our weekends. Week after week the attraction and the fondness that we felt for each other had developed into a closer relationship. This past weekend, while we were together at Kit's wedding, we acknowledged that we really and truly cared deeply for each other. So I guess I can sum it all up by saying that, 'We simply fell in love.'"

"Sounds to me." Bob responded, "You rose to love more than falling in love."

"I like that perspective," I answered.

Bob then inquired, "Didn't you tell me that Paul is a pilot?"

"Yes. He is." I confirmed. "And a very good one in my opinion."

"Does he have his own plane?" Bob asked.

"No. Paul has rented a plane whenever he has flown from Chicago to Grand Rapids. Upson/Ross has a corporate plane, but he can't use it for personal reasons," I explained.

Bob then asked me, "Are you aware that Bill Stevenson plans to sell his horse farm and move his horses to a farm he plans to buy in Ocala, Florida? As you probably know, he's a retired airline pilot, and has a landing strip and a hanger right on his farm. Seems to me this could be the ideal arrangement for you and Paul. If Paul had his own plane his commute back and forth from that farm to Chicago would be quite simple. Maybe you and Paul should consider buying it."

This news came as a big surprise. I was not aware that Bill Stevenson had decided to sell his farm and move to Florida. His farm was a showplace, with an attractive ranch home and a huge, impressive horse barn. The horse barn had a lot of stalls, a spacious combination office and tack room, and a large indoor arena for showing horses or for exercising them when the weather outside was bad. There was a smaller barn, which I assumed was where hay was stored and where he kept tractors and other equipment needed to operate the farm. White painted fences enclosed the fields where the horses grazed, and in addition to all this, there was a landing strip and a hanger for his plane. This had unbelievable possibilities, and I could hardly wait to tell Paul. I was so excited that I was actually trembling.

I went back to my office and fortunately reached Paul on his cell phone. He had been to the Stevenson farm three times, as that is where we had gone to go horseback riding. The first time just Paul and I went there riding, but we had taken Alicia there twice. So Paul was not only familiar with the Stevenson's Horse Farm, but I also distinctly remembered his commenting on how impressed he was with the place.

My voice must have been bubbling with excitement when I told Paul this news as he said to me, "Hold on, Colleen. Let's settle down and talk reasonably and calmly about this. I could come up with the money to make a down payment on the farm, but buying an airplane is another matter. Airplanes cost a lot of money.

"I'll buy you a plane as a wedding present," I quickly answered. "I've got more than a million dollars in my trust. So I can afford to buy you a plane."

"*You have what?*" Paul asked.

I'd never told Paul about my trust or my stock market investments. Money was a subject that up until this time we had just never discussed. "This is incredulous," Paul said, "I had no idea you had so much money in a trust account."

"Well I didn't intentionally keep that information from you Paul," I explained. "It's just that I never think about the trust. I know it's there if and when I need some money for a special purpose. But I should also tell you that I've got about a half a million dollars in stock in various companies, and I'm a part owner of the Castlewood Country Club which my brother Danny operates."

All of a sudden it seemed quite strange that Paul and I had actually never talked about or discussed our financial resources. I'm sure he took it for granted that I had a good income as a veterinarian, and I reasonably assumed that he was well paid as an executive with Upson/Ross. But I didn't know what his actual salary was, or how much stock he owned in his company. We should have talked about our financial resources when we decided to be married, but we just hadn't done that prior to this phone call.

"Well I'm just amazed." Paul commented. "I'm certainly willing to consider making Bill Stevenson an offer if we mutually agree that it's the right thing for us to do. Try to arrange a time for us to meet with him this coming weekend. I think we should consider this possibility carefully, but not make a hasty decision. After all, this is the first thing that's come along that seems like it would make it not only simpler but also easier for us to spend the weekends together. But there may be other options we need to consider as well. In the meantime, I'll try to find out where I could hanger a plane in the Chicago area and get some cost information. A lot of thoughts are going through my mind and I need to sort a few things out to see if buying Stevenson's Horse Farm would really make sense for us to consider. We'll talk again tomorrow night, and I'll try to have answers to a few things that I'll tell you about then."

That evening I told Mom and Dad about my day…including the talk I had with Bob Cunningham. I also told them that I had learned that Bill Stevenson was going to sell his farm and that Paul and I might consider buying it. Mom had a lot to tell me as well, as she had been busy making phone-calls most of the day regarding the arrangements for my wedding. She told me that she had talked with Danny and Abby and they had offered to have the wedding reception and the dinner at the Castlewood Country Club. As a wedding present, they would like to provide the reception, all the refreshments and the dinner in appreciation for everything I'd done for them. "Your father and I," Mom said, "Want to buy your wedding dress, the flowers, and the wedding cake…and also pay for whatever band you select to have play for the dancing."

Hearing all this not only made me feel very, very good but also very, very grateful.

Mom also had some suggestions, which I thought made good sense. She made the observation, "There will be a number of people coming from out-of-town to attend your wedding. There's Paul's mother and his friends in Chicago, his two sisters, Aunt Amy and her family from Baltimore, and there's probably others that will want to stay overnight somewhere. It would make it much more convenient for them if you and Paul were married in the big Lutheran church in downtown Grand Rapids. Guests could stay Friday and Saturday nights at the Amway Grand Hotel, which is just a few blocks from the church. After the ceremony, the out-of-town guests could go to Castlewood by taxi to get to the reception and the dinner. They wouldn't even have to rent a car unless they preferred to have their own transportation. The church is old, but very impressive and it's available Saturday, October 15, if that date suits you and Paul. I think that's about the earliest date you can realistically consider for your wedding in order to have time to get the invitations printed, addressed and mailed."

I asked Mom to go ahead and confirm the October 15 date with the church and to order the invitations. I was sure the date would be acceptable to Paul, as he had already agreed to be married in a Lutheran church. Paul and his family, I had learned, were Episcopalians. That night I went to bed even earlier than usual because I was simply exhausted. But I didn't sleep well. Probably because there was so much to think about. My mind kept jumping from one thing to another.

Fortunately, the next day the clinic was back to a more normal routine, and I had a few welcome breaks during which I made some personal phone calls. I called Ukadean, Joyce Kallman, Papa John, Abby and Danny as well as several others. I just wanted to share my happiness with everybody. That evening, Paul and I talked for a long time on the phone. I told him about the church in Grand Rapids and that October 15 could be the date for our marriage. This was OK with him, and he thought my brother Danny and his wife were being most generous in underwriting the cost of the reception, all the refreshments and the dinner as a wedding present.

Paul had important news to tell me as well. He had checked on the prices of planes and explained that a Beechcraft Bonanza, fully equipped, would cost around $350,000.00. That would be his preference should we decide to buy a plane. He also informed me that there was a small private airfield in Prospect Heights that had a hanger available where he could store the plane during the week. And this airfield was not far from the Upson/Ross plant in Northbrook. "As you know," Paul told me, "I own a condo in Highland Park, which I think I could realistically sell for about $450,000.00. I'm usually there now just on weekends. If we should decide that buying Bill Stevenson's farm is the right thing for us to do, then there'd be no reason to keep the condo, even though it's paid for. I can always stay at my mother's home in Lake Forest if bad weather should keep me from flying to Rockford, or if I had to stay over some Saturday for a business reason. My mother would welcome that arrangement."

"You now seem much more receptive to the possibility of buying Bill Stevenson's farm," I said to Paul. "I'm pleased that you're willing to consider buying it for our home, but I'd like to have you share with me your reasons for doing this."

"First of all," Paul explained, "The commute from the farm near Rockford to the air field in Prospect Heights by plane wouldn't take much longer than it does now for me to drive from my condo to our plant by car. I usually spend Monday mornings in the office and I'm there most Fridays. In between, though, I'm normally out of town. The commute by plane would be considerably more expensive than by car, but I love to fly, and we could use the plane for other trips besides my flights back and forth to work. I believe you'd be happier living in the country, rather than in a big city. You enjoy horseback riding and Alicia could have her own horse. She'd obviously be eager to spend a lot of time with us if that became a reality. I've never lived in the country, and it would be an entirely new experience for me. That possibility intrigues me because it could be a good diversion separating me from the pressures of my business. Bottom line, yes, I think we should seriously consider trying to buy this horse farm."

"However," Paul quickly added, "there are important things we need to know before we can make that decision. I noticed that the horse barn has a lot of stalls. We need to find out how many horses Bill Stevenson boards, what he charges for this service, and how much help is required to run the farm. When we went there to go riding I noticed there was a man giving a riding lesson and there were other people busy cleaning the stalls. Is there someone that could manage the farm, and actually run the place when you and I are not there during the week? I'd like to see a profit and loss statement, maybe even tax returns, if they'll show them to us. That would reveal how much income there is, and whether the Stevenson's make or lose money operating the farm. Hopefully, we'll be able to get answers to these and some other questions I have when we meet with him this weekend."

Paul was able to take Friday of that week off from work, and arrived at my home mid-morning. First we went to the courthouse to get our marriage license. After lunch, we went to a jewelry store where Paul bought my engagement ring and our wedding rings.

Later, we drove out to the Stevenson Horse Farm. We just sat in Paul's car and looked at it from across the road for a long time. We tried to contemplate what our lives would be like if we lived there. The Stevenson farm was on a paved road, and while sitting there looking at the place I had an interesting and intriguing idea. The home and the barns were close to one hundred yards back from the road. On the north side of the buildings was a large fenced-in pasture that came all the way out to the road. I thought to myself, "Why couldn't I take the front part of this pasture and build a clinic here if I do take the practice over when Bob Cunningham retires?" The fence could easily be moved back, and there would be plenty of land right next to the road to build a new clinic with adequate parking. The building the Cunningham Veterinary Clinic now occupied was close to fifty years old. It had been well maintained over the years, but the layout was not ideal for serving our clientele. We had all the latest equipment, but that could be moved to a new location. I could either sell the present building, or maybe Bob Cunningham would want to keep it and rent it to some other business. I knew he already had several real estate investments and this idea might possibly appeal to him."

When I told Paul what I was thinking he laughed and said, "That's what I call a big idea that really deserves serious consideration."

I then explained to Paul what Bob Cunningham and I had discussed as the basis for my taking ownership of the clinic when he decides to retire. "We'd have the property appraised, "I told Paul, "and would have to mutually agree on a purchase price for the business based on that appraisal and the book value of the equipment. Bob tells me that he does not expect to receive any factor for goodwill because of what I have contributed to the business. I would pay Bob a consulting fee, for which he would spend a certain number of hours at the clinic every month, and also be on call if I needed him. He's a very fair person and is pretty well off financially. I know he owns several commercial properties in town, as well as an apartment building, so he doesn't need to be a tough, hard-nosed negotiator when I buy the clinic."

Paul and I did a lot of talking that Friday because we had plenty on our plate to consider prior to meeting with the Stevensons the next day.

Saturday morning, September 10, Paul and I arrived at the Stevenson's Horse Farm promptly at 9:30 a.m. We met Bill's wife, Stella, and while having coffee and donuts in their kitchen, learned that she had been an airline stewardess. That was how she and Bill had met. Stella and Bill were in their early seventies, and had two married daughters who lived in Florida. They also had five grandchildren they were extremely proud of, and we had to listen to them brag about each grandchild's achievements. We were surprised when we learned that Stella and Bill went to Florida right after Thanksgiving and didn't return home until April. Once or twice a month, Bill flew home just to check on things but he only stayed for three or four days. Usually he flew his own plane but sometimes took a commercial flight…depending on weather conditions.

"We're able to do this," Bill explained, "Because we have a very dependable and competent farm manager. His name is Jim Morrison…maybe you know him, Colleen. He lives in town and his wife works at the shoe company. I believe Jim attended Rockford High School about the same time as your brother Danny."

"I don't believe I know him," I responded, "But Danny probably does."

During this meeting we learned that the barn had forty-four box stalls. Thirty-eight of the stalls were rented to individuals who boarded their horse at the farm. For this service they paid $400.00 a month. Their horses were fed twice a day, and turned out to pasture twice a day. The Stevenson's owned six horses which were used for riding lessons, or rented by the hour to people who wanted to go horseback riding. Jim Morrison, who managed the farm, not only gave riding lessons, but could also shoe horses. He received a salary of $48,000.00 a year, but contributed about $11,000.00 a year in income to the farm by giving riding lessons and shoeing horses. Four other people worked part time at the farm and were paid at an hourly rate. They used a landscape service to mow the lawn, care for the shrubs and trees, and plow the snow in winter. "Years ago," Bill informed us, "I cut the grass, pruned and mulched the shrubs and pushed the snow around…but it just took too much of my time. Stella loves flowers, so she still takes care of the flowers as well as our vegetable garden."

We talked at the kitchen table for more than an hour before the four of us went for a tour of the farm. The first place we went on the tour was the big horse barn. "The riding arena," Bill told us, "is 100 feet wide by 300 feet long." It was huge! There was even an air-conditioned viewing room where people could sit and look down at the riders in the arena. It was located in the front part of the barn, and was reached by going up a flight of stairs. Paul and I had not been in this viewing room before. Plus there was an additional large outdoor riding arena located in back of the horse barn.

Our tour of the barn ended up in the combination tack room and office, and there Paul and I were introduced to Jim Morrison. "I was a senior when Danny was in the ninth grade," Jim explained, "so I didn't know Danny personally, but I am well aware of his football and track achievements." Although I had never met Jim before, he knew that I was a veterinarian. And both Jim and Bill Stevenson were acquainted with my grandfather, Papa John, as they had bought horses from him. "Your grandfather," Jim commented, "is a man I really respect. He's a good, honest man who knows horses."

There was so much for us to see and talk about that before we knew it was 1:30. Stella invited us to have lunch and we accepted. Jim was included, so our discussion of the farm operation continued right through lunch, as Paul and I asked question after question. Paul had questions about liability, insurance, taxes and marketing. My questions mostly concerned the care of the horses. Bill told me that when a horse needed to be cared for by a veterinarian they usually called one with a sizable equine practice, although he sometimes called Bob Cunningham. However, he always brought Prince, his Dalmatian, to the Cunningham Clinic when he needed treatment. Bill Stevenson and Bob Cunningham had known each other for many years.

Paul and I left the farm late that afternoon both feeling somewhat overwhelmed. We fully realized that if we decided to buy this farm we would be taking on one heck of a lot responsibility, and that we couldn't possibly operate it without very capable help. Jim Morrison assured us that he wanted to continue working as the farm manager. That was reassuring, and would definitely be an important factor if we decided to make an offer to buy the farm.

Paul and I were told that the farm was profitable, but we wondered if the income was sufficient to cover the expenses of the Stevenson's lengthy stay in Florida, or if their income from social security and investments made this possible. The Stevenson's were unwilling to provide us with an operating statement until such time as we submitted a written offer. It was good to know that the farm made a profit…but how much profit?

The Stevenson's asking price for the farm was $2,250,000.00 and they had not listed it with a Realtor as yet. They were trying to sell it themselves, and had placed advertisements in a magazine offering estates for sale, and in a trade publication that reached people who raised horses. They did not reveal what response they had received from this advertising. The price they were asking for the farm was actually less than what Paul and I had guessed they were selling it for. That evening Paul and I talked long and hard as to whether or not it made sense for us to try and buy this farm. And we carefully reviewed our financial assets to see if we could really afford to buy it. Paul said that in addition to the $450,000.00 he thought he could realistically sell his condo for, that he could raise another $300,000.00 to apply against the purchase. I told Paul that, in addition to buying the airplane, I would be willing to sell all the stock that I owned, which would amount to a little over $500,000.00. This gave us $1,250,00.00 to apply against the purchase price of the farm. We thought we could easily get a mortgage for the balance, or perhaps the Stevenson's would let us pay off the balance with a land contract.

The next day, when we shared everything that Paul and I had discussed with my mother and father, they said they'd be willing to help us buy the farm. "The money is there in our trust, and it's going to be yours and Danny's someday," Dad said, "and if we can help you now while we're still alive so much the better. We helped Danny buy his home in Grand Rapids and the golf club he wanted, so we should help you get the farm you and Paul want. Your mother and I have a good feeling about your buying the Stevenson's farm. Obviously we'd like to have you living fairly close to us, and I should tell you that Papa John is really excited about the possibility of your buying that farm. He's always admired that particular farm. If this goes through, and you ever need to buy or sell horses, you'd be wise to have him involved. Papa John is the best horse trader I've ever known."

Armed with the knowledge that we had the financial wherewithal to buy the Stevenson farm, Paul and I decided to tell Stella and Bill that we were going to make them an offer. We called and told them that we were going to do this, and that we'd have my attorney prepare the offer. Stella and Bill were delighted to learn this and said they'd provide us with an operating statement as soon as they received our written offer.

The offer Paul and I decided to make was for $1,800,000.00. We expected…actually we hoped…that Stella and Bill would counter by reducing their asking price so that hopefully our negotiating would result in our paying around $2,000,000.00 for their farm. We were sure that they had considerably less than that amount invested in the place, but it could not have been replicated for that amount of money in 1994. However, we reasoned that there weren't many potential buyers with the resources to buy the farm, and fewer still who would be interested. The universe of potential buyers was quite small, and we believed that worked to our benefit.

After we made the phone call to the Stevenson's late Sunday afternoon, Paul left to return to his condo in Highland Park. Early Monday morning I called our family attorney, Doug Graham. First I informed him that I was going to be married in October and that my future husband and I had decided to make an offer to purchase the Stevenson Horse Farm. Then I asked Doug to prepare a letter presenting our purchase offer. Doug said he'd prepare the letter that day, and that I could pick it up at his office on my way home from work. I also asked him to FAX a copy of the letter to Paul at his office. Late in the day, Paul called to tell me that he had received and reviewed the letter. He said he would sign it and have his secretary return his copy to me by Express Mail as he was leaving that evening for Denver.

On Thursday evening of that week, September 15, I presented the purchase offer letter, which was signed by both Paul and me to Stella and Bill Stevenson. After reading the letter Bill stated that he was quite disappointed with our offer. "It's not acceptable," he said. "The price we have decided to sell our farm for," Bill explained, "is a very realistic figure based on the income the farm produces. Stella and I," he told me, "want to retire to Florida, and we have an option on a small farm near Ocala. If we weren't under any time pressure I'm sure we could sell this place for considerably more than our asking price. However, we will provide you with an operating statement, just as we promised, since you've have made us an offer in writing. Maybe after you've reviewed this statement, you'll consider upping your offer."

I felt slightly embarrassed as it seemed to me that Stella and Bill were somewhat offended by our offer. It was actually $450,000.00 below their asking price. "I'm going to Chicago this weekend," I informed them, "and Paul and I will carefully review the financial information you're providing. Obviously we are very interested in buying your farm, but there's also a limit as to how much we can afford to pay for it."

The next day, early in the afternoon, I left the clinic to drive to Chicago. I arrived at Paul's condo in Highland Park around 6:00 p.m. The traffic driving there that Friday afternoon was something else! This was the first time that I had been to Paul's condo, as I had stayed at his mother's home in Lake Forest on all my previous visits to Chicago. Now that Paul and I were engaged and would soon be married, it didn't seem inappropriate for me to spend the weekend at his condo. Besides the two of us had already spent a night together when we went to Kit and Dick's wedding in Lapeer.

Paul's condo was on a golf course. From his patio he had an open view up and down a wide fairway, which provided a feeling of spaciousness. Yet there was privacy due to the way the condos were constructed, and because of the landscaping. After I arrived, we had a quick tour of his condo and then sat on the patio sharing an excellent bottle of Cabernet Sauvignon. Paul brought out some cheese and crackers and some munchies so we sat there a long time relaxing and slowly sipping the wine. We discussed the possibility of buying the Stevenson farm, where we should go on our honeymoon, and various other subjects.

The operating statement that Bill Stevenson provided revealed that their gross income from the farm was just over $192,000.00 for 1993. After deducting all the expenses they netted $59,000.00, which was actually a much better profit than what Paul and I had guessed. We decided that Stella and Bill obviously had other sources of income, as it would require more income than $59,000.00 to maintain their lifestyle. But it was very encouraging for us to know, especially since we would not have to depend on the horse farm for our total livelihood. We decided we could up our offer...but we were not sure how much higher the offer should be.

Then we started talking about where we should go on our honeymoon. Paul told me that Boston was one of his favorite cities, and he suggested we fly there. "We could stay three or four days in Boston, then I'd like to rent a car and drive to Boothbay Harbor, Maine," he said, "and spend a couple of days there. The scenery is spectacular, and I think you'd really like it. In October the weather should be idea, and there won't be the crowds of tourists that you have to contend with in the summertime."

"I've never been to Boston or to Maine," I answered, "and I'd really like to go there." (I remembered that Gene and I had planned to go to the east coast for our honeymoon, but I didn't mention that to Paul).

We had a delicious and quite romantic dinner at the golf course clubhouse that evening. Paul was a member of this club, and he introduced me to some of his friends who were also having dinner there.

On Saturday morning, September 17, Paul and I prepared breakfast together and when we finished eating, we left to pick up Alicia at her mother's home. This would be the first time that I had been with Alicia since Paul and I had decided to get married, so I was a little apprehensive as to what her reaction might be. I should not have been concerned though, because Alicia ran to me and threw her arms around me. I hugged her back and she was all smiles.

"Is it true you and my dad are going to have a horse farm?" Alicia asked me.

"I sure hope so," I told her. "and you'll have a horse of your very own if your daddy and I are successful in buying it."

That statement I think clinched our relationship, because every time Alicia looked at me during the day she had a smile on her face.

The three of us bummed around all that Saturday. I got to see a lot of Highland Park, and by the end of the day I was well acquainted with the town. Alicia showed me her school and we did some shopping. That evening Paul, Alicia and I went to Paul's mothers home for dinner, and I received an exceptionally warm welcome from Connie. She seemed genuinely pleased that I was going to become her son's wife. Her graciousness and her comments made me feel really good, because I wanted her to accept me and I wanted us to be friends. We were off to a wonderful start.

Alicia spent Saturday night with us at Paul's condo and on Sunday morning the three of us had breakfast on the patio. It was a pleasant day to be outside, and after breakfast we shared the *Sunday Chicago Tribune* newspaper while finishing a pot of coffee. Later we went to the outdoor swimming pool at the clubhouse and went swimming. Late in the afternoon, I said goodbye to Paul and Alicia and headed for my home...arriving there that evening just before dark. What a super weekend it had been!

Paul and I had decided to up our offer for the Stevenson's farm to $1,950,000.00, and on Monday I called our attorney and asked him to prepare a new letter with this offer. He FAXED the revised letter to Paul. Paul signed it and returned it for my signature, and on Thursday evening I went to the Stevenson's farm to present the letter to them. They seemed a little encouraged that we had increased our purchase offer but were, as I expected, noncommittal.

With our wedding now just a little over three weeks away, Paul and I decided that we'd put the possibility of buying the Stevenson farm on hold unless they came back with a counter offer. However, I did contact a Realtor to find out if there were any other farms for sale in the area. There were a couple available. Paul spent the weekend at my home and on Saturday we looked at the two farms that were for sale, but quickly decided they were not what we wanted.

The wedding invitations had been printed, and 147 of them mailed to the list of relatives and friends that Paul and I were inviting to attend our marriage, the reception and the dinner. I was so anxious to be married to Paul that I was not just counting the days, but several times I stopped to figure out how many hours it would be before we would be married. Thankfully, I was quite busy, because so much was happening. In reality time was passing very fast.

That special day...the day that Paul and I were married...Saturday, October 15, finally arrived. A great many of the arrangements for our marriage were handled by my mother, as I worked at the clinic right up until two days before my wedding. I thanked her frequently but she simply told me, "It was a labor or love."

The wedding ceremony went perfectly. A lot of attention, though, went to Jennifer Malone and Alicia Ross who served as flower girls...each carrying a basket of rose petals which they sprinkled down the center aisle of the church preceding me to the alter. John Malone was our ring bearer, and he was cute as could be in his little tux carrying our wedding rings on a small velvet pillow.

What I remember most…my most vivid memory…was when the minister said, "I now pronounce you man and wife. Paul you may kiss your wife." We kissed! Then the minister asked us to turn around and face our wedding guests. When we did this he announced, "I am pleased to present Mr. and Mrs. Paul Ross." Everyone then stood and clapped their hands as we walked slowly down the aisle accepting handshakes and kisses all along the way. That's when I really knew that I was now a married woman.

Following the ceremony at the church the wedding party…consisting of the bridesmaids, the ushers, the flower girls and our ring bearer…left for the Castlewood Country Club. After we arrived there, a photographer took lots of pictures of us both outdoors and indoors. This took several hours to accomplish. In addition to taking pictures of the entire party, photos of various groups were taken of me with my Maid of Honor, Ukadean, as well as the bridesmaids, which included Abby and Danny's sisters Nancy and Susan. Also some photos were taken of Paul with his best man, who was his uncle Harold Ross along with three of his close friends who served as ushers…Chet Craft, Jack Higgins and Keith Evans. The flower girls and the ring bearer were also included in some of the photos, so that Paul and I would have an album with a variety of photos of the entire wedding party as a record of our marriage.

At 6:00 p.m. the wedding party formed a reception line in the spacious lobby of the Castlewood Country Club and for the next hour we welcomed our wedding guests. Over and over I heard the word "congratulations" and received many kisses both on my lips and on my cheeks. I appreciated every single one of them.

Abby and Danny spared no expense in providing the food and refreshments for the reception and for the dinner that followed. The hors d'oeuvres served during the reception were simply fantastic. The dinner was a gourmet event, and our guests raved about the food, which was served with champagne and various fine wines. Several times during the evening, Paul and I sincerely thanked Danny and Abby for their generosity. That evening, Danny more than repaid me for the financial support I gave him when he needed help. I thought, "What goes around, comes around, be it good or evil."

It was a wonderful and truly happy day and evening for both of us, and for our families. Everything was perfect, including the weather. Prior to and during the dinner there were many toasts. Paul and I cut the wedding cake, dessert was served and we danced until midnight. We then said goodbye to those who were still there celebrating our marriage and left for the Amway Grand Hotel in Grand Rapids, where we spent our wedding night in a beautiful suite. The love and desire that Paul and I had for each other was consummated that night. I was glad that I had waited to give myself completely to my husband. It was truly meaningful to me, because Paul was the first man that I had ever sexually loved. And I believe it was very special for him, because he knew that he was the first man that I had ever loved completely.

Sunday morning we had breakfast in our suite, which I really enjoyed. At noon we checked out of the hotel and went to Abby and Danny's home and left our wedding clothes…my gown and Paul's tux…at their house. After a short visit with my brother and his family, Paul and I went to the Grand Rapids airport and then flew to Boston for our honeymoon. We stayed in Boston for three days…walking everywhere, which was a good thing. The walking enabled us to burn calories from eating so much rich, good food in Paul's favorite restaurants. These included an Italian, a Greek and several American restaurants. We walked the freedom trail, and visited many of the important historical attractions. One morning, we took a taxi to nearby Cambridge, as Paul wanted to take me on a tour of the Harvard campus. That's where he received his MBA. Paul was certainly right about the weather and the crowds, because October turned out to be the perfect time to be in Boston.

Thursday, October 20 was my 30th birthday. After an early breakfast, we left Boston in the car Paul had rented and headed for Boothbay Harbor, Maine. Along the way we stopped in Kennebunkport for lunch and at the L.L. Bean store in Freeport to do some shopping. Paul bought me boots at L. L. Bean for a birthday present. When we arrived in Boothbay Harbor, I was really impressed because it was everything Paul had described it to be and more. This picturesque seaport looks and feels like an old New England village.

We stayed at an inn located on a wharf right on the waterfront. Paul had reserved a special suite at this inn with luxurious appointments and a private balcony. We quickly unpacked, and then sat on the balcony watching boats of every size and description move through the harbor. The fresh, salty air blowing off the ocean was really invigorating, and I was so happy and grateful to be able to enjoy this place on my birthday while on my honeymoon. That evening Paul took me to a restaurant where we celebrated my birthday with champagne cocktails, and I actually ate two lobsters. This was one special birthday.

The inn where we were staying served a fantastic continental breakfast, and that's how we started each day. On Friday and Saturday we walked all over the town, checked out some interesting shops, and ate our fill of fresh-off-the-boat seafood. We spent Sunday morning sitting on our deck soaking up the sunshine and watching all the activity in the harbor. Sunday afternoon we took a three-hour whale-watching cruise off the Maine coast. Then, on Monday morning, we left the inn and drove to Portland. From there we flew to Detroit, where we changed planes…arriving back in Grand Rapids that evening. Paul stayed overnight and for the first time slept in my bedroom.

My bedroom was no longer just my bedroom. It was now *our* bedroom!

While having breakfast the next morning, Paul and I gave my Mom and Dad a rather enthusiastic recap of many of the things we did and saw in Boston and Boothbay Harbor. I noticed that Mom and Dad were smiling all the time we were talking, as it was obvious to them that we'd had a great honeymoon.

After breakfast I kissed my husband goodbye, as he had to return to Chicago and I had to go back to work at the clinic. Ours was going to be mainly a weekend marriage, except for those weeks when we could take our vacations together. Whenever possible, though, I planned to take Fridays off from the clinic in order to spend a long weekend with my husband. For the time being, we would have two residences…his condo in Highland Park and my parents home near Rockford. I knew in my "heart of hearts" though that someday Paul and I would have our own home.

The next significant event in my life…and Paul's…occurred a few weeks later on Friday, November 25, the day after Thanksgiving. Paul and his mother arrived late Wednesday afternoon as we had invited Connie to spend the Thanksgiving weekend with us. Our farm market was closed on Thanksgiving Day, and Mom had hired two people to operate the market on Friday, Saturday and Sunday so that she could have her weekend free of that responsibility. All the apples in our orchards had been picked by early November, so there was not the hustle and bustle that went on every day when the apples were being harvested.

On Thanksgiving Day there were 14 people gathered round the long table in our kitchen. This included Connie Ross, Abby, Danny and their children Jennifer, Julie and John, Sarah, Andy and Becky Zondervine, Papa John, Mom, Dad, Paul and I. Becky had come home for the weekend from Glen Ellyn.

Mom and I, with some help from Connie, prepared the traditional Thanksgiving dinner and the smell of the savory goodness of the turkey and all the food cooking filled the house. By the time we ate, everyone was so hungry that each of us ate far more than what we would have normally consumed. Fortunately the weather was mild, so when the meal was finished and the kitchen cleaned up we all went for a walk in the orchards. Danny took a lot of pictures with his camera and Andy Zondervine had his video camera to record the day. It was a happy, delightful occasion. I thought a number of times during that day how much we had to be thankful for, and I mentioned that to Paul while we were walking. We were holding hands when I said this to him, and he squeezed my hand in confirmation. Paul then leaned close to me and softly said, "I love you." His saying this so spontaneously filled my heart with joy. I quietly responded, saying, "And I love you!"

The best was yet to come though, as Bill Stevenson called me Friday morning. He asked if it would be convenient for Paul and me to come to his house as he said that he and Stella were willing to negotiate the price they were asking for their farm.

Paul and I arrived at the Stevenson's home shortly after noon, and met with them in their living room. Bill informed us that in late September they had listed the farm with a Realtor but had protected us in the listing, because we had made an offer to purchase the property prior to the listing. This meant we would not have to pay any Realtor commission if we were the buyers. Bill then went on to say that they had decided to offer the property to us for $2,100,00.00. "Stella and I realize it will take time for you to sell assets," Bill said, "in order for you to make the down payment. We're planning to leave next week for Florida, and would really like to have this wrapped up before we leave. We need to finalize the purchase of the farm we have an option on, and our goal is to move there next spring. You could take possession of our farm the first of April, as we would move to Florida the latter part of March."

Paul asked, "Are you taking your six horses to Florida, or do you plan to sell them before you move?"

"We're going to sell four of them," Bill informed us, "but we are going to keep two of them…the two horses that Stella and I especially like to ride."

"Does your asking price include your tractors and the other equipment in the storage barn?" Paul inquired.

"We thought we would sell all the farm equipment including the tractors with an auction," Bill replied, "but that's negotiable."

Paul then asked Stella and Bill to excuse us for a few minutes so that the two of us could go outside and discuss their new offer privately.

Paul and I then went out in the front yard where we could talk without being overheard. The first thing Paul said to me was, "What do you think?"

"I think they're really, really anxious to sell," I responded. "Apparently we're the only potential buyer they have, and I'm willing to bet that we've made the only offer they've received. Let's offer them $2,000,000.00, which must include all the farm equipment. The horses we could purchase separately, after having Papa John check them over. I don't know about you, Paul, but I can hardly believe we're so close to acquiring this place. I'm trying to stay calm and maintain a poker face, but my excitement is hard to control. This would be a wonderful place for us to live and I hope you feel the same way."

"I do," Paul answered, "and I agree that we should offer them $2,000,000.00 and hang tough. If they think that's the maximum we can handle, then I think they'll accept our offer."

When Paul and I went back in the house we told Stella and Bill that we were willing to go to $2,000,000.00, which had to include the tractors and other farm equipment. There was some additional discussion, but when we refused to budge or consider any other options, Stella and Bill finally accepted our offer. We had correctly analyzed the situation, and we were able to buy a farm that would have cost considerably more than $3,000,000.00 dollars to replicate. The deal was confirmed with handshakes.

On Saturday afternoon, we arranged for a tour so that Connie, my Mom and Dad, Papa John and Danny and his family could see what would soon be the Ross Horse Farm. They were really surprised at what a beautiful place it was, and they were absolutely delighted that Paul and I were going to be living there.

On Friday of the following week, Paul and I signed a legal offer to purchase the Stevenson's farm. Our attorney was present, along with Stella and Bill and their attorney. I withdrew $100,000.00 from my trust for the down payment. Paul and I agreed to pay $900,000.00 by December 31st, and the balance of $1,000,000.00 on or before March 31, 1995. This was a good arrangement. It gave Paul four months to sell his condo and plenty of time for me to sell the stocks I owned. I was also pleased to learn from Paul that Connie was going to give us some money to help us buy furniture for our new home. The final closing on the farm was scheduled for late March of 1995.

I had just experienced an incredible week. My life, I thought, had soared to a fantastic high. First, I had shared Thanksgiving with those who were near and dear to me. Many families are not that fortunate. Then Paul and I were able to buy the Stevenson's Horse Farm. Life is about transition, and the purchase of this property was going to be a life-changing event for Paul and I. When we moved there next spring, we would have a home of our own to share. "Life," I told Paul several times, "couldn't get much better than this!"

Our lives, after that particular week, returned to a more normal routine with Paul and I spending weekends together and attending to our careers the days in between. In December, Paul arrived at my home two days before Christmas and stayed until January 3rd as the Upson/Ross plant was closed the week between Christmas and New Year's. We made the $900,000.00 payment we owed the Stevenson's before years end, and celebrated New Year's Eve at the Castlewood Country Club with Abby and Danny. In 1994, New Year's Eve fell on a Saturday so there were lots and lots of people celebrating. Paul and I joined them but we had more reason to celebrate than most people! In all my life I don't believe I'd ever been so happy.

In early January 1995, Mom and Dad departed for their condo in Orange Beach. This year I was home alone as Papa John went with them to Alabama. Paul sold his condo in February, and had to vacate it before March 31st. Talk about perfect timing! Mom, Dad and Papa John returned home mid-March, and the closing on the Stevenson's farm took place on Friday, March 24. Stella and Bill left the next day for Florida. Paul and I also bought the four horses the Stevenson's wanted to sell. Papa John and I checked them over carefully, and determined that the price they were asking for them was very fair.

Paul and I decided to redecorate our new home. We hired Emily Baker, an interior decorator, which turned out to be a smart move. However, the redecorating took more than a month to finish, as we either put hardwood floors or new carpeting in every room in the house. The kitchen and the bathrooms were totally redone, and every wall was repainted. The finishing touch was the furniture and the furnishings making it a warm, comfortable home. The interior decorator we hired did a fantastic job because the final result was a charming home that Paul and I moved into the middle of May. We now had our own home, actually much sooner than I thought it would ever happen.

Later in May, Paul brought his daughter Alicia with him for the weekend. This was the first time she had been to the farm since Paul and I had bought it. When she saw her bedroom she was thrilled, and said she wanted to move there permanently. I knew this was not going to be possible but I thought to myself, "I'm going to let her father handle this situation."

We also told her she could have her choice of any of the four horses we bought from the Stevenson's. One of them would be designated as her horse, or we would buy her another horse if she preferred. Alicia said she wanted to ride each one of them before making that decision. She spent every weekend with us that summer, and after Alicia had ridden all four of them several times, we ended up buying her a two-year-old gelded quarter horse. Fair enough, I thought, when we bought her the horse, because she really wanted a horse that was hers alone to ride. I remembered that I was eleven years old, the same age as Alicia, when my grandfather gave me Star. No one ever rode Star but me. Alicia named her horse Lucky, because she said, "I'm so lucky to have my own horse."

Paul took delivery of our Beechcraft Bonanza in late July and he absolutely loved that plane. When he and Alicia arrived at our farm early Friday evening I'd usually be waiting for them at the hanger. Sometimes on a Saturday or a Sunday, we'd take a short flight somewhere, usually landing at a small airport where there was a good restaurant nearby. After having lunch or dinner we'd return to our farm. I was learning a lot about flying a plane from Paul, and he encouraged me to take lessons and become a pilot.

On Sunday, October 15, Paul and I celebrated the one-year anniversary of our marriage. It was incredible, I thought, how fast the year had gone by. Weeks fly by, then months quickly disappear as well, when every day is packed with activity.

We really wanted to have Thanksgiving dinner at our home, but Mom and Dad insisted that we celebrate this special day at their house. Mom said most likely this would be the last Thanksgiving celebrated in the Malone family home, as the company that bought the 580 acres of the farm for a housing development now wanted to acquire the remaining 300 acres. Mom and Dad were seriously considering selling the orchards, as they were both 59 years old and Papa John was 82. They told me that if they sold the farm, including the house, the market, barns and the orchards, they would buy a condo in Grand Rapids and spend about eight months there and the other four months at their condo in Orange Beach. Sounded like a great plan to me. It would be a life style I thought they really deserved after many years of hard work and some of the difficult times they had gone through.

After several months of negotiations, the real estate developer did acquire the remaining 300 acres of the Malone family farm. The developer told Mom and Dad they could remain in their home for up to a year if they wanted to, but they had no intention of doing that. Once the property was sold...and since they'd no longer be raising or selling apples...they wanted to move out. And they did move in April of 1996...to a large comfortable condo in Grand Rapids. Danny took a few things from our family home and I took a few items as well...but most of the furniture, tools and lots of other stuff went to the Salvation Army. Mom and Dad did a good job of "slimming down" and Mom decided she wanted all new furniture for their new condo.

Paul and I recognized our one-year anniversary as the owners and operators of the Ross Horse Farm with a family dinner on Sunday, May 26, 1996. My family, as well as Connie and Alicia, were present and everyone enjoyed a delicious chicken dinner. Paul marinated the chicken for six hours prior to barbecuing it. The marinade was a recipe he found in a magazine that combined white wine, rosemary, lemon and olive oil and it turned out fantastic. Paul relished all the compliments he received, and I suggested he should do this more often now that he was a celebrated chef.

In spite of our demanding careers, Paul and I managed to have a number of long weekends together that spring, summer and into the fall. He often arrived at our farm on a Thursday evening and didn't fly back to Chicago until early Tuesday morning. I arranged to take either Friday or Monday off from the clinic with the cooperation of Bob Cunningham. While we did a little supervision of our farm on the weekends, it was really Jim Morrison who managed it for us. Many of the people who boarded a horse at our farm had complimentary things to say about Jim, because he took care of any concern or problem they had immediately. "And he's not only efficient" they said, "but also very polite." Since Jim was doing such a good job taking care of our farm, we decided to take care of him with a raise as well as frequent expressions of appreciation.

For the second anniversary of our marriage, Paul and I decided to celebrate with a ten-day safari in Africa...something that both of us had always wanted to do. We flew to Amsterdam on Friday, October 11 and arrived in Nairobi, Kenya on Saturday. We were welcomed with a cheerful *Jambo* (hello in Swahili). On Sunday, we drove to a large ranch where we saw lots of elephants and a rhino. That night we slept in a luxurious tent. The next day we enjoyed sundowners in a gazebo overlooking a watering hole where we watched gazelles, warthogs and zebras come to drink. On Tuesday (our second anniversary) we went to the game-rich Samburu Reserve where we saw all kinds of game and bird life, including the flightless Somali ostrich. From there we flew across the Great Rift Valley to the Maasai Mara Game Reserve where we stayed three days. We saw prides of lion, cheetah, giraffes, topi antelope and a leopard feeding on its prey. On Saturday, we returned to Nairobi where we had fun shopping for some souvenirs at the bustling City Market. Sunday, we flew to Amsterdam where we connected with our flight back to Detroit, arriving there Monday afternoon. We were home again that evening. after sharing an incredible adventure in Africa.

Two months later I learned that I was pregnant. I believe I got pregnant the night Paul and I spent in the luxurious tent in Kenya. We wanted to have a baby and now…after trying for five months…I was finally pregnant. My gynecologist said the due date for delivery was mid-July, 1997.

Our families celebrated Christmas and New Years' together then Mom, Dad and Papa John left in early January for Orange Beach, Alabama.

And then it happened…a horrible, unbelievable tragedy. Abby was killed on Saturday, February 22nd, in the parking lot of a grocery store.

She was walking to her car carrying a bag of groceries when a car slowly pulled up beside her. A man in the passenger seat reached out and grabbed her purse, which was hanging from her left shoulder. The purse strap didn't break and Abby was jerked forward, losing her balance. She fell hitting her head on the pavement with such force that she was apparently stunned and laid there. The driver stopped the car and put it in reverse. A loud thump was heard when the rear wheel of the car ran over her head. She was fatally injured. The man in the passenger seat then jumped out of the car and grabbed Abby's purse. They sped away but there were four people who witnessed the robbery and her murder. It was also recorded on a security camera in the store's parking lot. Abby was pronounced dead on arrival at the hospital.

When Danny got to the hospital and was informed that Abby was gone, he collapsed. Several hours later he called to tell me what had happened and I just couldn't believe this was really true…Abby couldn't be dead. I started sobbing and had to hang up the phone. Paul was home for the weekend, but wasn't in the house when Danny called. When Paul came in the house and found me sobbing, he put his arms around me and held me for a long time. Thankfully, he was there to console me, but he was also distressed and crying as well. Paul loved my family. Holidays and birthdays were always family affairs, and in between those occasions, we frequently had dinner together.

Mom, Dad and Papa John flew back from Orange Beach on Sunday. On Monday, Danny, supported by Mom and Dad and Abby's parents, made the arrangements for Abby's funeral. Tuesday evening, as well as Wednesday afternoon and evening, there was visitation at the funeral home. The funeral service was held on Thursday morning, February 27, at a large church in Holland. The church was filled to capacity. Not an empty seat…and people were even standing in the side aisles.

Danny asked me to speak at Abby's funeral service. My first reaction was that I couldn't do this because I was sure I'd break down and start crying. I relented though, as Danny really wanted me to present personal reflections about Abby. He asked Becky, and a neighbor who was a close friend of Abby's, to also do this. I made some notes but decided I needed help. So I turned to the pastor of our church for his advice. He suggested that I simply speak from my heart and talk about the person that Abby was...about her kindness, her goodness and her love for her family. He also gave me a poem to read if I wished to do so.

At the funeral service, when it came my turn to speak, I first described how Abby and Danny met. "I introduced them when Danny came to visit me while I was a student at Hope College," I said, "And I believe they fell in love the very moment they were introduced. Their love for each other never dimmed, but grew stronger with every passing day. Abby was the kindest, sweetest person I have ever known and to have her life taken from her the way it was is incomprehensible."

I ended my reflections about Abby by reading the poem my pastor gave me. It was written by an unknown author, and was titled "To Those That Love Me."

I am with you always
When I am gone, release me. Let me go.
I have so many things to see and do.
You mustn't tie yourself to me with tears Be happy that we had so many years.

I gave you my love, you can only guess How much you gave me in happiness.
I thank you for the love each have shown, But now I travel on alone.
So grieve a while for me, if grieve you must.
Then let your grief be comforted by trust.
It's only for a while that we must part So bless the memories within your heart.

I won't be far away, for life goes on So, if you need me, call and I will come.
Though you can't see or touch me, I'll be near.
And if you listen with your heart, you'll hear My love around you, soft and clear.

And then, when you must come this way alone, I'll greet you with a smile and "welcome home."

When I returned to my seat Paul took my hand, leaned close to me and whispered, "I'm so proud of you." I forced a smile, but I soon started to tremble. I had steeled myself to make it through my remarks and the poem I read, but now my emotions were erupting beyond my control. I clinched my teeth, pressed my lips tightly together, and briskly shook my head from side to side all to no avail. I started weeping as quietly as I could, while a flood of tears streamed down my face. Paul put his arm around me and pulled me close to him. It took a moment or two, but after I released my pent up emotions. I slowly regained my composure.

Following Abby's funeral service at the church, we went to the cemetery where she was to be interred. It was a bitter cold and windy day. Instead of having a graveside service, a brief one was held inside a chapel at the cemetery. After that, those who wanted to returned to the church where the funeral service had just been held. A luncheon was served in the church's community room. It bought back memories of the day my fiancé Gene Morris was laid to rest, and the meal that followed. I couldn't eat then nor could I eat anything this day. I felt so sorry for Danny and for what he was going through. My heart ached for I knew his life…and his children's lives…were going to be totally changed. He no longer had a wife and Jennifer, Julie and John no longer had a mother.

I overheard Danny tell someone, "My life consists of two parts. The first part of my life was Abby. The second part will be without Abby. I hate to think what the second part of my life is going to be like without my Abby."

CHAPTER 7

The Trial

The two men responsible for Abby's death were arrested in late March in Chicago. One of the witnesses to her murder got the license plate of the car driven by the culprits, which was a brown 1989 Pontiac sedan. A man who lived in Benton Harbor, Michigan owned the car. He first claimed that his car had been stolen, but when he learned that there was a $50,000.00 reward for information leading to the arrest and conviction of the two men responsible for Abby's death, he quickly changed his story. The owner of the car then told police that he had loaned his car to the two young men who committed the crime, and even told police exactly where they were hiding out on the south side of Chicago. Supposedly they were his friends, but when it comes to money there's no honor among thieves.

Benjamin "Bear" Bugalski and Morris Kane were the names of the two murdering thieves. After they were apprehended, their names and pictures were in the newspapers and on television. Both had long arrest records for purse snatching, shoplifting and larceny. Bugalski was 26 years old and Kane 28. They were Caucasian, and both had served time in prison. The lead detective told Danny that they were heroin addicts and both had the aids virus. Stealing was how they got the money they needed to buy heroin, as neither one was employed. They were two pathetic and despicable individuals.

After they were returned to Grand Rapids, Danny attended their appearance in court when they were arraigned and charges filed against them by the prosecutors office. Bugalski and Kane were each represented by court-appointed attorneys. They were charged with second degree murder, robbery and parole violation. There was also a warrant out for their arrest for another crime they were suspected of committing. Bail was denied, and they were remanded to jail to stand trial for the charges brought against them. The judge also decided that there would be one trial but with two juries.

Danny told me they were a disgusting looking duo. They had thin bodies, long scraggly hair, and lots of tattoos. He said they seldom looked up at all during the arraignment. My brother had presumed that Bugalski would be a big guy with the nickname "Bear", but he was actually only about five feet seven or eight inches tall. Kane was about the same height. "Kane's name," Danny commented, "Should have been spelled C-A-I-N as he looked like the devil incarnate."

Their trial was scheduled to start Monday, October 6, 1997 so there was nothing that any of us could do in the meantime but go about our normal schedules.

My Mom and Dad and Abby's parents really pitched in to help Danny and to comfort ten-year-old Jennifer, nine-year-old Julie and seven-year-old John. Danny got his children up, dressed, fed and off to school each morning. In the afternoon, either my Mom and Dad or Sarah and Andy Zondervine were at Danny's home to greet their grandchildren when they arrived home from school. The children were usually fed a snack, after which Mom and Dad or Sarah, depending on whose day it was to be at Danny's house, prepared their dinner. My parents and the Zondervines cooperated and worked out a schedule to do this, and it provided a loving family atmosphere which Danny and his children really needed with Abby no longer a part of their lives. Mom and Dad or the Zondervines always stayed for dinner and occasionally I joined them as well.

In April, I had an important meeting with Bob Cunningham regarding the commitment that I had made to take over the clinic when he retired. Paul and I had discussed this situation a number of times, and we finally came to the conclusion that this was something I just wasn't going to be able to do. When I made this commitment to Bob I was single, and owning the clinic was the career path that I wanted to follow. Now I was married, expecting a baby in July, and had two nieces and a nephew that I felt needed some of my attention. In addition, I wanted to take at least six months off from the clinic when my baby was born. When I informed Bob that he was not going to be able to depend on me to take over the clinic when he retired he took it very well. Actually much better than I thought he would, considering the serious discussions we had held about my doing this during the years we had worked together.

In this same meeting, I also told Bob that Paul and I planned to have two children, which meant that there would be periods of time when I was going to have to put my career on hold for a while. "When our children are older and in school," I explained, "Then I would like to work on a regular basis…but only for four or five hours a day…as I don't want to stop being a veterinarian."

"Your decision doesn't come as a big surprise," Bob told me, "and things will work out for both of us I'm sure. Several years ago, when we first talked about your succeeding me as the owner of the clinic, I was seriously thinking of retiring before I was sixty years old. Now that I'm nearing that age, I'm not at all sure that I want to do that. What would I do with all my free time? This is a busy, successful practice and I enjoy doing what I do. I'm going to add another veterinarian to the staff as a result of your decision. The opportunity for that person to take over the ownership of the clinic in a few years should make the position especially appealing…particularly for a young veterinarian with a few years experience. I'll always be glad to accommodate you, Colleen, as to whatever days and hours you want to work at the clinic. You're a very capable and competent veterinarian, and I definitely want to keep you on the staff."

I thanked Bob for his consideration, and for his kind words but most of all I felt really relieved to have this matter resolved.

The due date for the delivery of my baby was Sunday, July 20. I was able to work at the clinic until Friday, July 11 and I looked very, very pregnant. As the saying goes, "I was big as a house." Everybody that saw me during the last two or three weeks of my pregnancy thought I might go into labor at any moment. Thankfully I did so on Saturday, July 19, right on schedule, when Paul was home for the weekend. Paul drove me to the hospital and was present for the delivery of our son, Michael Edward Ross.

Paul jokingly suggested that we should have named our son Frederick Paul Ross so his initials would be FPR…for Fast Pain Relief…the product that brought Paul and I together. That idea didn't fly.

The summer of 1997 was certainly different for me. I had a baby to care for, and I was not reporting to the clinic five or six days a week as I had been in the past. Every day was busy, and thank goodness I was used to an early to bed and early to rise schedule. Mom came occasionally to provide a helping hand, but I really managed to do everything pretty much on my own. Paul did take a week's vacation when our baby was born, and he was a great helpmate. That week quickly passed, though, and after that he was only home on the weekends. However, whenever Paul was home, he pitched in doing his share in caring for Michael, even changing his diapers when necessary. Whenever I saw him do this I usually told him, "You're a very good daddy."

Weeks, then months, quickly passed that summer and early fall, and it was time for the trial of "Bear" Bugalski and Morris Kane to start. Jury selection took close to two weeks as two juries were necessary for the trial. They would both be tried at the same time, but there would be one jury specifically for Bugalski and the other jury assigned to Kane. An unusual arrangement.

I wasn't able to attend the trial every day. When I could go, my mother came and took care of Michael, but I was only able to stay in the courtroom for a few hours. My first impression when I saw Bugalski and Kane was actually quite different than how Danny had originally described them to me. When I first saw them in court, they were clean shaven, hair short and neatly cut, and dressed in suits with ties. Quite a transformation had taken place as they actually now looked quite respectable.

However, there was plenty of evidence to convince the juries that these were the two young men who were guilty of killing Abby when they stole her purse. There were four witnesses who identified Bugalski and Kane as the ones who were responsible for her robbery and murder. Videotape from the store's security camera clearly identified Kane when he got out of the car to take Abby's purse. In addition police had gotten a search warrant to search Bugalski's mother's home, and they recovered Abby's purse there. He had given it to his mother as a present. Abby had an engraved pen and pencil set in her purse that Danny had given to her, and they were found among Kane's things. I quickly became convinced that these two young men were incorrigible, and the best thing that could happen would be for them to spend the rest of their lives locked up in prison, where they could not prey on society.

The trial lasted one and a half weeks and both were found guilty. Bugalski, who was the driver of the car, was sentenced to life in prison, and Kane was sentenced to thirty-years in prison. With good behavior Bugalski might possibly be released in twenty-five years, and Kane perhaps in fifteen to twenty years. But I wondered if either one of them would live that long, since they both were infected with the aids virus.

We didn't celebrate after the trial. My family, Abby's family and our friends all just felt relieved that the trial was over and done with, and that justice had been served. Nor did it give us any more closure, or ease our sorrow, as we still missed Abby terribly. It would take a long, long time for our hearts to heal, because all of us who knew and loved Abby would never ever forget her.

Paul and I invited our families to come to our home for the traditional Thanksgiving dinner. Paul took the entire week off, but flew to Chicago on Wednesday to bring his mother and daughter back to our home where they would stay through the weekend. On Thanksgiving Day, Mom and Dad arrived early in the morning as Mom and I, with assistance from Connie, prepared the feast that we would enjoy later in the afternoon. Danny and his children came mid-morning, followed by Papa John and the Zondervines...Sarah, Andy and Becky. After the usual welcoming hugs and kisses, everyone went to the horse barn.

From the moment Alicia arrived until she left to return to her mother's home late Sunday afternoon, she spent almost all her time in the horse barn brushing, riding or feeding her horse. She was crazy about her horse, Lucky. Papa John and my dad helped Jennifer, Julie and John each saddle a horse and they all went riding...including Papa John. Mom, Connie and I took time out from preparing the dinner, which was well under control, to go watch the five riders in the barn's indoor exercise ring. After a short warm-up they decided to ride outdoors, as it was an unusually mild day for late November. It was interesting to see the four children riding off with my 84-year-old grandfather. We watched until they were out of sight on the trail we maintained between the fenced in pastures for horseback riding.

Mid-afternoon, we gathered in our dining room for dinner. The four children ate at the kitchen table, as our dining room was only big enough to accommodate the nine adults and Michael in his high chair. Before the meal, Andy asked the blessing and it was a meaningful prayer that he gave. There were teary eyes when he thanked God for the life of Abby, and for the joy and the love she gave this family and especially to her husband and children. Then Paul carved the turkey, and we had a delicious dinner with a choice of either pumpkin or apple pie for dessert. The first Thanksgiving dinner at the Ross Horse Farm was such a success that I figured it would become an annual event.

While we were having dinner, Sarah and Andy invited all of us to come to their home for dinner on Christmas Day. Everyone accepted. Then Danny reported that the Castlewood Golf and Country Club was having an outstanding year, and to celebrate he invited all of us to the club for dinner on New Year's Eve. That was a wonderful offer, which none of us refused. Both Andy and my Dad were directors of the corporation that owned Castlewood, and they were pleased to hear that the club was going to exceed the prior year, both in income and profit. There were many things to be thankful for this day.

The Castlewood golf course was not only now rated as one of the best courses in the state, but also in the Midwest. Danny had invested heavily in improving an already good golf course…making it a beautiful and challenging course to play, with huge, well-maintained greens that were as smooth as the surface of a billiard table. Membership in the Country Club had more than doubled since Danny took charge, which was due not only to the improvements he had made, but also to the outstanding, well-trained staff of enthusiastic employees he had developed. Danny had applied the service lessons he learned while he was with Zon's Thrifty Marts. These included such things as rewarding members of the staff for good performance whenever he witnessed it or learned about it from a member of the club. And these rewards for good performance were generous.

The Castlewood Club House had also been significantly improved, and had been enlarged and redecorated. However, the most talked about improvements were the men's and women's restrooms on the main floor, next to the main dining room. They were simply incredible. They were spacious, with black marble floors, pink marble walls and impressive fixtures. Soft music played in the background, and during the dining hours in the evening there was even a uniformed attendant present to hand you a fresh, soft white towel to dry your hands. The famous Roman Baths had nothing on these facilities. They were in a class by themselves.

The huge kitchen with all its shining stainless steel was a sight to behold, and it was under the command of a chef that Danny had recruited from a well-known Chicago restaurant. The time, effort and money that Danny had invested in his enterprise was really paying off, as there was now a waiting list of people who wanted to join the Castlewood Golf and Country Club.

My father had never played golf until after he retired and he and my mother had moved to their condo in Grand Rapids. Danny then provided Dad with a good set of clubs, as well as lessons from the club pro, so he was enjoying the game and playing quite well, according to Danny. Andy, however, had played golf for many years, as had my husband, so the four of them talked seriously about playing a round of golf together next summer…something which they had never done before. I really hoped this foursome would be able to do that.

Christmas and New Year's of 1997 came and went, and the New Year…1998…was soon underway. I was scheduled to start working again part time at the Cunningham Veterinary Clinic in January, but decided to put that plan on hold. Bob Cunningham had hired another vet to assist him, and the two of them were handling the workload OK without me. I was thoroughly enjoying staying at home and being a mother, so I was glad that I could delay resuming my career as a veterinarian a little longer.

My father was born on January 20, 1936, so we recognized his 62nd birthday, as well as a six-month birthday for our son Michael, on Sunday, January 18 at our home. It was a bitter cold day with lots of snow on the ground but it was a warm, delightful and happy day in our home when these two birthdays were celebrated. In our family, birthdays always received special attention and there was one to celebrate almost every month of the year. Dad's in January, Danny's in March, Paul and my Mom's in April, John's in May, Jennifer's in June, Michael's in July, Alicia in August, Papa John's in September, mine in October, Constance in November and Julie's in December. Celebrating our birthdays together, as well as sharing the dinners served on all the traditional holidays, certainly contributed to the closeness that existed in our family.

Saturday, February 14, was Abby's birthday, and in 1998 she would have been 35 years old. I thought about her frequently that day and I knew that Danny and everyone in our family did so as well. Her birthdays were always kind of extra special because Abby was born on Valentine's Day. How appropriate, it seemed to me, because she was truly a sweetheart of a person. A few weeks later on Sunday, February 22, I thought about her a lot again as it marked the one-year anniversary of her death. It was horribly unfair that her life had been cut so short as a result of the stupid, senseless actions of a couple of heroin addicts. Abby didn't live long enough to see her children graduate from high school, go off to college, marry and have children of their own. How sad! But the world keeps on going, even though her participation in it unfortunately lasted for far too few years.

In the spring of 1998, I started working again at the Cunningham Veterinary Clinic…but only for five hours a day on Mondays, Tuesdays and Wednesdays. Mom usually came and stayed with Michael, but sometimes I took him to the clinic with me. I put a playpen in my office where he could play and nap, and he received plenty of attention from the staff. Far more attention than he really needed.

May 26th marked the third anniversary of our owning the horse farm. We had experienced surprisingly few problems in the past three years, thanks to the capable management of Jim Morrison. All the stalls that we wanted to rent were taken and the bookkeeping service we used was doing a good job of billing, collecting and depositing the rent money as well as handling our payroll. Thank goodness the Ross Horse Farm operation was well under control, as Paul and I both had careers that took a lot of our time.

Our home sits about a hundred yards from the big horse barn. Consequently, the renters of the horse stalls seldom ever bothered us when they came to ride their horses or to pick them up in a horse trailer to go ride somewhere else.

We had a strict policy that horse trailers could not be left on our property. The Stevenson's had strongly advised us not to allow the stall renters to leave their trailers on the property. "Do it for one," Bill had cautioned, "And you'll soon have a dozen or more lined up in front of, or around the barn. Then people will have to park their cars or their pickup trucks some distance away from the barn because of all the trailers.

We had followed Bill's advice, but occasionally someone would come to our house…even after Jim Morrison had explained that they could not leave their horse trailer on the property…to try and get either Paul or me to agree to let them do this. Our answer was always, "Sorry, we just can't accommodate you. If we allow you to do this then we'd have to do it for everyone who rents a horse stall, and we'd soon have a whole bunch of trailers parked permanently around the barn."

This certainly wasn't a huge problem, but it was probably the most serious issue that Paul and I had to contend with in the three years that we'd owned the farm.

Actually, 1998 turned out to be a very pleasant year. Everything went especially well for Paul and me and for our family. No unpleasant surprises, no crises nor unusual difficulties. Michael was a year old in July, which was the most significant of all the birthdays we celebrated that year. Our lives were flowing along from day to day, highlighted with regular family get-togethers and occasionally there was some special event for us to attend. Paul, Dad, Andy and Danny did manage to play golf together twice that summer, and once in the early fall. In October, Paul and I celebrated our fourth wedding anniversary and our family came to our home again on Thanksgiving. That Thanksgiving was much like the year before except that when we sat down for dinner I announced that Paul and I were going to have a baby next May.

As soon as I made the big announcement that I was pregnant, I got hugs and kisses from Mom, Dad, Papa John, Connie, Sarah and Andy. Danny squeezed me so tight that I thought he was going to break one of my ribs. Even Alicia, Jennifer and Julie had to give me a nice hug, probably because they thought they should do what they saw the adults doing. John and Michael, though, just sat quietly in their chairs and watched the entire proceedings. I suppose they were wondering, "What's the big deal? Let's eat."

Christmas and New Year's soon followed. On Christmas Eve, as we did every year, we attended the service at our church. The next morning Michael, to his delight, discovered that Santa Claus had stopped at our house during the night. On Christmas day our family exchanged gifts. However, we never exchanged expensive gifts, nor were we supposed to receive more than one gift from another family member. Years ago we had mutually agreed that our giving of Christmas presents should be symbolic. Christmas giving was really for children, and for those less fortunate.

As we did the previous New Year's Eve, Paul and I enjoyed dinner with our family at the Castlewood Country Club. This year, though, Danny brought his three children. He said he wanted Jennifer, Julie and John to be with him. I jokingly told Danny, "I think what you're really doing is keeping them up late so they'll sleep in tomorrow morning."

"You've got a point there," was Danny's reply, "Because I'm counting on that happening."

We had a great time, and at midnight everybody locked arms together and sang *Auld Lang Syne*. After which everyone loudly shouted, "Good bye 1998. Hello 1999!"

Shortly after that everyone departed for home.

CHAPTER 8

Danny's Tragic Death

Early in 1999, we hired an architect to plan an addition to our home. Over the past three years, Paul and I had had lots of company. In addition to the frequent visits of Alicia and Connie, Paul's sisters and their families had visited us several times. Other guests included some of Paul's old pals and their wives, as well as our mutual friends from Metamora, Kit and Dick Dixon. My nieces Jennifer and Julie and nephew John also occasionally stayed overnight. Paul and I had the master bedroom, Alicia had her own bedroom, and Michael's bedroom was the former guest bedroom. Our den had a couch that opened up into a bed, but we really needed more bedrooms in order to accommodate our company. And we loved having company. So Paul and I decided to add a wing to our home, which would have three bedrooms and two baths.

We approved the plan the architect created, got several bids from contractors, and hired one to do the construction. Fortunately and thankfully, our home improvement project was virtually complete by the end of May, when Emily Abigail Ross was born on May 30, 1999.

Michael was just 22 month's old when Emily was born, so I really had my hands full with two babies to care for. Without a doubt, my career as a veterinarian was on hold indefinitely. Mom gave me a helping hand whenever she could. However, she had a standing commitment to go to Danny's home either two or three days a week in the afternoon where she prepared dinner for him and his children.

My niece Jennifer talked her father into buying her a horse, which of course was stabled at our farm. We saw Jennifer frequently that spring and summer, and fortunately she and Alicia got along famously. They were great buddies and shared a love of horses. The two of them spent much of their time caring for and riding their horses, but they also provided me with welcome assistance in the kitchen, as well as help caring for Michael and Emily. They were now both old enough, Alicia was 15 and Jennifer 13, to accept responsibility, and they both did so…usually without my even having to ask. I really appreciated these two willing and capable helpers.

That fall we had devastating news that had a major impact on our family. Early in November, Danny had a physical exam at his doctor's office, as he had not been feeling quite normal. His doctor sent him to a hospital for additional tests, including a cat scan. The cat scan revealed that he had a mass or tumor in his intestines, and he underwent surgery on Tuesday, November 16. The tumor was removed, along with a large section of his bowel and a small section of his liver. After the operation mom and dad talked with the surgeon and my mother called to tell me the dreaded news…*it was cancer.* The tumor removed from Danny's stomach was malignant.

By the weekend, Danny was home recuperating. Starting in mid-December, he was going to have to undergo a minimum of ten chemotherapy treatments…one every four weeks…using very strong chemicals. Everyone in our family was stunned and deeply concerned. We were well aware that should the chemotherapy fail to eliminate all the cancer cells from his body, it might reoccur. I prayed hard and often that this would never happen.

We all tried especially hard to make our family celebration of Thanksgiving and Christmas just as enjoyable as they had been in previous years. However, we couldn't help but feel somewhat subdued because of what Danny was going through. Knowing that his life might be in jeopardy if the chemotherapy treatments didn't destroy any cancer cells remaining in his body, couldn't help but somewhat subdue the joy we should have felt on these occasions. There was a feeling of apprehension that I could sense hanging over our family gatherings like an unseen cloud. Danny, though, was upbeat, cheerful and…if he had dark moments…he sure didn't show it when we were together at Thanksgiving and again on Christmas Day.

The millennium was a big deal in the news media, and especially on the television news programs leading up to New Year's Eve. We did not go to the Castlewood Country Club this year to celebrate the end of the 20th Century. Instead Paul, Alicia, Michael, Emily and I had dinner at home. After Paul and I put Michael and Emily to bed we stayed up to watch television until well after midnight, and it was fascinating to see how the turn of the century was being celebrated around the world. It was a quiet, interesting evening. I was glad Paul and I were able to share it with Alicia, as I knew it was it was a memorable event for her. At least she claimed that it was!

The weather was unusually mild on Friday, December 31, 1999 and what little snow was on the ground melted. This wasn't at all normal for this time of the year. I couldn't help but wish, "Why can't everything just be normal, including the weather/"

Mom and Dad said they were not going to their condo in Alabama early in January as they had been doing for a number of years. Danny, though, insisted that they not change their plans because of him, as either he or a nanny that he would hire could be at the house when his children came home from school. He informed us that he fully intended to go back to running the Castlewood Country Club in January. The club was open year round for lunch and dinner, even though the golf course was closed for the winter. Somewhat reluctantly Mom and Dad, as well as Papa John, did go south for nine weeks.

After two chemotherapy treatments, Danny started losing his hair. By March 8, his birthday, most of his hair had fallen out and he started wearing a beret. I noticed that he had also lost weight, as he certainly looked thinner.

Danny's 38th birthday was celebrated with a big party at the Castlewood Country Club, which his family attended along with some of his friends and the club's staff. When Danny thanked everyone for coming to his party, he said, "The extent of the support and the compassion that I've received is just incredible, and I'm truly, truly grateful. You have no idea how wonderful it is to know that so many people care about you. I've received hundreds of cheerful notes and cards with get well wishes and I know that many people are praying for me. It's really overwhelming. It gives me hope, and I know and believe that hope will help me heal. Thank you so much for caring."

Our family was together again a few weeks later on April 23, which was Easter Sunday. Julie had recently gotten her own horse so the three girls—Alicia, Jennifer and Julie—really wanted to come to our farm for Easter so they could spend some time riding their horses. After attending church services, everyone arrived in the early afternoon. The spring weather that Sunday was just delightful, and the temperature was in the high 60's, a great day to be outdoors in the warm sunshine.

Late in the afternoon, we enjoyed our Easter meal of baked ham with sweet potatoes, which was the traditional fare for our family. Everyone ate heartily. I was counting on some leftover ham and sweet potatoes, but there wasn't any.

The summer of 2000 was not much different from the prior year, except Alicia spent the entire summer with us. We had a party to celebrate her 16th birthday on Thursday, August 17. The next day she got a Michigan drivers license, and on Saturday her father let her drive our car for several hours. She first drove up and down the blacktop landing strip on our farm, and later on backcountry gravel roads with Paul as her driving instructor. Learning to drive a car that day was an experience Alicia said ranked as one of the most exciting events of her life. Later, Paul told me privately that it was pretty scary at times…especially when they were passing other cars on the gravel roads.

In September, Danny finished the chemotherapy treatments and that was a welcome and noteworthy milestone for him. I prayed hard and often, as I knew everyone in my family was also doing, that the chemotherapy had eliminated all the cancer cells so that Danny would have a full and long life.

By Thanksgiving, Danny's hair had grown back and he really looked like his old self. We enjoyed having the family for dinner again at the Ross Horse Farm, and Thanksgiving and Christmas were really special. Three-year-old Michael tried very hard to stay up Christmas Eve to see Santa, but he fell asleep before midnight. On Christmas morning, the cookies he put out for Santa to eat were gone…but they were replaced with some interesting toys. Emily was confused as to what the occasion was all about, but was delighted with the doll and teddy bear she got from Santa.

On New Year's Eve, Paul and I went to the Castlewood Country Club for an early dinner with our family. Danny and his children, Mom and Dad, Papa John as well as Sarah and Andy Zondervine were all present. We took Michael and Emily with us, but left right after dinner so that we could put our children to bed. After they went to sleep, Paul and I sat in the den and watched television. As soon as the lighted ball finished its traditional drop on the top of the One Times Square Building in New York City, marking the end of the year 2000, we kissed each other goodnight and went to bed.

As they usually did every year, Mom, Dad and Papa John went to Orange Beach, Alabama early in January 2001, and stayed there until early March. I was still a stay-at-home mom, and had decided that I would not resume by career as a veterinarian for a few more years, probably not until Michael and Emily were in school. There was a comfortable routine to our lives. Paul was home every weekend, but usually left Monday mornings to return to his work. He sometimes arrived home on Thursday evening, but usually it was on Friday morning. So we often had three-day weekends together. And when he took his vacations, we stayed at home. Paul traveled so much for his business, that he relished the time he spent at our farm. Besides, we both felt that Michael and Emily were still too young for vacations. The longest trips we took were to visit Paul's mother in Chicago, where we would usually stay either one or two nights. Connie gladly served as a baby sitter for Michael and Emily in the evenings, so that Paul and I could go have dinner at a restaurant and see a show. I looked forward to these enjoyable two-or three-day trips, especially because of Connie's afternoon teas and the opportunity for Paul and I to have a night out on-the-town together.

On September 11, Paul was in California for a meeting when the terrorists struck and destroyed the twin towers in New York City by flying two commercial planes into them. They also crashed a plane into the Pentagon, and another one into a field in Pennsylvania. It was horrible! I, like all Americans, knew the world had changed forever, and that our country was in another war.

Paul wasn't able to return to Chicago in the Upson-Ross plane until Thursday evening of that week He arrived at our home Friday morning, and I was waiting for him with Michael and Emily in tow, when he landed his plane on our farm's landing strip. As soon as he got out of the plane, we held each other for a long time. There was a sense of insecurity that now existed...a new threat to our way of life...that everyone recognized. There were also feelings of anger and disgust that Islamic terrorists were able to kill so many innocent people. 9/11 was the main focus of everyone's life, especially as we watched the news day after day on television.

The year-end holidays...Thanksgiving, Christmas and New Year's...were observed and celebrated by our family exactly the same way that we always celebrated them. We were all a year older, with the changes in age most notable in 4 ½ year old Michael and 3 ½ year old Emily. This year, Michael had a list of things he wanted Santa to bring him for Christmas. What he wanted most was a bike. On Christmas morning Santa delivered a bike as well as some other toys Michael had on his list. He was so thrilled and excited when he saw the bike that he screamed with joy. Then he just sat quietly in awe for a long time, carefully studying his bike. I believe he thought he was now a big boy because he had graduated from his tricycle to a small bicycle, even though it had training wheels.

The week between Christmas and New Year's was always a special week for me, mainly because Paul was always home for that entire week. It was a time that we used to do some shopping together, either for clothes for our children or things for the house. Plus we would dine out a few times for lunch, which was a welcome break for me.

This year on New Year's Eve, our family again had dinner together at the Castlewood Country Club. Michael and Emily behaved quite well during dinner, to my relief. This year we kept them up a little past their normal bed times, so that Paul and I could dance together a few times. However, it was not really all that late when we arrived home. Like an old married couple, Paul and I again stayed up until midnight just as we had done the year before and watched on television the celebration taking place in Times Square in New York City. Right after we watched the lighted ball drop on top of the One Times Square building, confirming the end of the year 2001, we turned off the TV and headed for bed.

The year 2002 started off bitter cold with not much snow on the ground. The war in Afghanistan highlighted the news, as the coalition forces had successfully driven most of the Taliban from that country. We had retaliated against the evil forces that had attacked our country and who were dedicated to trying to destroy our way of life.

Early in January Mom, Dad and Papa John left for Alabama to escape from Michigan's harsh winter weather…just as they had been doing for a number of years. The operation of the Ross Horse Farm continued along day after day in its regular, normal way. Paul's company was doing well, and he loved his job. There was an order and a consistency that made my life comfortable and secure. I thanked God every day for my good life, and for my many blessings.

On Friday, March 8, Paul and I hosted a birthday dinner for Danny at our home. Mom, Dad, and Papa John had just returned from Alabama so they were present along with Danny's and our children. I served a pot roast, which I cooked in a Dutch oven along with the potatoes, carrots and onions…a favorite meal of Danny's. Mom provided the birthday cake. Danny had a big smile on his face all evening long, but I sensed that he really didn't feel good. He didn't say anything about how he felt, but my intuition told me that he was not feeling as well as he pretended.

A few weeks later, we learned that a blood test and another cat scan had revealed that Danny had cancer in his intestines again. He underwent surgery and we were all once again devastated to learn that, in addition to another malignant small tumor, the cancer had spread to the lining in his stomach. It was horrible news, and it meant that Danny would have to have more chemotherapy treatments. In addition, we learned from the surgeon that the odds of Danny surviving for more than a year or two were not very good. I wish the doctor had never told us this.

I tried very hard not to break down and cry, but nearly every time I thought about my brother the tears welled up. Sometimes when I was alone I just let myself go and had a good cry. "Why did this happen to Danny?" I asked myself this question over and over, even though I knew there was no good answer. I liked to think that life's predictable and safe, but in reality I really knew that we don't actually have total control of our lives. Things happen beyond our control that severely impact our lives, and there's nothing more upsetting and discouraging than when someone we love is seriously ill or injured or, worse yet, dies. Life is wonderful, precious, glorious and at times quite fragile.

Week by week, Danny grew weaker and the chemotherapy treatments only seemed to drain more of his strength away. He no longer could manage the Castlewood Country Club, and Andy Zondervine stepped in to supervise the operations. Mom and Dad spent a lot of time with Danny, and I went to visit him at his home several times a week.

On one of my visits Danny said to me, "I think my real calling in life was to create a family. Because of my cancer, I've thought a lot about my life and my successes, as well as the mistakes I've made. My athletic accomplishments, my business career and everything else fade in comparison to what Abby and I achieved in creating three wonderful children. I cherish the time I spend with Jennifer, Julie and John and when I woke up this morning they all three climbed into bed with me. Cancer didn't seem all that important when I heard them say to me, "*I love you daddy.*"

The last month of Danny's life…May, 2002…he received very competent and compassionate hospice care at home. Hospice nurses provided him with hands-on care, emotional support and assistance with daily tasks. Jennifer, Julie and John moved to my home, but I took them to see their father every day. I could see his strength and life ebb away week after week.

Danny passed away peacefully during the night on Friday, June 8. He was just 40 years old. It was not unexpected when Dad called on Saturday morning to tell me that Danny had died during the night. Even though it was not a surprise, it was still a shock. I started sobbing when I heard the bad news, and continued crying for a long time even after I had finished talking with my Dad. I heard the distress in my fathers voice and knew that he and mother were suffering intense sorrow. Paul heard me crying and came and put his arms around me and held me for a long time. Thank goodness the rock of my life…my husband…was there to hold and comfort me that awful Saturday morning.

Mom and Dad made all the arrangements for Danny's funeral service on Saturday afternoon…including selecting his casket. This had to be heart breaking for them. Mothers and fathers shouldn't have to bury their children, but there are times when this difficult task falls on the parents. Danny's funeral service was held the following Tuesday morning at the same church where Abby's funeral had taken place. The church was filled to capacity. It was actually a nice spring day, but a pall of clouds stretched across the sky…making the day seem even bleaker than it actually was. Two close friends of Danny's and Andy Zondervine gave eulogies, but the only words I really remember was when Andy Zondervine at the end of his remarks said, "I know that Abby and Danny are together again."

In the weeks before Danny passed, he put all of his affairs in order. He asked Paul and I to adopt Jennifer, Julie and John, and we agreed to do so. The home in Grand Rapids was listed for sale soon after Danny's death. Jennifer, Julie and John's clothes and other belongings had already been moved to our house. It was fortunate that Paul and I had added the three bedrooms to our home, as they were all now taken by our three additional children. The Ross Horse Farm was now their permanent home. At least it wasn't a strange place for them, as all three had frequently stayed overnight with us.

It was really a difficult period for our family but especially for Jennifer, Julie and John. Two days after her dad's funeral, we had a birthday dinner party for Jennifer, as we wanted to have things seem as normal as possible. It was her 16th birthday. She was unusually quiet, which was understandable, and she wept several times. Her father had written her a letter to be opened on her birthday. When she finished reading his letter, she put her head in her hands and started weeping. I put my arms around her and tried to console her saying, "Everything is going to be OK." That was the best I could come up with…even though things were not really OK, and probably wouldn't be for a long time. Jennifer didn't share the contents of the letter with us, nor did we suggest or ask her to do so. Whatever Danny said to his daughter in the letter was private.

Early Friday morning, Paul flew to Chicago and brought Alicia back for the weekend. My three big girls spent the afternoon taking care of their horses, and also went for a long ride on the trail beside our farm. On Saturday morning, Paul took Jennifer to the landing strip on our farm so that she could have her first lesson driving a car. As he had done with Alicia, he let Jennifer drive the car for an hour or so up and down the landing strip and practice stopping, turning and backing up. Later he let her drive on the backcountry roads, which he told me went quite well. He thought Jennifer was going to be a good driver because she was very attentive and very cautious.

The next few months were sometimes difficult, but things went reasonably well. I found that the busier I kept Jennifer, Julie and John the better. In August, I registered them in our local schools. They would now be riding buses to school, whereas they had walked to their schools when they lived in Grand Rapids. It was a new experience, but they adapted to it without any problem.

Sunday, October 20, 2002 was my 38th birthday. I got up extra early to bake a streuselkuchen, which my mother had taught me how to do, but mine never seemed to taste quite as good as when she made it. My three big girls…daughters Jennifer and Julie and stepdaughter Alicia…pitched in to help me prepare breakfast. Alicia had arrived on Friday with her Dad, as she wanted to participate in the celebration of my birthday. Alicia was now a freshman at Northwestern University. The three girls were lots of help and didn't need much, if any, direction from me. Everybody had a job to do. Alicia made the oatmeal while I scrambled eggs and cooked some sausage patties. Julie set the table while Jennifer poured the juice, milk and coffee. When we finished eating, the four of us pitched in and quickly cleaned up the dishes and pans so that we could get to our church in time to attend the 10:00 a.m. service. My birthday dinner was planned for late in the afternoon when Mom, Dad, and Papa John would be joining us.

As soon as we arrived home after attending the church service, everyone quickly changed clothes and went off to the horse barn. Jennifer, Julie and Alicia were eager to ride their horses. It was a beautiful fall day with some crispness in the air, so the bulky sweater and knitted cap I was wearing felt good. I stood by the fence that enclosed the outdoor exercise ring and watched my three big girls as they cantered their horses around the ring. I felt proud watching them as they were actually very good riders. My little daughter Emily was sitting beside me in her stroller, watching with fascination as her big sisters rode their horses around the ring. John and Michael were off riding their bikes, either up and down our front drive or on the landing strip. Paul was with them.

As I stood there by the fence watching the girls, I suddenly remembered that Saturday in 1980, just a few days before my 16th birthday. It seemed like it was only a few years ago, but in reality 22 years had gone by. Could I really be 38 years old today? Could Jennifer actually be 16? Yes, she really was! I vividly recalled getting up earlier than usual that Saturday so many years ago to go ride my horse Star, and I remembered Papa John bringing me a hot cup of coffee to drink. I thought about the big breakfast Mom served after I returned home from riding Star, and the discussion we had during breakfast about the crucial football game that was played later that day. That football game seemed so important at the time. And I wondered what ever happened to Star after I sold him when I went away to college.

How my life had changed in the past few years! It was hard to believe that, after being single until I was thirty years old, I now had six children…two of my own, three adopted and a stepdaughter. And I loved them all.

I looked up at the sky. It was slightly overcast with big puffy clouds. Here and there I could see patches or pieces of the sky through openings or breaks in the clouds.

And then I heard it. It was startling. I could hear Danny's voice and his words as clearly and as distinctly in my mind as if he were standing beside me. "*Take good care of my children,*" Is what I heard Danny say to me, followed by "*Give them lots of love and guide them well.*"

I turned and quickly looked to both sides to see if someone was standing next to me. There wasn't. Only Emily sitting quietly in her stroller, totally absorbed watching Alicia, Jennifer and Julie riding their horses. Then I looked up at the heavens and there was a bright shaft of sunlight beaming down through an opening in the clouds. It was an awesome experience, as I actually felt and believed that Danny's spirit had spoken to me.

I stared up at that shaft of sunlight for a few seconds, then I answered my brother saying, "*I will Danny. I will.*"

About the Author

This novel springs from Mr. Baker's early experience as an advertising copy-writer, and his knowledge of business gained during his later years managing the advertising and public relations programs for companies in a wide variety of categories. He is a graduate of the University of Missouri School of Journalism and holds an honorary doctorate degree in Business Administration from Cleary University. He has written magazine articles, a history of a cement company and his autobiography "A 50-Year Adventure in the Advertising Business." He founded the E. W. Baker, Inc. Advertising Agency in Detroit in 1964. The agency was acquired by The Omnicom Group in 1990. The E. W. Baker agency was then merged with DDB Needham Worldwide, after which Baker served as chairman and CEO of that agency's Detroit office. His knowledge of the apple industry is both personal and professional. His agency handled the advertising of Michigan Apples for twenty-two years, and he owned and operated Baker's Apple Orchard for twenty-seven years. During his career he served a number of different organizations as a volunteer. In 2001 the National Association of Parks recognized him as the Volunteer of the Year.

978-0-595-39923-9
0-595-39923-1

Printed in the United States
63785LVS00010B/82